VISIONS *of* HOPE

A NOVEL

To Edna –
May all your
dreams come true
Love
Candace

Candace Murrow

Singing Tree
PUBLISHING

ISBN 978-0-9827881-2-7

Library of Congress Control Number: 2010911718

Singing Tree Publishing
www.candacemurrow.com

Book design by Kathryn E. Campbell
Printed in the United States of America
Gorham Printing, Centralia, Washington

For Gary, Mom, and Jo Ann

and to the memory of my kitty muse, Bear

ACKNOWLEDGMENTS

Deepest appreciation to Sue Atwood, my dear friend, for being available through all the rewrites to offer early editing support. You're the best.

To Victoria Tennant and Deborah Sicignano: Thanks for your encouragement and for your invaluable assistance in birthing this book into the world with the special work you both do.

And to Barbara Fandrich, my editing pro, who helped shape the novel just right: Thank you.

Special thanks to Lena Karunamaya, whose supportive coaching and intuitive insights inspired me.

As always, big hugs to my sister, Jo Ann Ableman, and her family. Thanks for your love and support.

With love to my mother, Frances Clogston, for being there to encourage me. You hold a special place in my heart.

To Gary, my beloved husband and best friend: You are my rock. This project couldn't have happened without you. Thank you for everything and more.

Forever grateful to the Creative Spirit for constant guidance and inspiration.

VISIONS *of* HOPE

ONE

A whispering crept into Libby's dream. The whispers grew louder until the crying out of her name scattered the dream and pulled her out of a deep sleep, startled her, woke her. An icy draft swept through, and the warmth of the summer night vanished in an instant, causing her to shudder.

She clutched the covers to her chin, fighting the urge to open her eyes, but the urge to look grew stronger. She peered at the corner of the room. There, in a glowing light, the remnants of a blue mist trailed away, leaving no discernible image, no clue to her unexpected waking.

She reached for the lamp's ceramic base and fumbled for the light switch. No breeze from the opened window rustled the curtains. No shadows quivered in the corner. The room was eerily still.

She grasped her clothbound journal. This was not the first time she'd had this mysterious flight from sleep. She paged forward and spotted two entries: June 21, July 10. On a blank page she penciled in the date and time, July 20, 4:00 a.m., made a notation, and set the book aside.

Sleeping now was impossible. The incident had unnerved her with an urgency she could not explain. She slipped her robe over her silk pajamas and padded toward the kitchen in search of something to settle her anxiety.

She switched on the stove light, opened a drawer nearby, and rummaged through the spare change, paper clips, and pencils until she found a stray cigarette. She positioned it between the fingers of her left hand, reached for a book of matches, then paused and recalled her doctor's words.

To ground herself, she breathed in the tobacco odor, as stale as it was, and massaged the cigarette between her thumb and forefinger all the way to the living room. Being surrounded by the familiar—the beige couch, the oak furniture, the cozy window seat with its oversized pillows—further steadied her in the present.

She sat in her rocking chair, prepared to wait for daybreak to fully illuminate her Pacific Northwest retreat. Already the veil of night was lifting, flushing the walls in a pale light.

Just as she began to relax, a creak and snap of the floorboards drew her attention to the hallway. Expecting nothing less than another otherworldly experience, she calmed at the sight of her friend, Ellen Davis, emerging from the shadows in her pink nightgown, fluffing her cropped hair.

"Did I wake you?"

Ellen stationed herself with fists on hips, eyes skewered on Libby. "You've had one of those visions again, haven't you?" She pulled the hassock close, her gaze settling on the cigarette. She snatched it out of Libby's hand and set it on the end table.

"I wasn't going to light it," Libby said. "But if these unrelenting visions keep waking me up, I'm not promising anything. I have a business to run and a good night's sleep is essential."

Ellen clucked her tongue while rubbing Libby's hands. "They're like ice. My goodness, it's the middle of summer. Do you want to talk about it?"

"Same as last time, only the feeling is getting stronger."

"I can tell that. You're so chilled."

Libby shuddered again, thinking about the totality of the incident. "There's something about it, Ellen. I can't describe it, except to say something or someone desperately wants to break through."

"Who do you think it is?"

"I'm not sure yet," Libby said. "I haven't had anything like this happen for years, not since I worked with the police. But during that time most of the information came to me in dreams. Now my dreams seem to be manifesting outwardly."

"What do you think it means?"

"It might have something to do with a client," Libby said. "I don't sense it has anything to do with me directly, but it's too soon to tell. I'll have to wait for the entity to manifest to know for sure."

"I don't know how you handle all this psychic stuff. It's a wonder you're still sane. Let me get you some tea, warm you up." Ellen extended her hand to Libby.

Libby gladly followed Ellen through the great room into the kitchen where Ellen snapped on the overhead light.

"In high school you were always there for me when anything like this happened, remember?"

"Someone had to take over for your mother," Ellen said, "but this entity stuff makes my skin crawl." She filled the teakettle with water and placed it on the stove to heat.

Libby retrieved the chamomile teabags from the pantry and placed them in the cups Ellen had taken out of the cupboard.

Ellen took hold of Libby's hands. "They're getting warmer."

"The energy has dissipated, and I'm fine now, thanks to you." Libby gave her a squeeze. "You know, Ellen, it's nice having you here, even if it is only for the reunion."

"You were in bed last night when I got back from decorating. I want to know what the doc said."

Libby splayed the fingers of her right hand. "Five years now. I've reached a milestone. It looks good as far as he's concerned."

"That's so great." Ellen returned Libby's hug. "You're free now. So what are you going to do, bed every eligible man in town?"

"Ellen."

"You know what I mean."

"I feel great physically. I've expanded my consulting business, and I'll probably take on more clients, do more readings."

"How boring," Ellen said. "What about men? You've been so, you know…"

"Celibate?"

"Well, yes, and alone, to yourself."

Libby replaced the tea box in the cupboard.

"All men are not like Dan," Ellen said.

"I know, but I'm not interested in starting up anything new." Libby smoothed the wrinkles of her robe on the left side.

Ellen eyed Libby. "It's your breast, isn't it? You're afraid they won't be able to love you the way your breasts look now."

"That's something I have to consider, Ellen."

"It's not that bad."

"How can you say that, with all the scars and they don't even match in size anymore."

"Whose do? But I wish you had taken better care of yourself, especially when you were married to Dan."

"I should've never married him, and I should've been more proactive about getting regular breast exams."

"You could always have reconstructive surgery. You know there are options out there. Why don't you talk to your doctor again?"

"Ellen, let's just drop it. I've got my business. That's all I need."

"But Libby…"

Libby pressed a finger to Ellen's lips. "What about you? Have you decided to leave Mel?"

The kettle's shrill whistle interrupted them. Ellen poured the water into each cup and returned the kettle without answering her.

"Well?"

"I'm still thinking about it," Ellen said. "The kids are in college. They don't need family like they used to. But I'm not sure. It's such a big step."

"I don't know how you can forgive him for all he's put you through."

"Do you mean the women or the gambling?" Ellen lowered her voice, almost to a whisper. "Sometimes you have to make sacrifices because of the kids. I guess that's what I've been doing."

"Oh, Ellen. I'd love to have you back in town. In fact, you can stay here as long as you want to."

"You're a doll, you know that? We'll see, after the reunion."

"How are the preparations going, by the way?"

"It's hectic," Ellen said, "but things are getting done. Still, I'm wondering if I should have volunteered. It's so much work, especially with my living an hour north of here. I'm so glad I could stay in Harbordale with you these last few days."

"You were always into everything in high school, all the clubs, cheerleader. I envied you back then."

"Cheerleader, hah! Look at me now." Ellen aimed her index fingers at her body. "Size 14. You, on the other hand—"

"Oh, right. I've got a figure like my mother. Narrow shoulders, skinny legs, hips that could bear a litter."

"You have a poor image of yourself, Libby. You do take after your mother, but she had a fabulous figure."

"At least she had children."

Before Libby could turn away, Ellen cupped Libby's face. "You can still have kids, honey. Don't give up that dream."

"At forty-three? I still have to be vigilant about the cancer. Besides, look at the legacy. Mom died of breast cancer. So did Aunt Lolly."

"But you didn't."

"I know, Ellen, but it's too late for children, and men."

"It's never too late." Ellen took a cautious sip of her tea. "Have you decided to go to the reunion?"

"I suppose, but I'm not looking forward to it. The past is better left alone."

"Oh, don't worry about the past. It's been twenty-five years. People grow up, lose their memories as they get older. They won't be thinking about you and your psychic gift. They'll be worrying about how they look."

"I know, but—"

"I'd hate to see you miss out on new opportunities. Mister Right could show up. Who knows?"

"So who's the psychic now?"

"You always told me you can't read your own future. Maybe I need to step in, give you a nudge."

"I'm not looking, and that's that."

"Maybe I'll look for you." Ellen jutted her chin.

Libby responded to Ellen's playful look of defiance with a good-natured shove. Ellen picked up her teacup and strolled out of the kitchen.

Libby loved Ellen for looking out for her, but even with the best of Ellen's intentions, and after all Libby had gone through—the scarring cancer, the abusive marriage—there was no way she would be nudged into any situation she wasn't ready for.

T W O

Kipp Reed checked the clock on the dashboard. The time was six-thirty. If he hurried, he could make it to Harbordale in forty-five minutes, an hour max. Not one to worry about speed traps, he pushed the accelerator of his Jeep, swung into the fast lane, and sped up to seventy-five miles per hour. Even though flying down I-5 was not an issue, being late was, especially to his twenty-fifth high school reunion.

He hated the thought of waltzing into the room and being stared at by his old classmates, even though he'd spent most of his adult life working as a reporter on national TV. Maybe it had something to do with his new, more secluded lifestyle, working as a freelance journalist. Maybe it was because of Kelly. The thought of answering questions about his daughter nauseated him. He hoped Charlie Bender, his closest friend, would be sensitive enough to leave the subject alone.

Whatever the reason, tonight he wanted to blend in and not become a spectacle, yet he chuckled to himself because he could remember a time he would have loved the attention, especially with a twenty-three-year-old model on his arm. Those days were long gone, and he mused how life's circumstances had taken him in such a different direction. Why was he even going to this reunion?

By the time he parked at the Harbordale Inn and saw people moving toward the entrance, he'd made up his mind to make the best of the evening and enjoy himself. Before joining the others, he undid the top button of his shirt and loosened his tie. The hell with it. He flung the tie into the backseat and grabbed his sport jacket. He slipped on his jacket on the way to the door.

The hotel held a spectacular view of a sprawling lake that emptied into Puget Sound, but for the most part Kipp ignored the view and went directly downstairs. A white banner, decorated in red lettering, hung over the entrance to the ballroom: HARBORDALE VIKINGS 25th REUNION. Tables and chairs hugged the sides of the large, dimly lit room, and people gathered in small groups or milled around in the center. From a quick scan Kipp guessed about half of the two hundred fifty seniors who had attended the public school, the only high school in Harbordale, were present. Sounds of the chattering crowd turned Kipp's stomach queasy, and he wished he'd stayed home.

As soon as he moved through the doorway, an anorexic woman in a low-cut dress charged him. "Kipp Reed!"

Kipp smiled and searched his memory for a name to put with the face.

"You don't remember me, do you?" His puzzled expression compelled her to continue, "Jan Pierson. Math class, junior year?" She tapped at her name tag.

He nodded but grasped for more information. She, however, seemed undaunted by his lack of recognition.

"Well, I remember you. Who wouldn't? Your face has been all over the TV. But I haven't seen you on the news lately. Where have you been? My goodness, you look as handsome as ever."

Kipp spied a group of men huddled next to a bar on the far side of the room and saw his escape. "Will you excuse me, Jan?" He made an effort to slide past her.

"Oh, sure, but you need this." She located his name tag on a table nearby and reached for his shirt in an attempt to pin the tag on his pocket. Kipp picked the tag out of her hand. "If it's all the same to you. Thanks anyway."

"Sure. Whatever."

He relegated the tag to his jacket pocket. When he reached the bar, a group of four men greeted him with handshakes and slaps on the back.

"Damn. Practically the whole team's here tonight," said a man with thinning blond hair, taller than Kipp. "I never thought that would happen, especially with you traveling all over the world, Reed. You were the only one of us who had any smarts."

"Put on a few pounds, eh Bill?" With a playful touch, Kipp fisted Bill Turner's belly.

"Yeah. Pam cooks too good. I wouldn't be able to get off the ball if my life depended on it."

"So, where's Charlie?"

"He stopped by earlier. Said he had some paperwork to catch up on. How 'bout a Bud?"

Holding the cold bottle of beer helped ease the rising temperature caused by the gathering crowd and the August heat. While listening to his buddies hash over the good old days of football, Kipp scanned the room to see if he recognized any other classmates. When a lull in the conversation arose, he gestured toward the entrance. "Who's the woman in the white suit?"

"You don't recognize her?"

Kipp took a swallow of beer, his gaze on the woman.

"That's Chicken-legs McGraw." Bill flapped his arms like a bird. "Cluck, cluck, cluck."

The other men laughed while Kipp squinted to get a better view of her. "You've got to be kidding. She never looked like that."

"She shed that long hair and filled out in all the right places, if you know what I mean."

"I can see that," Kipp said. "What's her story?"

"Don't you remember what happened our junior year?"

"You'll have to refresh my memory."

Bill leaned in. "Remember the fire incident when she told the principal there was going to be a fire the night of the homecoming dance? No one got hurt because they were prepared? We started calling her—"

"The Witch of Harbordale High. I remember," Kipp said. "What's her story now?"

"You mean besides the sexy bod? Pam heard she went to graduate school, got an MBA. Does some kind of counseling. That's all I know."

Kipp eyed Libby until several of his classmates surrounded him, vying for his attention.

⁓

Libby clutched a glass of iced tea and wished she could leave. She'd moved away from the crowd, found an empty chair near the door for a quick exit if need be, and waited for Ellen, who was flitting from one person to another. Classmates wandered by and glanced her way, but no one approached her. Either they didn't recognize her, or they remembered her reputation. The lighting was dim, but not that dim.

She tried to get comfortable, but she still felt as though she were in a fishbowl. When Ellen joined her, Libby voiced her distress. "This must be what the Salem witches felt like."

"You're nuts," Ellen said. "They're looking at you because you're so damn stunning in that white suit with your black hair. They probably don't even recognize you."

"I didn't have time to change," Libby said. "I barely got back here from Seattle in time for this thing. I don't know how you battle that freeway up north all the time."

"Don't change the subject."

"What?"

"The subject of how stunning you are. People are probably intimidated by you."

"You're full of it, Ellen. They remember things."

"So what if they do? Come on. I'll walk you around."

"No, thanks. The energy in this place is chaotic. I feel better seated."

"Suit yourself. I'm going to talk to that hunk over there." Ellen nodded toward the group of men gathered by the bar.

"What hunk?"

"The cross between Clint Eastwood and Robert Redford. The one with the reddish-blond hair. Kipp Reed. Don't you recognize him?"

"No."

"Oh, that's right. You didn't have a TV back then. He was a reporter. I don't know what he does now. He kind of dropped off the radar screen. He was the Viking quarterback and a buddy of mine. Don't you remember?"

"I do now. He and his friends used to heckle me."

"Maybe they did, but I remember Kipp as a really nice guy. I'm going to say hi. Want to come?"

When Libby leaned back and folded her arms, Ellen marched off.

❧

Kipp looked up in time to see a woman in a black sheath bounding his way. Before he had time to make a move or say anything, the woman gave him a quick hug.

"Hey, buddy, remember me?"

Kipp stepped back and looked her over. "Ellen West, or used to be West. You look the same."

"Oh, don't give me that bullpucky. Look at me." She held her arms out and shifted her gaze to her body.

For a moment he was at a loss for words. But always the consummate diplomat, he told her she looked great.

"I'll take any compliment I can get," Ellen said. "Hey, do you remember the time we collided at the Madison game when you were running toward the sidelines? You slipped in the mud and slid right into me. I thought I'd been hit by a truck."

"I can't say I remember that, but I hope I apologized."

"Apologize? It upset you about as much as it did me. Those were the days. Say, what have you been up to lately?"

Kipp dreaded the questioning. He opened his mouth to answer but was interrupted by a woman intent on speaking to Ellen. Thinking this was his way out of the situation, he prepared to turn back to his buddies, but the woman made her departure in time for Ellen to return her attention to him.

Ellen smiled at Kipp. "So where's the missus?"

"There is no missus."

"Really. Well, why don't you come say hello to a friend of mine? We'd like to hear what you've been doing with your life." She looked in Libby's direction, but Libby's chair was vacant. "I wanted you to meet Libby, but she must have gone to the ladies' room. I'll go check. Be back in a flash."

Kipp watched Ellen breeze through the room and out the door. This whole reunion thing was beginning to feel stifling. He ran his hand under his collar where perspiration had formed.

"That Ellen is still a card," Bill said. "Want another beer? You might need one before you meet the infamous Libby McGraw."

The thought of that panicked Kipp. He wasn't in the mood for talking to a nutcase or witch or whatever she was. "You know, I think I'll run over to the station and find Charlie."

"You don't have to leave. Charlie might show up later. Come on. Have another beer."

"I'll be back. I'd like to talk to Charlie in private." Kipp shook hands with his buddies and strode toward the door of the ballroom. On his way outside he saw neither Ellen nor Libby.

He removed his jacket and unbuttoned his shirt down to the middle of his chest. The breeze was light but provided little relief from the heat that had persisted into the evening. A few classmates, whom he didn't recognize, stood smoking nearby.

Just as he reached his car, a silver Accord headed in his direction. As it slowly passed by, he made eye contact with a woman in a white jacket and dark chin-length hair. He nodded to her before sliding into his seat. So that was Libby McGraw. Without a doubt, even if the woman was a nutcase, she was rather well put together.

Kipp drove through the main part of town, down the same streets he'd driven as a teenager, past the old Penney's store, now an office building, past Starbucks where Miller's Department Store used to be. Restaurants had come and gone since Kipp lived in town; nothing stayed the same.

He recalled the hours driving with his buddies on Friday nights after the games, following girls and keeping one step out of trouble. He wondered whatever had happened to some of his old girlfriends, although he had seen one of them tonight: Jill, with her husband Fred. It all seemed so long ago.

He drove into the parking lot of the Harbordale Police Station and parked near the entrance to the one-story building that had to be as old as Kipp, its rough exterior badly in need of paint, the shrubbery surrounding it dense and overgrown.

The town's forty thousand inhabitants had yet to pass a levy to replace the building and its overpopulated jail. Over the years other more pressing projects had taken precedence, such as the updated sewage plant and the new high school building.

Detective Charlie Bender, whose six-foot five-inch frame towered over Kipp's medium height, moved aside to let Kipp enter the station. Behind the counter the desk sergeant, a young man with a crew cut, was sitting under a flickering fluorescent light.

Charlie slapped Kipp's shoulder and led him into a secured area past several empty cubicles to an office at the end of the hallway.

"Man, is it good to see you. Come in and sit down." Charlie pulled up a metal chair for Kipp in front of the coffee-stained desk. He sat in a swivel chair and pushed his mug aside. "Does it take a reunion to get you down here?"

Kipp glanced at the only folder on Charlie's desk. "Why aren't you there with the old gang? It doesn't look like you've been working that hard."

"I see those jokers around town. Besides, it's not the same without Patty. I don't want to have to answer questions about the divorce."

"I can understand that," Kipp said.

"How's your mom and dad? They still in Florida?"

"Yeah. Your folks still doing okay?"

"They're slowing down, but they're still in the same house."

"Do you remember how much time I used to spend there?"

"Do I? It was like your second home. Have you seen your folks lately?"

"We don't communicate much."

"It hasn't changed?"

"They're still upset about my quitting the TV job," Kipp said. "And now, Kelly."

Charlie rose to full stature. "Do you want coffee?" When Kipp responded with a shake of his head, Charlie sat again. "Have you heard anything more about your daughter?"

"Nothing."

"No leads? Nothing's been happening?"

"They say they're doing what they can, but they've got a million missing kids. Kelly's on the registry—"

"I meant the dick. You hired a private dick, didn't you?"

"Yeah, but nothing came up. I'm at a loss."

"What about Tanya?"

The sound of his ex-wife's name and the subject of his daughter's disappearance had produced a sinking feeling in the pit of Kipp's stomach. The drab walls, the stuffy odor, and the institutional feel of Charlie's office reminded him of all the other police stations he'd frequented in his search for Kelly. Or maybe it was the lone African violet on the windowsill, the only sign of life in this place, that spurred the urge to bolt. "I think I better go."

When he made an effort to stand, Charlie asked him to wait. "Listen, I don't know if it will do any good or not, but some police buddies of mine up north gave me the number of, I don't know, a person or organization that helps find missing persons. They're psychics."

Kipp pushed up from his chair, the tension in his neck adding to the nausea he felt.

"Wait a minute, Kipp. Hear me out." Charlie rounded the desk as Kipp neared the door. "It's been a while since they told me this, but these people were instrumental in getting important clues that led to finding some kids. We never used their services, but we never had to, yet."

Kipp waved a dismissal. "I'll talk to you later." He walked out of the room and advanced down the hallway, anxious to get outside, Charlie's footsteps padding after him.

Charlie put his hand on Kipp's shoulder and stuck a business card in Kipp's shirt pocket. "It never hurts to keep an open mind, Kipp, my man."

After Kipp was settled in his car, he retrieved the card out of curiosity and snapped on the overhead light. The name of the business was: New Horizons, Intuitive Consulting. He relegated the card to his jacket pocket, alongside his name tag. To Kipp, the subject of his daughter made the reunion seem frivolous, and returning to the hotel to converse with his high school buddies lost any appeal it may have had.

He turned off the light, started the engine, and steered the car onto

I-5 North. In thirty minutes he would exit onto Highway 16 toward Port Anderson.

✖

By the time Libby veered off Slater Road toward Jackson Point, five miles northeast of Harbordale, it was getting dark, and the homes, scattered along the wooded route, provided the only light along the way. Beyond the crest of the hill, she turned onto her private gravel road. Just before her driveway a black-tailed deer darted in front of her headlights and bounded into the forest, one of those lovely perks for those living in the woods.

Above the treetops the stars were beginning to colonize the night sky. The air was too stagnant for this late at night.

Once inside, Libby switched on a lamp, draped her jacket over the rocking chair, and kicked off her heels. The high ceilings, white walls, and light décor normally gave the room a cool feel, but the sun, shining through the skylights, had baked the room all day long. Too late to bother with the air conditioner, she dampened a washcloth in the bathroom and dabbed her face.

Wired from the day's activities, she decided to wait up for Ellen. She set a glass of water on the coffee table next to the overstuffed couch.

More than happy to be seated in her own house, she leaned her head back to rest. No sooner had she closed her eyes and taken a few deep breaths then she drifted into a dreamlike state. In her mind's eye a picture materialized: sitting across from her in the baby blue recliner in her office, a man with blondish hair removed his wire-rimmed glasses and wept. Startled, she tried but couldn't make a connection to any person or circumstance she was aware of, and she brushed the image off as a silly daydream.

She curled up on the sofa and dozed until she felt a scratchy sensation on her arm and realized Ellen was laying a blanket over her. "When did you get home?"

"Just now. I'm sorry I woke you."

Libby pushed the blanket aside and massaged her neck, stiffened from resting her head against the decorator pillow. "What time is it anyway?"

"Two-thirty. I stayed and helped clean up. Made sure everyone was taken care of."

"You're such a mother hen. You were always looking after me and everyone else."

"That's me. Good old Ellen."

Libby scooted over and made room for her on the couch.

"What happened to you tonight? I went looking for you. You up and disappeared," Ellen said.

"I couldn't stay. I was too uncomfortable and too tired."

"You missed your chance to meet Kipp."

Libby gave Ellen a disgusted look. "I guess I sensed it was a good time to leave."

"He's not married," Ellen offered, but Libby had already crossed the room before Ellen could elaborate. Ellen scurried down the hallway after her. "I didn't have a chance to ask for any other pertinent details. He left early, too."

"Just as well. Good night, Ellen." Libby fled to the sanctuary of her bedroom and closed the door, away from Ellen's prattle about Kipp.

But Ellen's comments jogged her memory and reminded her of the eye-to-eye contact she'd made with Kipp in the parking lot. She recalled his wire-rimmed glasses and suddenly made the connection to the image that had surfaced before she fell asleep: the weeping man with the wire-rimmed glasses.

Though she was at a loss as to how or when, she sensed meeting Kipp Reed would not be a lost opportunity.

THREE

On Monday morning Kipp rose early, showered, dressed, grabbed a cup of coffee, and wandered toward the second bedroom of his two-bedroom house, the room he'd converted into a study where he could do his freelance work.

The phone rang, and he returned to the kitchen to answer it. Jerry, his friend and editor of *New World Magazine*, was on the line.

"I was just going to call you," Kipp said. "I finished the article, and I'll send it today."

"Great. I'm glad I caught you. Are you on a new assignment yet?"

"I've got something in the works, but it's not definite. I have to give them my answer soon. But actually I was thinking about taking a break."

"You need to keep working, Kipp, and keep your mind off things."

"That's easier said than done."

"I've got an assignment that will definitely keep your mind occupied. In fact, it will make your head spin."

"What's the subject?"

"We want to do an investigation on psychic phenomena, ESP. Who has it, and who doesn't. Who are the real psychics, who are the fakes, and how you tell the difference. That sort of thing. We want a fresh slant. You could even write it from a skeptic's point of view. See what you find out. What do you think?"

Kipp thought back to the reunion and the talk about someone being a psychic or a witch or something, and what a huge coincidence this was. "That wouldn't be so hard, writing it from a skeptic's point of view. But the subject really doesn't interest me."

"That's not the answer I was hoping for."

"Can't you find someone else to write it?"

"Everyone's on assignment," Jerry said. "Let's just say by asking you I'd be calling in a favor. Remember your first break?"

"You're going to call that one in, are you? In that case—"

"This stuff's hot, and you really would be helping me out."

Kipp growled under his breath. "All right. I'll do it."

"You're a pal. I'll fax you the guidelines this afternoon."

"When's the deadline?"

"Three months, tops."

"Three months. Do you have any suggestions on where to start? I mean, this isn't my thing."

"You're the investigative journalist. Interview some psychics," he told Kipp before hanging up.

Kipp pressed the top of his shoulder where his knotted muscles ached, unsure whether the pain was due to the tension that had settled there since his daughter's disappearance or to his new assignment.

When he went into the study to ponder the direction he would take the article, he noticed his sport coat, draped over the computer chair, and remembered the business card Charlie had given him. He fished the card from his pocket. "Intuitive Consulting." Hell of a coincidence. Might as well start there. In the kitchen he poured a fresh cup of coffee, sat at the breakfast counter, picked up the phone, and prepared to make the connection.

The phone rang four times before switching to an answering machine.

A woman's voice began, "You've reached the business of New—" Then someone picked up: "New Horizons."

"Hello. My name is Kipp Reed, and I'm a journalist doing an article on ESP for *New World Magazine*. I got your number from Detective Bender of the Harbordale Police Department. I was wondering if I might interview you or one of your associates." Kipp paused.

"Kipp… I mean Mr. Reed, you want to interview Elizabeth."

"Do I know you? Your voice sounds familiar."

"I don't think so. I'm the secretary here," the woman said. "Can I make an appointment for you? What day would you like to come?"

"Would tomorrow be too soon?" In the background he heard papers shuffling.

"She has a full day tomorrow. How about Wednesday at two?"

"Fine. Where are you located?"

"Harbordale." She hastily gave Kipp the address and ended the call before Kipp could ask another question.

He examined the card, then the address, and wondered who this Elizabeth was. Since the location was Harbordale, he speculated the business might be connected to Libby McGraw, but he dismissed the idea, because anyone who went to graduate school, as Libby allegedly had, would be far too intelligent to be involved in such flaky dealings as ESP.

FOUR

When Libby arrived home from another appointment in Seattle, the aroma of freshly-brewed coffee permeated the house, and Ellen greeted her with a glass filled with ice cubes clinking in a rich brown liquid.

"You're back so soon, Ellen. I'm so glad." Libby accepted the glass of iced coffee. "I could get used to this. Do you want to be my house husband?"

"I don't have the right equipment. You'll just have to settle for a good friend who will be staying with you for a while."

"You decided to leave Mel?"

"I'm just taking some time out. A couple of weeks, if that's okay with you."

"You know I'd love to have you here as long as you want. I told you that when I gave you the extra house key."

"I just wanted to make sure before I brought my suitcase in," Ellen said. "By the way, Kipp Reed called and made an appointment for Wednesday afternoon."

Before Ellen could open the screen door, Libby latched on to her arm and dragged her back into the room. "Your suitcase can wait. What's this about Kipp Reed?"

"While you were out, your business line rang, and I answered it. I didn't want you to miss a client. I was just going to take a message and—"

"Why would he want an appointment?"

"He's writing an article on ESP and—"

"You told him he could interview me?"

"Sure thing."

Libby noticed Ellen's self-satisfied grin. "Didn't he know it was you?"

"He was almost on to me, but I didn't give him time to think about it. I said I was your secretary."

"And does he know it's me he's coming to see?"

"I only gave him the name Elizabeth." Ellen started toward the door.

"Wait a minute," Libby said. "You set this up, didn't you?"

"I couldn't have dreamed this beauty up. It just fell into my hands." The screen door slammed shut as Ellen escaped outside.

In her bedroom Libby slipped on a pair of shorts and a baggy top, grumbling to herself. There had to be a way out of this situation. No way would she see Kipp Reed.

Ellen ventured in, sat on Libby's bed, and watched her hang up her skirt and blouse. She ran her hand over the mauve quilt and glanced around at the teak furniture and the Georgia O'Keeffe prints. "You've got such great taste. You could have been an interior decorator."

"Right now I wish I were," Libby said. "Did you get a number where I could reach him?"

"Kipp?"

"Did you get it?"

"No."

"Ellen…"

"What do you want his number for?"

"To cancel. Or have you call and cancel."

"Why?"

"First of all, I don't want to do any interviews. And secondly, I don't want to entertain Mr. Reed. How did he get my number anyway?"

"From Charlie Bender."

"How did he get it?"

"Didn't say. You know your reputation precedes you."

"That was a long time ago. I haven't done any police work lately."

"Who knows? Word gets around." Ellen rounded the bed and began to sift through Libby's closet. "Let's pick out what you're going to wear. A woman must be prepared at all times."

"For what, may I ask?"

Ellen gave Libby a look of disbelief. "It has been a long time, hasn't it? For anything, silly. Let's see." She held up a red sundress. "This is a cute little number. Shows just enough to leave him wanting more."

"For goodness sake, Ellen, this is an interview, not a seduction." Libby snatched the dress from Ellen and stuck it back in the closet. "Are you sure you didn't call him?"

"Like I said, I couldn't have planned this if my life depended on it." Ellen twirled around with her arms spread. "It just danced into my lap like a little angel."

Libby marched out of the room to get a glass of water, wondering how to get out of the appointment.

That night, she tossed and turned into the morning, her stomach in knots. Kipp Reed had imprinted himself in every thought, in every dream, in every feeling she'd experienced throughout the night. Each time she made a case against him coming to see her, his expression convinced her otherwise. He seemed anguished, at times pleading. Why would that be? His demeanor in her dreams did not fit the circumstance of their upcoming meeting, which was an innocuous interview. Nevertheless, she could think of no way out of seeing him.

The feelings associated with him were intense and urgent, same as the energy of the visions she'd had the last couple of months. Could they be connected? She sensed they were, and if so, she'd have to put her own dis-comfort aside. The more he came into her mind, the more convinced she became there was a reason for their meeting, but the reason eluded her.

Drained from thinking about the situation, she meandered into the living room and separated the curtains to assess the weather. A light cloud layer covered the morning sky, giving the forest a gray cast. Sunlight was trying to worm its way through, but to no avail, a welcome relief from the past week of abnormally high temperatures. Libby thanked the gods for the change, even though gray skies were far too prevalent in the Pacific Northwest.

⚮

On Wednesday afternoon Libby was in her office going over a few notes she'd prepared for her next workshop when a car came up the driveway, tires grinding on gravel.

Ellen burst through the doorway. "He's here. Let me look at you. Beige slacks, crisp white blouse. I don't know why you didn't wear that red sundress. Oh well, you still look fabulous. I'm going to slip out the back and walk in the woods for a while so you two can be alone. Don't want him to know it was me on the phone. Too tacky." She pulled Libby from the chair. "Okay now. Go get 'em girl."

Ellen left Libby standing in the middle of the room in a state of anxi-ety. Just as the back door slid shut, the doorbell rang. Replacing the but-terflies in her stomach was an army of ants.

When she opened the door to let Kipp in, a woman's image flashed in front of her, then faded, sending a shiver through her body. No time to give the vision a second thought. She blinked her eyes and focused on Kipp, who with a briefcase in hand was staring a hole right through her.

This close to him for the first time, she caught a glimpse of the sea green eyes she remembered from years past. Dressed in jeans and a polo shirt, he had the build of a man who might have done some serious jogging.

"It's you. You're the Elizabeth."

She was sure he took a step backward. "If you'd rather not stay..."

He hesitated a little too long in Libby's judgment. "Maybe I shouldn't."

She cringed, thought about agreeing with him, but a voice inside her head rang through: *Make him stay. Make him stay.* And the knot returned to her belly. Whenever it came to her clients or friends, and sometimes to herself, she heeded the voice. She opened the screen door, touched his arm. "Please come in."

He glanced at her hand, an awkward grin developing. His expression puzzled her, but she didn't press for an explanation.

She observed him cautiously inspecting the room, eyes narrowing, as if he might find something strange or bizarre—a skeleton or a shrunken head.

He refused her offer of lemonade and followed her to her office. She sensed him sizing her up. In one second she hoped she looked adequate, and in the next second she chastised herself for even thinking about her appearance.

Clients who came for readings always sat in the baby blue recliner. She took the computer chair. She preferred to sit with her back straight because the energy flowed better that way.

To ease his confusion, she asked him to sit in the recliner. He sat on the edge and looked around, as if on guard, ready to leap up at the first sign of anything weird or out of the ordinary.

Libby always kept the lighting dim while doing readings, but she realized that might be another cause of his obvious discomfort. He seemed nervous, edgy. She had a tendency to pick up on other people's energy, but at the moment it was unclear whether the anxious feeling belonged to him or to her.

She opened the curtains wide and snapped on the overhead light. She wished she had spritzed the room with lavender oil, an action that would have relaxed them both. She sat and crossed her legs. "So, you're doing an article on—"

"ESP and the people who have it. For *New World Magazine*."

"Why do you want to interview me?"

"Charlie Bender gave me your card. I didn't know it was you when I called."

"Or you wouldn't have come?"

"That's not what I meant. I just never expected—"

"To be in the same room with someone like me?"

"It's just that this psychic stuff gives me the creeps, and I'm not exactly wild about doing this article." He sucked in a breath, seemed surprised by his own response. "I'm sorry. I don't know why I said that."

Libby knew why. More times than not, the truth tumbled out in her presence, and she felt the need to come to his rescue. "Most people don't understand it. It's natural to feel the way you do." She uncrossed her legs and shifted in her chair. "Why don't you just ask me a few questions?"

❧

Kipp groped in his briefcase for his notebook, his pen, and the recording device. He skimmed the first page of the notebook, but he could not stop thinking about his inexplicable blunder and how unprofessional he'd sounded. It had to be her eyes, those translucent blue eyes that seemed to draw a person into this crazy world of hers.

He wished he could glance at his watch without her noticing. They had only been in the room five minutes, and he wanted to flee. Why had he let Jerry talk him into this madcap assignment? The only thing to do was to go forward and get out as quickly as possible. "Do you mind if I record?"

"No, but I'd rather you not use my real name. I'm not looking for any publicity."

"Fair enough." He flipped on the handheld recorder. "Would you mind scooting your chair closer so your voice will come through?"

As Libby wheeled her chair directly in front of him, he got a whiff of a heady rose scent, causing him to lose control of the recorder and it fell to the floor. He bent sideways to pick it up, all the while feeling like an idiot. Once he had everything in place, he cleared his throat twice to regain his focus. "Why don't we begin with you? What do you call yourself, professionally?"

"I'm an intuitive counselor."

"Meaning…"

"I give one-on-one personal clairvoyant consultations. I also do intuitive training for individuals, as well as businesses."

"What does a psychic know about business?"

"I have an MBA, and I give workshops to teach people how to use their intuition for making business decisions."

Kipp's brow wrinkled. "Business and intuition. Now those are strange bedfellows."

"Not really. We all have the ability to tune in to our inner guidance to make good choices; even business people have this ability. I teach them how to tune in. Would you like to learn?"

"No, thanks. So how long have you been able to do this ESP stuff?" Again, how unprofessional. "I mean, how long have you had this ability?"

"Since I was a little girl. At first it manifested in my knowing when there was going to be a death in the family. Maybe a few weeks before."

"That must have frightened your parents."

"Not really. My grandmother had the gift, too."

"And not your parents?"

"It skipped a generation."

Kipp took a moment to make a few notes, trying to disregard the rose scent that was not so easy to ignore. "Why do people come to you for consultations?"

"It gives them insights into their personal issues. It helps them see things differently. I guess you could say I'm kind of a counselor, only I never tell people what to do. I give them information and let them do with it what they will. I help clarify things."

"I can't say I buy into any of this, but how do you get the information? Do you use tea leaves or read palms?"

"Sometimes I hear words in my head, or I see pictures in my mind, or sometimes I just get strong feelings. Sometimes it comes in dreams."

"How do you know you're not crazy?"

Libby smiled. "I used to think I was. I went through a period of time when I denounced everything. That's one reason I went to college and got my MBA. I tried to bury it, but I kept having dreams and strong feelings about people. That's when I began working with Dr. Grant at UCLA. He helped me learn how to deal with my gift. He tested me and proved to me I wasn't insane."

"Is he someone I could contact?"

"I don't know what he's doing now. I haven't had any contact with him in years."

"Why's that?"

"Off the record?"

Kipp turned the recorder off.

"Let's just say he was married and our work brought us too close, so I left the study."

That bit of information piqued Kipp's interest, but he decided to stay in the professional arena and turned the recorder back on. "How do you know the information you get is the truth?"

"I don't for sure. I'm not 100 percent accurate. I just get the information and give it to the client. They let me know if it rings true. Plus, I see things in patterns, how the road looks at this point in time. But things can change. People have free will."

Kipp forgot about his discomfort and leaned back in the recliner. "I have to tell you, this all sounds like smoke and mirrors. I'm not sure I buy any of it."

Libby grinned. She did not look surprised.

"You look like you've heard this before," he said.

She touched his knee. "Why don't you let me give you a reading, and you can judge for yourself."

Kipp sat up with a jolt. "I don't think so."

Libby leaned toward him and held on to his arm. He stared at her beautifully sculpted nails, then up at her face, and immediately relaxed.

"Be the investigator," she said. "Prove me wrong."

Something in her expression challenged him, yet he found himself mesmerized by her whole being. It wasn't that she was a picture of perfection. Her nose had a slant to it, a tiny mole hugged the corner of her mouth, and her smile revealed a crooked front tooth. But it was the overall package, something that transcended earthly beauty. Finally, he broke the trance.

"I figured if you were a psychic, you'd already know all about me."

"I get impressions, but I don't tune in to specifics unless I have permission. Psychics have ethics, too."

Libby backed her chair away from Kipp and turned her attention to her appointment book. "How about coming Friday morning for that reading?" She wrote on the back of a business card and handed it to him, then wrote down his phone number.

He glanced at the card. He had an appointment for Friday at ten o'clock, even though he couldn't come to grips with why he was agreeing to see her again.

From the security of his car, he gave her house a furtive glance before heading down the driveway. There was something about the woman. He couldn't put his finger on it. She seemed normal, even delightful, except for the one thing he could not give credence to: her psychic ability. On

Friday he would discover if this psychic thing was even an issue.

Anxious to get home to go over his notes, he sped over the back roads past a small industrial park housing a warehouse for one of the huge box stores. When he merged onto the freeway, he was thinking back on the interview. It seemed half the questions he'd planned to ask had floated away, and instead he'd agreed to a reading, allowing her to delve into his personal life, and that was the last thing he intended to do.

By the time he'd crossed the Narrows Bridge and rounded the curve toward Port Anderson, he made up his mind to call Libby and cancel out of the whole damn thing—interview and all. He would go with the information he had, and he would never have to see her again.

He entered his house and wasted no time in digging through his briefcase to locate Libby's business card, but to his surprise and dismay, he discovered he'd left his recorder behind. He'd set it on her desk when she handed him the appointment card. Now what was he going to do?

He thought about asking her to send it to him, but he could not imagine telling her he wanted to cancel out and in the next breath asking her to package it up for him. He could ask her to drop it off at the police station, give it to Charlie, but he didn't want Charlie to know he had actually contacted her.

He retrieved a beer from the refrigerator—something he normally wouldn't do in the middle of the day—went back to the living room, stared blankly out the window to his backyard, and tried to work up the courage to call her, when the phone rang. It was Libby McGraw.

"I wanted you to know you left your recorder here, in case you were wondering what happened to it."

Now was his chance. He could cancel and ask her to, to do what?

"You can get it Friday when you come for your appointment."

Hearing her voice again, he lost his train of thought and said, "I just realized I left it, and fine, I'll see you Friday."

She hung up, and he stared at the phone, wondering what just happened to his resolve. It was that woman, he concluded. There was something about that woman.

❧

Ellen met Libby in the living room with two cups of tea and motioned for her to sit. "Tell me all about it. I've been out here, pacing for an hour."

"I'm sorry I kept you waiting. I had a phone reading right after Kipp left."

"You're door was closed. I figured you were busy. Come on, spill."

Libby rested her feet on the coffee table. "It was rather a short interview. He didn't ask many questions. I was surprised."

"I don't care about the questions," Ellen said. "I want to know how he acted around you."

"What do you mean?"

"Oh, come on, Libby. You know. Did he flirt with you? Does he want to see you again?"

"Ellen, this was business, nothing more."

"What did he say to you?"

"He just asked questions for the magazine article. That's all."

"And you didn't flirt a little, help him along?"

"Ellen…"

"Oh, all right." Ellen folded her arms in defeat. "So, how did the interview go?"

"It went okay. He's a bit of a skeptic, so I talked him into coming back for a reading."

Ellen clapped her hands. "I knew it. I knew it."

"What am I going to do with you? It's just business."

"Maybe. But it's a start," Ellen said. "He wouldn't come back unless he was interested. You've got to admit, he's got that sexy, rugged thing going for him, like a man who's been outdoors wrestling wild beasts, don't you think?"

"He's attractive."

"Come on, Libby. He's more than attractive. He reeks sex appeal."

"Why don't you go after him if you're so smitten?"

"Maybe I would if things were different and I was single and fifty pounds lighter. But I'm not. Besides, he and I were like brother and sister in high school. I still think of him that way." She aimed a finger at Libby. "I want you to have him."

Ignoring Ellen, Libby began thumbing through the nearest magazine.

"Why are you so stubborn? He's single, he's interesting. He's for the picking. Why don't you go after him, or at least show an interest?"

Libby set the magazine aside. "We've been over this before, Ellen."

"I know. It's the cancer, isn't it?"

"That, and my gift. I don't want to spend the rest of my life trying to prove myself to someone, let alone a born-again skeptic."

"Why don't you just go on a date, have some fun? You don't have to look so far ahead."

"He's not even interested in me. He still thinks I'm a nut."

"How do you know? Have you asked him?"

"I don't have to. I can feel it. He could barely look me in the eye when he got here." Libby paused. "Oh my gosh, I just remembered the vision."

"What vision?"

"When I answered the door, the figure of a woman flashed in front of me as soon as I saw Kipp."

"Do you know who it was?"

"No, but my sense is that it's connected to whatever has been waking me up at night. Those visions must be connected to him."

"Oh boy, this is getting good. Maybe you'll find out when he has his reading."

"Maybe." Libby's thoughts were drifting to Kipp.

"I want you to tell me everything when I get back Monday."

The word Monday filtered into Libby's awareness, and she refocused on Ellen. "Where are you going?"

"Home, so you and Kipp can be alone."

Libby glared.

"Just kidding," Ellen said. "Jennie called. Summer quarter is winding down, but she's decided to work through to fall quarter. She's coming home for the weekend, and I'm driving up north to pick her up on Friday. So I'll be home all weekend. Back on Monday."

"Are you going to tell Jennie about the separation?"

"I haven't decided. I'll play it by ear."

"Have you talked to Jason?"

"Jason who?"

"Oh, Ellen…"

"Computers and school. That's all he has time for. He's not coming home from Stanford either. I doubt if he'd notice anything his mother does. He's becoming his father's clone."

"What about Mel?"

"What about him?"

"You'll have to spend time with him."

"You mean, bedroom time? So what. I could use a little roll in the hay after all this talk about you and Kipp." Ellen patted her heart and sighed.

Libby huffed, "There is no me and Kipp."

FIVE

On Thursday Kipp tried to make sense of the notes he'd scribbled during the interview and cursed himself for leaving his recorder behind. He pounded out what he could decipher, but recalling the feel of Libby's hand on his knee and the intoxicating rose scent, which seemed as real now as it was then, he pushed away from his desk.

He wanted to pace, but he could barely maneuver around the stacks of books and papers and the crumpled Pepsi cans scattered about. He thought about calling his editor and begging off the assignment, but he couldn't think of a reason Jerry would buy, save coming down with the plague.

He picked up the pop cans on his way to the kitchen, tossed them into the recycling, and checked the refrigerator for something to eat. Macaroni and cheese and leftover spaghetti held no interest, plus he was too restless to cook.

He grabbed his wallet and keys and drove down the hill to The Fish and Ale, a local hangout by the bay. On summer days the salty air drifted into the restaurant and commingled with the odors of fried fish.

Kipp sat at the bar and ordered a basket of fish and chips, the house specialty, to go. Sam, the owner, a middle-aged man with an abundance of dark curly hair and mischievous eyes, wiped the counter in front of

Kipp and asked how things were going.

"To tell you the truth, Sam, I can't seem to get a certain woman out of my mind."

Sam grunted. "Woman problems, huh? Right up my alley."

"It's not what you're thinking. This woman is smart, attractive, and under any other circumstances, I'd be interested, but she is also a professed psychic."

"Yeah, so?"

"She seems to have a way of making me do things I don't particularly want to do."

"That sounds like every woman to me, psychic or not." Sam chuckled.

"This is different. It's like I'm determined not to see her, then I hear her voice and I'm a goner."

Sam grinned. "You've got the bug, man."

"What are you talking about?"

"The love bug. You're halfway there."

"You have an overactive imagination. Did anyone ever tell you that?"

Sam laughed all the way into the kitchen. When he returned with Kipp's order, his face was still lit up with an impish smile. "Yep. You've got the bug."

Kipp slid a ten across the counter. "You should be paying me for the entertainment I'm providing you. You're enjoying my predicament way too much. But, Sam, you're way off base."

As he wove his way around tables filled with the dinner crowd, he heard Sam shouting after him, "Give her my regards."

At home Kipp wolfed down the coleslaw and the ale-battered fillets and chucked the fries. He had worn himself out worrying about seeing Libby again and decided to turn in early. He set his glasses on the nightstand and tugged the disheveled covers toward the headboard.

His fatigue was overwhelming, but when he closed his eyes, sleep became a stranger. Libby's face was as clear as if she were in the room. He rolled onto his stomach, punched the pillow over his head, and hoped for the best, but in the morning the truth was evident: Libby had been on his mind, and he was as tired as the night before.

On this Friday morning he'd planned to get up at seven, but he'd dozed on and off, and now it was past eight. At least he wouldn't have time to think it over, and as he got into his car, he was resigned to making the best of an undesirable situation.

On the way down the freeway, it dawned on him he may have worn the same shirt he had on Wednesday, but then he recalled that shirt was blue, not green. Why did he even care? One thing he knew for sure: an apology was in order for his despicable past behavior.

Towering firs and alders lined the winding driveway to Libby's house. He inched the Jeep forward with the thought that a person could lose themselves, living alone in these woods. Still, the surroundings were beautiful, especially with the sun glistening through the trees.

Libby was on the porch, watering petunias in colorful flowerpots, wearing a dress that matched her unusual blue eyes. Approaching the porch steps, he was too anxious to return her smile. Small talk was impossible. He refused her offer of iced tea, even though the lump in his throat was thickening.

In her office—he in the recliner and she in the desk chair—she handed him his recorder and told him he could tape the session if he was so inclined.

"First, I need to clear something up," he said, causing her to tip her head in a puzzled manner. "It's about high school. I want you to know I'm sorry for how I treated you, the name calling and everything."

"Oh."

"When I came here Wednesday and discovered you were the Elizabeth from high school, I felt terrible about it. I didn't realize—"

"That's why you were having such a hard time looking at me?"

He answered with a sheepish grin.

"And I thought I disgusted you."

"Oh, no. Far from it. I'm just nervous about all this."

Libby touched his arm in that tender way of hers. "Please don't be. I'll try to make it easy on you."

"Like that's supposed to help."

"Really. There's nothing to be afraid of," she said. "Let's get started. Why don't you lean back and try to relax as much as possible. You can close your eyes if you want. What I'll do is tell you what I see, give you my interpretation. You let me know if it rings true or not, but don't tell me too much, just yes or no. I'll ask for more information if I need it. Are you ready?"

He gave her a sharp affirmative nod, but in reality he wanted to get as far away as possible. Many times in his career he'd been placed in dangerous situations—war zones, earthquake disasters—but nothing matched the angst he felt in this moment. He fiddled with his recorder while Libby dimmed the lights. To satisfy himself no tricks were involved, he kept his eyes open.

"I'd like to say a silent prayer before I begin." Her eyelids fluttered shut, and she inhaled deeply.

On edge, yet curious, he stared at her and waited for her to speak. If nothing else, she was fascinating to look at.

"Will you state your full name?"

"Kipp..." His voice cracked, and he cleared his throat. "Kipp Sanders Reed."

She took another deep breath, her eyes closed. "You love the outdoors, the wide open spaces. Traveling has been a way of life for you. Is that correct?"

That was nothing profound, but he answered in the affirmative.

"I sense that you are very independent, you like to take charge of things, but you can be a bit stubborn at times. Is that true?"

Again, nothing profound, and he answered yes.

"I see you as a child, walking alone. You are an only child. Your parents live far away from you, and I feel there is a great distance between you, not only in miles, but in the way you interact. Is this correct?"

"Yes and no."

"Are you an only child, and do they live far from you?"

"Yes."

"Are you estranged?"

"No."

"I don't see you having much contact with them."

"It's been a while. That's all."

"Hmm… I feel there's something else there, but let's move on." She paused for a moment. "It feels to me you've lived a whole lifetime in a short period of time. Does that make sense?"

"I don't know. Maybe." He wondered where she was going with this line of questioning.

"It seems your life has changed in the last few years," she said. "What I'm seeing is you holding an inflated balloon. It represents your life. It's like you lived your life large in every way, but the balloon punctures, and the air has come out of it. I see you on a path with a fork in the road. You've had to make an important choice. Is that so?"

Kipp shifted uncomfortably in his chair. Balloons, forks in the road. What she was saying was all so vague, yet so close to the truth. "Somewhat," he said.

"Who is the woman younger than you who is close to you?"

Kipp was silent.

"She has blond hair the color of straw. Very thin, very beautiful. The name starts with a D or a T."

"My wife, Tanya. My ex-wife."

"I feel there was a rift between you. Something happened. I see you both weeping. Was there a child?"

Kipp's stomach clenched. "Yes."

"I feel there was a loss. Did you lose custody?"

"No. I had custody."

"There's definitely a loss of some kind. I sense that… I see a child being ripped from your arms. I feel indescribable anger and sadness. You have been suffering from the loss of your child. You long for this child. Is that correct?"

Kipp's eyes widened. She'd jabbed the nerve that was so raw it stung with unbelievable pain. Tears flooded his eyes. It had been months since he'd cried openly, but opening the wound that had been sewn up for so long allowed the tears to flow with an ease that shocked him. He removed his glasses and wept.

The next thing he knew, Libby was handing him a tissue and telling him she understood. The touch of her hand on his was a shock to his system, his emotions laid bare. Anger rose from the middle of his belly with such force he jockeyed his glasses into place and leaped to his feet. "You don't understand anything."

She hastened to back out of his way. "I didn't mean—"

"You think you know everything, how I feel, you and your dog and pony show." His eyes burned from the tears and the rage. "You don't understand. You don't know anything. You're a quack, lady. You're a quack and a misfit."

He gathered his belongings—dropping his pen in the process and having to pick it up, juggling his notebook and recorder, stuffing it all into his briefcase—and stomped out of the room. He slammed the front door on his way out and never looked back to see if she'd followed him.

His tires sprayed gravel all the way to the two-lane highway. Tears streamed down his cheeks, and he was so bleary-eyed he had to pull over to the side of the road. In no condition to drive on the freeway, he picked up his cell phone and called Charlie.

Charlie was off duty and agreed to meet him on the outskirts of town at a hole-in-the-wall tavern, known for its dart tournaments and frequented by the after-work crowd. The short drive gave Kipp enough time to compose himself. In the parking lot of Barney's Place, he spotted Charlie's black pickup near the entrance, alongside three other vehicles.

Inside, a man and woman sat at the bar, and two younger men were playing a game of pool at one of two pool tables in the far side of the room. Barney's was less airy than The Fish and Ale and had the stench of cigarette smoke embedded in the walls from a time when smoking in public places was legal. Kipp stopped at the bar and paid for a draft.

Charlie waved from a corner booth. He had on a Mariner's tee shirt. "Hey, buddy, I already ordered onion rings and a couple of beers."

"Good. Two beers will do just fine."

"You sounded pretty shook up on the phone."

"Yeah, well, you don't know the half of it."

Charlie watched Kipp gulp down the better part of his beer. "What are you doing in Harbordale?"

"You're not going to believe this, but you know that business card you gave me with that psychic's number on it?"

"Yeah."

"The psychic happens to be Libby McGraw."

Charlie's eyebrows shot up. "No shit."

The waitress brought their order, and Kipp stalled until she left them alone. "I just came from seeing her."

"No shit."

Kipp explained about the article he was writing, his reason for seeing Libby, and the personal reading that had him so upset.

"You didn't go there to ask about Kelly?"

"No, but she knew all about her. At least she knew I'd lost a child. I didn't let her go any further."

"Why not?"

"I lost it." The gut-wrenching emotions threatened to surface again, and Kipp had to work at staying in control. He stared at his glass. "She poked around where she shouldn't have, and I lashed out at her, called her names. Then I took off. She shouldn't have gone there, Charlie."

When he looked up, Charlie was shaking his head.

"What?"

"When are you going to accept someone's help?"

"I hired a P.I. That didn't go anywhere."

"That's not what I meant."

"Then what?"

"Why didn't you give this woman a chance?"

"A chance to do what?"

"I don't know. Give you some emotional support. Maybe she can help you deal with this. I mean, you've been going it alone. Everyone leans on you."

"You mean Tanya."

"Who do you get to lean on?"

"I've got you, friend."

"You know what I mean."

"I don't know what you're getting at."

"I'm talking about letting her help in anyway she can. If you would have let her finish, maybe she could have given you some clues. If it were my kid, I'd do anything."

"That's not fair, Charlie."

"I'm sorry, man, but going to a psychic is just one more stone to turn over."

"Since when are you such a big fan of this psychic crap. You're a cop, for chrissakes."

"I don't know. I just think if she were my kid, I'd put my prejudices aside."

"Well, she isn't your kid. She's mine. And I'll do what I think is best." Kipp stood up while struggling to get his wallet out of his pocket. "I can see I'm not going to get any sympathy from you. And I don't need your advice." He threw a twenty down and left his friend at the table.

Charlie caught up with him outside and clamped onto his shoulder. Kipp was fighting back tears.

"Why don't you come to my place and chill out before you head home. You're in no condition to drive."

Kipp proceeded to jam the key in the lock.

Charlie clutched his arm. "As a cop, I'm not asking you. I'm telling you. I don't want you driving. Come on, I'll follow you to my house."

∽

After napping an hour on Charlie's couch, Kipp left for home. He'd told Charlie he felt better, but thoughts of his daughter never left him.

The emptiness he felt when he entered his house was like a boulder—hard, cold, and heavy. The light on his answering machine blinked on and off. The caller was Libby. "I wanted to make sure you got home all right," she'd said. The hypnotic sound of her voice flooded his mind with the feelings he'd tried so very hard to extinguish.

He erased the message and sank into his leather chair. Damn her. Damn the Witch of Harbordale High.

SIX

OVER THE WEEKEND Libby had no time to think about Kipp's outburst. She had phone readings to do and a workshop to prepare for. His anger did concern her, but she'd seen this reaction before and didn't take it personally. Even though she was tempted to call him whenever she had a spare moment, she talked herself out of it. She sensed he needed the space to be with his feelings.

On Monday Libby was in her office, checking her appointment book, and Kipp's name popped into her head. Should she call him? She closed her eyes and pictured his face. A sinking feeling, as if the energy in her body suddenly had more weight to it, gave her the answer she sought. She turned to the next page in her appointment book, preparing to make another call, when the screen door banged shut.

"Libby, it's me." Ellen appeared in the doorway, dressed in a tee shirt and shorts unflatteringly too tight.

"Come in, Ellen. I didn't hear you drive up."

Ellen plopped in the recliner and propped up the footrest. "So, how'd it go?"

"You mean with Kipp."

"Who else?"

"Let's just say it was very enlightening."

"What did you find out?"

"That's client privilege. You know I can't divulge any information about him."

"Not even to little ol' me?"

"Not even to little ol' you."

"Can you tell me anything at all, like how long he stayed?"

"Not very long."

"Why not?"

"Let's just say I hit a nerve."

"Really. You do have a way of doing that. So, when's he coming back?"

"I don't expect him anytime soon."

"Oh… you hit a giant nerve."

Libby nodded.

"Why don't you call him?"

"I don't think that would be wise."

"I could call him and feel him out."

"I really think he needs time to take it all in."

Ellen squeezed her chin and narrowed her eyes. "Hmm…"

"Leave it alone, Ellen, and tell me about your weekend."

"You mean with Mel, the man from hell?"

"If that's what you want to call him."

"I do and I don't. Jennie and I had a blast together. We went shopping and did a lot of talking."

"About the separation?"

"Yup."

"How'd she take it?"

"She loves her dad, you know, so it's going to be hard on her, but she seemed to understand. She knew more than I gave her credit for."

"And what about Mel?"

"He stuck around all weekend. We took Jennie out to dinner and had a great time. That's the good part."

"And the bad?"

"He doesn't want a divorce, but he's more than okay with me staying here for a while. It makes it so much easier for him to stray in all the wrong places."

"I'm sorry, Ellen."

"Don't be."

Libby wheeled her chair directly across from Ellen and held her hands. "Do you want to know what I think?"

"Shoot, kid."

"I think as soon as you make up your mind what you want to do, and I mean do for yourself, the world will open up to you."

"You are always the optimist." Ellen disengaged from Libby and pushed the footrest down. "So, what's on your agenda this week?"

"I have a few phone readings, then I'm off to Denver on Friday to participate in an intuition workshop. I'll be home Sunday evening."

"What about Kipp?"

"Would you forget about Kipp? I have to call some clients. Why don't you see if I have anything in the fridge for lunch, and I'll help you in a minute?"

After Ellen closed the office door, Libby took a moment to reflect on Kipp's reading. She'd trained herself to let go of her client's issues, but Kipp's reading troubled her. She knew he had lost a child, but the abrupt ending stopped her from pursuing the details. Even so, the pain he displayed, albeit through the lens of anger, was clue enough to know the facts of the matter were not pleasant.

❧

The next morning, when Libby entered the living room, Ellen was sitting in the rocking chair with a wadded tissue in her hand. As soon as Libby greeted her, Ellen fled to the kitchen.

Libby pursued her. "What's wrong, Ellen?"

"Nothing. Do you want coffee?"

Libby moved in range of Ellen's face. "You've been crying."

"It's nothing." Ellen filled the coffeemaker with water and measured out the coffee.

"You're always helping me. Let me help you for a change."

Ellen set the coffee can down. "I'm just in the dumps. Today I don't know what I'm doing. Maybe I should go home."

"Or maybe you should just give it more time."

"I don't know."

"Look, I have an idea. Why don't we go to the gym and work out?"

Ellen stared at Libby as if she'd suggested they drive to town naked in a convertible.

"It will do you good."

"You mean my fat figure."

"I mean emotionally."

"I haven't seen the inside of a gym since high school. I wouldn't have the guts. I didn't know you did anything like that."

"I got talked into a membership once. I go when I can. Exercise helps keep the energy moving."

Ellen glanced down at her body. "I can't go like this."

"People of all shapes and sizes go. Come on. It will give you a lift."

"I don't have a membership."

"You can be my guest."

"I don't have any clothes to wear."

"You brought sweatpants, didn't you?"

"Yes, but—"

"No more excuses."

"Don't you have work to do?"

"I'll rearrange my schedule. It won't be a problem. Let me make some phone calls, and we can get going." As she entered her office, Libby thought what a gift it was to be going to the gym. She could sweat out the pent-up energy she had regarding Kipp, because all night long she couldn't get him off her mind.

⁕

Libby drove down the country road to the edge of town, and within ten minutes they were at the Power House Gym. All the way in, Ellen had desperately tried to talk Libby into turning around, but Libby remained adamant that the workout would help Ellen's mood.

After signing Ellen in, Libby prompted her upstairs and instructed her on the treadmill, starting her at a low speed. Ellen complained for the first few minutes, but then Libby noticed the old Ellen returning; she was laughing and joking as usual, back to her old self.

An older woman in yellow sweats was reading on an elliptical machine, and a young man in shorts was working up a sweat on the Stairmaster. Because it was a weekday, the gym was less crowded.

Fifteen minutes later Ellen stopped to get a drink of water and was stooped over a water fountain. A petite, ponytailed woman, dressed in a black shirt and running shorts, came from the weight room and tapped her on the back. The loud, driving music drowned out their voices, but they chatted as if they'd known each other for years. Libby thought she recognized the woman from high school. They finally wandered over to Libby. She got off the treadmill, wiped her forehead with a towel, and waited to be introduced.

"Do you remember Jill Mason?" Ellen said. "She was a year behind us. She was a cheerleader like me, and she married Fred Foster. You remember Fred."

"He was in my English class."

"Boy, you've changed," Jill said. "You look great, Libby. It's Libby isn't it?"

"Yes, and you look great, too."

"I saw you at the reunion," Jill said.

Ellen elbowed Libby and gave her an I-told-you-so look. "How did you like the reunion, Jill?"

"I loved it. I got to see all those seniors, especially my old boyfriend, Kipp. Didn't he look great? I mean, he wears glasses now, but he still has that thick head of hair and those bedroom eyes." Jill fanned her face and blew out a breath. "God, was he a great lover. Oops... I'm telling on myself, what a bad girl I was. Well, we were all doing it back then. That's no secret."

"Tell us more," Ellen said.

This time Ellen received the elbow, but the jab didn't faze her, or Jill.

Jill's eyes took on a dreamy glaze. "We used to park down by the water near the old warehouse. You know, the old lovers' lane. He used to fly me to the moon. He knew just how to press the right buttons." She glanced around, then put her hand to the side of her mouth to shield her next words. "Boy, is he a stud, if you know what I mean." She giggled. "I shouldn't be telling you that, but we'll never see him again. I just can't believe I did it with a famous TV personality. My claim to fame."

"We better finish our workout, right, Ellen?" Libby placed her hands on Ellen's shoulders and directed her toward the treadmill.

"Sure enough. I've heard all I need to know. Nice talking to you, Jill."

"You, too." Jill strode toward the stairs.

With Jill well out of earshot, Ellen laughed so hard she couldn't place one foot in front of the other. Libby refused to look at her, and when Ellen tried to speak to her, Libby hushed her up and realized their workout was finished for the day.

Ellen held it in until they reached the car, then burst out laughing again.

"Why on earth did you egg her on like that? What she said about Kipp was so personal."

"Oh, Libby, lighten up."

"I didn't need to know that about him."

"Just look what you're missing." Ellen burst into another round of laughter.

Libby pinched Ellen's arm.

"At least we know why he broke up with Jill," Ellen said. "With a big mouth like that, nothing is sacred."

On the drive home Ellen jabbered about everything from her marriage to the price of underwear. The workout had done her a world of good. Libby tuned in now and then, but her mind unmercifully drifted to the picture of Kipp and Jill in a car on lovers' lane.

⚬⚬

Over the weekend Kipp wandered aimlessly around the house. He didn't shave, he didn't cook, he didn't see the light of day. For two days he refused to open the blinds. He hadn't gone through a state of depression like this since he'd first learned of Kelly's disappearance. It was unsettling, to say the least.

On Monday he felt like Punxsutawney Phil coming out of his den for the first time. He opened the blinds to the backyard. Though the cloud cover shielded the sunshine, he had to squint to get used to the light.

The initial pain, brought on by Libby's reading, had subsided, and he was more in control. He decided to quit brooding and do something productive.

He sat at the computer, but his stomach wouldn't stop growling. He was hungry for the first time all weekend. He prepared bacon and eggs and sat in front of the TV. The news took too much concentration, something he wasn't ready for.

He flipped through the channels and hit on a talk show in progress. While eating his breakfast, he listened intently to a psychic field questions from the audience about deceased relatives and relationships. The people seeking answers were emotionally affected by the experience; many tears were shed. His original reaction to Libby's reading had been the same.

Call-ins were encouraged, and Kipp was so engrossed in the show that he reached for his cell phone and punched in the 800-number. Once he got through to the studio, he asked how to know if a psychic was for real. The woman gave him a no-nonsense reply. She said, "If psychics are genuine, you'll know. They'll be able to get to the heart of the matter. They'll know how to help you see the truth."

Kipp hung up, more relaxed, and stared at the TV, but his thoughts were on Libby. She definitely got to the heart of the matter; she knew just where he hurt. Could she help him any further? How would he ever know for sure? He'd burned his bridges. Why had he been so stubborn? She said he was stubborn. Those were her words. He thought about the words he'd flung at her: quack and misfit. He had to apologize. If he could swallow his embarrassment and make the call, would she even forgive him?

For the next few days, he struggled with his decision to call. By Thursday night he'd mustered up the courage. Even if he never saw her again, he could at least express regret for his inexcusable behavior. He owed her that.

At eight he grabbed his phone, fully aware that she might hang up on him. Her phone rang four times before the recorded message switched on. He hung up, relieved she hadn't answered. His shirt stuck to his armpits.

He stalled an hour, telling himself he needed to calm down, then tried again. This time someone picked up. When she said hello, his heart skittered in his chest. "This is Kipp, Kipp Reed." The exaggerated pause convinced him she wasn't going to make it easy on him, might even hang up.

"How are you doing, Kipp?"

Her gentle voice reassured him enough to continue, "I wanted to... Could I take you out to dinner tomorrow?" He wondered where that question came from. He hadn't thought of dinner beforehand, but maybe that wasn't such a bad idea.

"I can't. I'm sorry."

Of course she couldn't. Why would she go out with him after the horrible way he'd insulted her?

"I'm going out of town for a workshop."

Maybe it wasn't as bad as he thought. "Can we meet for a drink before you go?"

"I'm leaving tomorrow afternoon."

Something, like an invisible jab in the back, pressed him forward. "I'd really like to meet with you. An apology is in order."

"There's no need for that, really."

"I think there is. I'd like to see you before you go. Could I meet you at the airport?"

A space of time elapsed, and Kipp was sure she was thinking of a way to let him down easy, and then she said, "I can be there early, say twelve-thirty. That should give me enough time to meet with you and get through security. My plane doesn't take off until three-fifteen. If you want, we can meet at Starbucks in the Main Terminal."

"Great. I'll be there."

"And really, there's no need to apologize." She hung up.

Freed from the suffocated feeling that had gripped him, Kipp felt lighter than he had all week. His legs began to relax and weaken. Then reality set in. Tomorrow he and Libby, this strange yet bewitching woman, would be face to face.

⚭

One look in Ellen's impish eyes and Libby immediately regretted having taken the call in the kitchen instead of in her office. Ellen was perched on a chair next to her.

"Was that who I thought it was?"

Libby refused to answer and strode from the room with Ellen on her heels.

"You know, the temperature is heating up again," Ellen said. "And I definitely mean heating up. I think that red sundress would be just perfect."

"And I think you should go to bed and let me get packed."

"Spoilsport." Ellen pranced from the bedroom, then looked in again. "Don't think too hard on what Jill said about Kipp's you-know-what."

Libby gave Ellen a killer look. "I think I liked you better when you were depressed. At least I got a break from this Kipp thing you're so stuck on."

"Something beyond *me* is drawing you two together. Fate or something. You have to admit that. But I get the credit. I thought of it first."

Libby waved her off and closed the door. If Ellen only knew how close she was. Libby and Kipp were being drawn together, but the reason was still unclear. Recalling her resolve not to get involved with anyone, she hoped the purpose of the mystery had nothing to do with her personal life.

⁂

Ellen insisted on driving Libby to the airport. She complimented Libby on her appearance and told her she looked sexy in the white linen slacks and lavender scoop-necked blouse. She instructed Libby not to be aloof, to give Kipp a chance.

Upon entering the terminal, Libby breathed easier. Being away from Ellen's incessant prodding, even if it was the friendly variety, was sheer relief.

Late summer crowds swarmed the airport, and she had to stand in the check-in line longer than usual. It was one o'clock by the time she neared their arranged meeting place.

Travelers were milling around Starbucks, but she didn't see Kipp. She had a sinking feeling he'd left and at the same time wondered why it mattered to her.

Then Kipp appeared from behind two chatty women pulling carry-on luggage. Today he had on a pair of beige slacks, not jeans, and a pale blue shirt with the sleeves rolled halfway up his forearms. She was relieved to see him.

He glanced at her blouse. "You look nice in that color."

"Thanks."

"I thought you weren't coming."

"I thought you'd left."

Libby agreed to accompany him to a nearby eatery where they ordered club sodas and he sat next to her at a table just outside the entrance.

He turned his glass around and around, sliding his thumbs through the condensation before looking at her. "I think this is where I say I'm sorry for being such a jackass."

"I told you, you don't have to apologize."

"Yes, I do. I said some awful things to you. I'm truly sorry. I had no right."

Touched by his sincerity, she placed her hand on his arm, then drew it back. "I accept your apology, but it really isn't necessary. It's normal to get emotional in those situations. I don't take it personally."

He stopped twirling his glass and smiled for the first time since they'd met up. "So, where are you going, if you don't mind me asking?"

"Denver. To a conference on intuition and creativity."

"Are you teaching or participating?"

"Teaching. Actually, there are a number of different topics being presented throughout the weekend. I'm just one of the presenters."

He questioned her more about the conference and she sensed a genuine interest. She asked him about his former job as a national news reporter and all the exotic places it took him. He was surprised she hadn't seen his face on TV.

As if on cue, a tall brunette, dressed in a flight attendant's uniform, came up to their table and asked Kipp for his autograph. He scribbled his name on a napkin and forced a smile. She acted as if she wanted to talk, but glanced at Libby and left.

"You must have been a famous TV personality. I'm sorry I didn't know."

His face turned a rich pink. "That never happens, at least it hasn't in a long time." He offered to buy Libby another club soda, but she refused. "Do you travel a lot?"

"Too much. But it's my bread and butter." She leaned forward, making an effort to peer into his eyes. "Are you going to be okay? After our session…"

"You brought up some things I didn't want to look at. I'd rather not talk about it, if you don't mind."

She sensed his pain was deeper than she'd imagined. Offering him another reading seemed warranted, but she decided to respect his wishes and leave the subject alone. She had a feeling he'd come to her when he was ready.

She glanced at her watch. "The time, it's gone by so fast."

He agreed, and as she pushed her chair away from the table, he stood and said, "Would you have dinner with me?"

He caught her off guard, and she grasped for an answer.

"Please, I feel like I need to make amends for my stupidity."

"There's no need," she said.

"Then let me take you out to dinner, as a friend."

She was about to decline when she stared into his eyes and saw the eyes of a man who had been beaten down, yet a man who showed tremendous strength and resilience. She found herself drawn to him. "All right."

"When will you be back?"

"Sunday night."

"May I pick you up at the airport, that is, if you don't have a ride? We could have a late dinner on the way back to your house."

"That's out of your way, and I don't get in until seven-thirty."

"I don't mind if you don't," he said. "I can stay at a friend's house if it gets too late to drive home. Please."

Reluctantly, she agreed and gave him the arrival information. He walked her to the security checkpoint, and they said their goodbyes. When she glanced back, he was still standing there.

SEVEN

Traffic crowded the freeway, and Kipp hated traveling this time of day, especially on Fridays. He tried to avoid the chaos whenever possible. Keeping his attention on the cars ahead gave him no time for frivolous thoughts.

An hour later the quaint town of Port Anderson and its snug little harbor came into view. He never tired of the scene from the top of the hill: the azure waters, sailboats moored at the marina, houses snuggled among the fir trees across the bay. Here, life was simple and less demanding—qualities that reminded him of the Connecticut town he'd lived in before he moved to the Pacific Northwest.

He approached The Fish and Ale and considered stopping in, but instead continued around the bay and up the winding road.

Entering his house was like a time warp. Its condition didn't match his new outlook on life. It looked like the home of someone who didn't care, someone who had no purpose: garbage on the counters, papers everywhere, clothes strewn over the furniture. What had changed for him? Libby came to mind. Though his week had been miserable, the short time they'd been together at the airport made him feel better.

He changed into shorts and a tee shirt, put on a Rolling Stones CD, and launched the task of cleaning up. The music blared. He was singing along, straightening piles, and was deaf to the phone until the fourth ring. He turned down the volume and caught the phone before it switched to the recorder. But the voice on the line jerked him out of his good mood.

"Have you heard anything?"

At the start of these conversations, her voice was always the same, matter-of-fact, as if she were reading a script.

"Nothing, Tanya."

"Are you doing anything or just lolling around?"

He ran his hand through his hair and prayed for patience. "I've done all I can do for now. There are no leads. When are you going to get off my back?"

She paused until he thought she might have hung up.

"There's nothing to tell you." He knew what to expect next.

"Why can't you do…" Her voice trailed off, and she began sniffling.

He squeezed his eyes shut and counted to ten, but she was still blubbering into the phone. He opened his eyes and sighed. "Don't cry, Tannie. We'll find her." He craved a break from always having to comfort his ex-wife, but he remained even-tempered. "Is there something I can do for you?"

"I'm going to Paris for a shoot, and I'll be gone all week. I'll be at the same hotel as before, and you can reach me there. If there's any news, please call me."

"I will."

The sniffling began again.

"Please, Tannie, don't cry. We'll find her. I know we will."

"I know. I know. But I can't talk anymore. It's all too sad, the divorce, everything. I love you, Kipp."

She hung up without asking anything about him, and their talks always made him lose the desire to do anything else. He shoved the newspapers off the couch and lay down with his hands behind his head.

He loved that woman once. He loved her so much it hurt, but to hear her say she loved him, after what they'd been through—the lies, the betrayals, the loss of their daughter—didn't evoke the same feelings for him. Each time she repeated those words of love, he numbed out.

He felt himself edging toward depression, but the thought of Libby offered him a lifeline. He recalled their airport meeting and remembered the arrangement to pick her up on Sunday. His attraction to her was perplexing, but the attraction was there. She was a contradiction—all business, yet tender-hearted. In comparison to Tanya, Libby was a vacation, something he desperately needed. For a moment he wished he could talk to her. Sunday seemed so far away.

౭ఴఴ

At ten o'clock in the evening Libby entered her hotel room and locked the door. She'd asked for nonsmoking accommodations, but a telltale hint of cigarette smoke lingered from the previous occupant, and she fought the urge to light up. She wondered if that urge would ever go away.

The room was similar to every other hotel room she'd occupied—queen beds, a desk and chair, a place to hang a few items of clothing with an iron tucked away on an upper shelf, and a full bath.

She broke open a package of salt she'd taken from the restaurant downstairs and sprinkled a light dusting around the perimeter of the room to ward off any negative energy. She spritzed lavender oil over her bed.

Drained from the energy of the crowds, she took a hot shower and changed into her nightgown. Although the temperature outside had climbed to one hundred degrees, the air-conditioned meeting rooms had been chilled all day. She looked forward to the warmth of the blankets.

Her workshop had been a success, and another teacher had asked her to co-teach the next day—something unexpected. She welcomed a good night's rest, but when she switched off the light and shut her eyes, Kipp's face appeared to her in the darkness. She hadn't had time to give him a thought until now.

He was going to pick her up at the airport tomorrow night, and she wondered how on earth he'd managed to convince her to go along with such an arrangement. Silently, she pleaded with him to get out of her mind and let her get the rest she needed to get through the next day.

Sleep did come, but very early in the morning she woke with a start. The time was three-thirty. She lay back and reflected on the dream that had awakened her: A man and a woman were strolling along, holding hands with a little girl between them. Then the man and woman started walking in opposite directions, thus pulling the girl's arms. Suddenly, the girl's arms broke off, and her body floated up and away, like a helium balloon.

The dream had to be about Kipp's child. When Libby's dreams were this vivid, they'd wake her to get her attention, and it meant she needed to take action, but she wasn't sure what her guides wanted her to do. Kipp had closed the door on further probing into his situation. As far as she was concerned, it was up to him to seek her help.

She lay still, hoping to get more sleep, but by five o'clock she knew the night was over, so she rose and dressed for the day. Her eyelids were puffed, her nose stuffy, her face drawn, and she dreaded having to teach, even if the class was only two hours long. These conferences were losing their magic, and she looked forward to the end of the day. But the end of the day meant Kipp would be waiting for her at the airport.

A twinge of excitement tickled her, as if some part of her were awakening at the prospect of having a man's attention. Her body was getting too carried away, and she vowed to control the unanticipated desire. Besides, Kipp was giving her a ride out of guilt and embarrassment, not out of interest or affection.

At the end of the conference, Libby spoke to a few friends and teachers and slipped out of the lobby as soon as possible. Not wanting to miss the flight, she packed her bag and caught a cab to the airport extra early.

She boarded on time, but the plane had technical difficulties, and it sat on the runway way beyond take-off time. Because of the busy summer season, every other plane was in service, and she had no opportunity to transfer to another flight. She wondered if Kipp would wait.

By the time the plane left the ground, Libby's blouse clung to her, and beads of moisture littered her brow. All she wanted to do was nap, but the cabin was overpopulated with boisterous teenagers, and the beverage carts clanked in the aisles.

She hadn't eaten since breakfast, and she'd promised to eat with Kipp. Exhausted, she wished she hadn't accepted the dinner invitation.

⚬⚬

Kipp checked the arrival times and discovered Libby's flight was delayed. Estimated arrival time was nine-thirty, and he had over two hours to kill.

Because of the late arrival time, he figured Libby might have chosen to eat earlier, so he went into a restaurant where people were chatting and lingering over meals, but when the waitress brought the menu, he changed his mind, suddenly worried Libby might wait to eat with him. He apologized to the waitress for taking up her time, sought the coffee stand nearby, and bought a blueberry muffin, a latte, and a Sunday paper. He absentmindedly ate his snack and lost himself in the events of the day.

At nine-fifteen he wandered to the area where he'd arranged to meet her. Travelers streamed by him, pulling carry-on bags, with jackets and tote bags draped over their arms. Several teenagers rushed by, causing him to step back out of the way.

All weekend he'd thought about Libby and about what their conversation would be like on the way home. He barely knew her, yet she'd already burrowed into his mind. She was different. She had an unusual and intimidating eccentricity, but he couldn't dismiss her.

At the sight of her up ahead, his thoughts scattered. As she came toward him, she was scanning the area but hadn't spotted him yet. The way she wore her hair, chin-length and curvy, and her choice of clothes, conservative yet bold, made her stand out; she was a classy woman. When he waved to get her attention, she smiled in recognition.

He took her carry-on bag and escorted her toward the exit to the parking garage. "Long day?"

"I'm so sorry you had to wait. If I'd known—"

"Don't worry about it," he said. "But I thought with your gift, you would have foreseen the delay." He hoped she would take that as a joke.

"You'd think so, wouldn't you? Oh well, everything happens for a reason. I might not have accepted your offer if I had known."

They walked down a long aisle of parked cars to get to the Jeep. He opened the door for her and stowed her bag in the backseat. He settled himself in the driver's seat and asked her if she was hungry.

"You know, I'm so tired I think I'd rather skip dinner. Would you mind just taking me home?"

"Of course. Why don't you put the seat back and rest?"

"If you don't mind." She struggled with the lever, but the seat wouldn't budge.

"It gets stuck. Let me help you." He leaned over to reach the handle, but adjusting the seat without touching her was like trying to hang a picture without touching the wall. His arm grazed her legs, and his face was level with her chest.

The airplane smell permeated her clothes, but it couldn't mask the perfumed scent of her body, that heady scent of roses. He felt a rush of energy in his groin and heat in his neck and face. He wasted no time straightening up. Libby put her fingers to her lips and quickly turned toward the side window to suppress a grin.

Leaving the airport, Kipp recovered enough to ask about the conference, and she chatted about the weekend. After they'd merged onto the freeway, she tilted her head back and shut her eyes. He drove a while, asked her another question, but she didn't answer.

He fiddled with the radio until he found the classical station, then lowered the volume. She shifted sideways and leaned her head against the seat, her eyes still closed.

He drove on. At one point he wondered if he wasn't interesting enough for her to stay awake, but he laughed at himself for having such a big ego. The truth was she was exhausted from the day.

Though it was dark inside the car, he couldn't help glancing at her. It had been a long time since he'd been this close to a woman he cared about. Cared about? Were those his thoughts? Wasn't he getting carried away? She hadn't shown the least bit of interest in him, and already he wanted to reach out and touch her, to hold her hand.

Earlier he'd admitted to himself Libby was different. That was true, but maybe he should qualify that and upgrade the remark to interesting. Yes, she was interesting—and so much more.

The traffic had eased up by the time he approached the outskirts of Harbordale. He exited the freeway and followed the meandering road to her wooded retreat. She stirred when he turned onto the gravel road and pulled up to the house. She straightened up and yawned.

Kipp lifted her suitcase from the backseat and walked her to the door. In the glow of the porch light, the lines around her eyes revealed her weariness.

"I was terrible company," she said. "I'm sorry about dinner."

"Asking you to do something after a long weekend wasn't a very smart idea," he said. "My fault."

"Thanks for the ride home." She reached for the doorknob.

"What about a rain check on dinner? How about tomorrow night or some other night this week?"

She hesitated. "I can't really think straight right now."

"I'll call you."

"Thank you for driving me home." She opened the door and slipped inside.

For a moment Kipp remained on the porch, mulling whether or not he'd been rejected. He wasn't sure. On the way down the driveway, he glanced back in time to see the porch light fade out.

Once he turned onto the main road, a hollow feeling washed over him, and going home to an empty house gave him no comfort at all. He reached for his cell phone and headed for Charlie's.

∽

Libby set her bag in the living room and took off her pumps. Today had been one of the longest days of her life. She tiptoed down the hallway in search of some peace and quiet in her nice warm bed. She clicked the bedroom door shut as quietly as possible so as not to wake her friend and snapped on the overhead light. Turning around, she let out a shriek.

On the end of the bed with her arms crossed was Ellen. "You're not going to get by me tonight. Not before I get the Kipp and Libby report."

"God, you scared me. If I wasn't awake before, I am now."

"Good. Start talking." Wrapped in her snuggly robe, sporting her furry slippers, Ellen looked as if she were ready and willing to stay up all night if need be.

"Can't this wait till morning?"

"Hah! That's a good one." She tugged Libby's shirt sleeve until Libby gave in and sat down.

"There's nothing to tell."

"Like I said, that's a good one. Now spill."

Libby relented and told Ellen about the late flight and the drive home.

"How romantic. You even fell asleep."

"It wasn't a date."

"The hell it wasn't. A dinner is a date. So, when is he taking you out again?"

"I don't know. I didn't commit to anything."

Ellen bumped up against Libby. "You didn't even encourage him? You're so exasperating."

"I can't get involved with him even if I wanted to. And I don't want to. He's a client."

"Not anymore."

"I have a feeling he'll be back for another reading, and I don't want any emotional issues to cloud my judgment."

"Why do you think he'll be back for a reading?"

"I can't tell you the details, but I had a dream last night, and I feel that it's very much tied to him, and he'll be back."

"Do you want to know what I see in your future?"

"Would it matter if I said no?"

Ellen took hold of Libby's hand and traced her finger along one of the lines. "This has to do with romance. I think he'll come back, and the two of you will fall madly in love."

Libby pulled her hand free and gave Ellen a push toward the door. "I need sleep, and you need to stop fantasizing."

"I don't care, Libby. I see love in your future. I do. I do. I do." Ellen danced out of the room.

Libby changed into her pajamas and crawled into bed. Her body ached from fatigue, but her mind would not shut down. She replayed the weekend, pondered the interesting people she'd met, and settled her thoughts on Kipp.

She had to confess his presence at the airport uplifted her, and she got a kick out of the embarrassing moment he'd suffered while adjusting her car seat. If she hadn't been so tired, she was certain she would have enjoyed his company. But maybe it was best they hadn't talked. Getting close to Kipp, or any other man for that matter, was not in her future, despite Ellen's delusions.

◌⁓

Charlie answered the door in plaid pajamas and bathrobe, his curly hair disheveled. Kipp apologized for the late hour, and Charlie informed him he didn't have to go into the station early and encouraged him to come in. He picked up the newspapers that were scattered over the couch and offered Kipp a place to sit.

Charlie settled in a recliner that looked as if he slept in it and swung the footrest up. "You like this neck of the woods, don't you? What are you doing here this time of night?"

"I'm sorry I was such an asshole the other day. I wanted to make sure we were still on speaking terms."

"If I remember correctly, we ironed all that out before you left, so cut the crap and tell me why you're really here."

"You could always see through me," Kipp said. "That's what I like about you."

"Want a beer?"

"No, thanks. I'm going to drive home."

"So, what's up?"

"Well…"

"Wait. Let me guess. Does this have anything to do with our Witch of Harbordale High?"

"The one and only."

"Did you take my advice and ask her to help you?" When Kipp wouldn't respond, Charlie slapped the side of his chair. "Damn. You're dating her, aren't you?"

"I wouldn't call it that." Kipp shared the circumstances surrounding his time with Libby and his need to make amends for the insulting remarks he'd aimed at her.

When he finished, a broad grin spread over Charlie's face. "So, what's your next move?"

Kipp stared at Charlie with an innocent look.

"Come on, man," Charlie said. "You hardly know the woman. You could have apologized over the phone. You wouldn't have made the effort to drive her home from the airport if you weren't looking to get to know her better. Shit. Anybody could see that."

"It didn't start out that way. I thought she was a nut, remember?"

"And now?"

"I don't know for sure. The more I'm around her, the more I think she's…"

"What?"

"Like everyone else."

"You mean normal?"

"More than normal. Interesting."

"And what about hot?"

"That, too," Kipp said.

"If you think about it, she's not a raving beauty," Charlie said, "but she's got some kind of thing going for her. I can't put my finger on it."

"Charisma?"

"Something like that."

Kipp sank deeper into the couch and heaved a sigh.

"Are you here to get my approval to go out with her? Like you need some kind of confirmation that it's the right thing?"

"I don't need that."

"It sounds like you want me to say I don't think you're crazy for wanting to date someone like her, being a psychic and all."

"Maybe I do."

"Well, I say go for it, man."

"She's not interested."

"How do you know that?"

"It felt like she was giving me the brush-off after I brought her home. She wouldn't commit to having dinner again. She said something about not being able to think straight and went inside."

"Since when would that ever stop you, my man? You've always got what you wanted with women. They drape themselves all over you."

"Not this one. She's independent."

"So was Tanya."

"Not in the same way," Kipp said. "Tanya was independent as far as her work, but once we laid eyes on each other, she clung to me like—"

"A vampire?"

Kipp knitted his brow. "This woman keeps her distance. I can't read her."

"You're just not used to rejection, pal. You've had it great with women ever since high school. Hell, ever since junior high. You can't stand one woman in the world not throwing herself at you." Charlie's body rocked with laughter.

"She's definitely not throwing herself at me."

"You'd like to move this relationship to the bedroom, and she won't cooperate." Charlie laughed again.

"Screw you, Charlie." Kipp made a move to get up.

"Wait. Sit down, sit down." Charlie motioned with his hand. "I was just having fun with you. You've sure lost your sense of humor these last few years, but I can see you're serious about this one."

"I like being around her, Charlie. I don't know why, but she has this calming effect on me. I haven't had that in a long time. After tonight, I don't know whether to back off or move ahead. I feel like a teenager again."

"Why don't you call her and ask her about Kelly?"

"Absolutely not. I can't go through another gut-wrenching session with her. I know where that leads."

"Quit thinking about yourself and start thinking about your kid."

"Again, screw you." Kipp made another attempt to get up.

"Dammit, Kipp, sit."

Stunned at the acid tone in Charlie's voice, Kipp settled back down.

"I'm sorry, buddy, but you're so pigheaded sometimes. Let's get back on neutral ground. Okay?" He lowered the footrest and braced himself on his thighs, his expression serious. "So, when are you going to give her the big guy?"

Charlie's question caught Kipp off center, and he broke out laughing. "You sonovabitch."

"In all seriousness," Charlie said, "call her in a couple of days."

EIGHT

ON THE DRIVE HOME Kipp considered Charlie's advice about Libby. He liked her looks, her business sense. Even her so-called gift was becoming less threatening. She was definitely a woman he could sink his teeth into—figuratively and literally. But why should he care about a woman who had shown little interest in him?

Also, there was the article to consider. Thinking about her in a romantic sense was not getting the article written. Time marched on, and Jerry would soon be demanding results.

He decided to quit acting like a teenager in heat and put his feelings for Libby aside. Charlie was right: Kipp had never begged a woman to go out with him. He was in no mood to start now. Where the hell was his dignity, for chrissakes?

He shed his clothes on the way to the bedroom and laid his head on the pillow at two in the morning. He drifted into sleep as soon as he closed his eyes, but his sleep was fitful. He tossed and turned, finally waking in a cold sweat. Every bit of warmth in the room had been sucked out.

He felt unsettled, agitated. An inner urge prompted him to sit up. Across the room a swirling image floated in the doorway. He blinked his eyes, squeezed them shut, opened them again. He could have sworn he caught a glimpse of his little girl, heard her wee voice calling out to him.

He threw off the covers and stumbled to the spot where he thought he saw her, his arms outstretched, feeling the space in front of him, trying to connect with whatever had been there. Nothing but the shadows, cast by the fire alarm's tiny red light, hovered in the hallway.

A chill swept up his spine. His body began to tremble uncontrollably. He staggered to the bathroom and leaned into the counter. It took several deep breaths to calm his throbbing heart. The moisture that had formed across his forehead trickled downward into his eyes. He wiped his face with a towel.

Never before had anything like this happened, not even in the days following her disappearance. He could have sworn he saw her shaggy blond hair and pudgy cheeks. He could have sworn. Then his logical mind took over. It was a dream. It had to be a dream.

He changed into a dry tee shirt, put on his glasses. Too shook up to go back to bed, he brewed a pot of coffee and wandered into his study to his computer. Work could always settle him.

He stared at the monitor, hoping to dispel the memory of the last ten minutes. After a few attempts at formulating a sentence, he gave up, parted the curtains, and waited for the morning light. He tried to blank his mind, but he couldn't shake the image of his daughter. His face was wet with tears, and the old questions came rushing back to haunt him. Who had kidnapped her, and why?

He had work to do, and thinking about Kelly wasn't going to bring her back or help him finish his assignment, so he went back to the computer and begged for inspiration to come.

On the edge of his desk was his recorder. He drew it closer, gave it a long look, and finally punched the on button.

Hearing Libby's voice irritated him. He wasn't sure why. He switched off the machine and shoved away from the desk. If he did nothing, he would think about Kelly, but his article had everything to do with Libby.

He felt trapped and cranky.

He powered down the computer, pulled on his jeans, and grabbed a long-sleeved shirt from the closet. He discovered his shoes in the kitchen where he had abandoned them yesterday. He poured a mug of coffee and stepped outside.

He rounded the corner of the house and aimed toward the woods. As he crossed the back lawn, the morning dew splattered his shoes. Early morning held a chill.

He stepped over the low wooden fence and entered the forested path that led to the hill overlooking the harbor. High up on the branch of a fir tree a robin chirped a morning song. A gray squirrel darted in front of him, then dove into the salal bushes. Taking this route early in the day provided him with a clear path and no distractions, a perfect setup to work out his personal problems. It had worked well in the past.

When he broke out of the trees into the clearing, the boats in the marina were already bathed in light. The bay, like a mirror reflecting back to him, rippled lightly near the shoreline. Kipp sat on a boulder at the edge of the hill and took in the view. The sun warmed his upper back. If this couldn't clear his mind, nothing could.

Not a day went by that he didn't think about Kelly, but in order to function, he'd compartmentalized the trauma. He'd constructed stone walls. But since he'd met Libby, those walls were crumbling, and he was starting to feel out of control.

What the hell was the dream about? It was so vivid. It seemed so real. Nothing like this had ever happened before, not until Libby. It was Libby's fault. She must have put some sort of spell on him.

He marched back to the house with renewed determination to put new mortar between the stones and triple them if he had to. He needed to regain control of his mind. He wouldn't let her win.

He spent the rest of the day mowing and raking the lawn and pulling weeds between the rhododendron bushes. The feel of the soft warm earth between his fingers soothed him. By evening he was aching for sleep, too exhausted to think.

He ate half a pizza and took a hot shower, then retreated to the bedroom. The room was stuffy. He opened the window to catch a draft, collapsed into bed, and immediately fell asleep.

It was still dark outside when he woke in another sweat. His first thought was the temperature of the room had increased, but his body was cold and shivery. The sheets were clammy.

He threw off the covers just as the moon peeked around a cloud, throwing light on the windowsill. The curtains fluttered wildly in the breeze. He rose to shut the window, but the branches on the fir tree next to the house were stone-still.

The hairs on the back of his neck quivered, sending a chill down his spine. The electricity in the room was palpable, as was the metallic taste in his mouth. He swore he could smell the scent of baby powder.

A whispery voice called out to him. His back muscles tensed. Again, the voice whispered. He spun around only to see the filmy outline of a blond little girl very much like Kelly. The moment he gasped, the girl vanished.

He squinted, trying to reconstruct her form, wishing desperately to see her again. The reality of the situation hit him square on: it was a ghost.

He switched on the bedroom light, followed by every other light in the house. He reheated the pot of coffee and drank every last drop.

What was happening to him? He analyzed every detail of the last forty-eight hours and concluded whatever it was had to do with Libby. The only person who could help him was Libby. He had no choice. He had to call her.

NINE

L IBBY RAN her palms through the air over her client's body, as if smoothing a sheet but never making contact. With eyes closed, Bert lay on his back, outstretched on the flat surface of a massage table. Libby made several passes before finishing the session.

When she placed her hand on his shoulder and whispered she was finished, he opened his eyes and sighed. "That was wonderful, Libby."

She slipped into the bathroom and rinsed her hands in the cool, purifying water. When she returned, Bert had turned onto his side.

"You're a jewel," he said.

At her desk she made a few notes while he attempted to sit up. "Don't get up too fast." She handed him a glass of water. "How's the knee?"

He edged off the table and distributed his weight on one foot, then the other. "Gone. I think it's gone. How do you do that?"

"I don't do anything," she said. "I'm just a channel for the healing energy that comes through."

"I don't know about any channel, but I'd say you're an angel."

Libby shook her head. "Oh, Bert."

"How much do I owe you?"

"You know the routine."

"Donations don't keep you in food and wine, dear. Why don't you let

me take you out to dinner? Since my knees are better, we could go danc-
ing and have a gay old time."

"Now, Bert, you know I don't date clients." She laced an arm around
his and escorted him from the room.

"Oh, hell, Libby, for once in your life break a rule."

"You sound like my girlfriend."

"Well?"

"You're old enough to be my grandfather."

"I can still make a woman smile." He winked.

When they reached the door, Libby gave him a peck on the cheek.
"Stay well, Bert."

"I'll be back."

"Drive carefully. And thanks for the fresh eggs."

Though the energy work relieved Bert's chronic pain for several weeks,
it hadn't healed it completely, and she could count on his return. He liked
being around her, and she often wondered if the pain was less severe than
he professed it to be.

As a rule, she charged for her services, but Bert was a family friend
and had recently turned eighty. She wanted to help him however she
could. The healing sessions fit the bill.

She wiped the sweat from her brow. The work always heated her, plus
the weather had shifted, and today promised to be a scorcher, with no
cool breeze for relief. She changed into shorts and a summer top and
welcomed the rest of the day to herself.

On Monday she'd had several readings, and she'd blocked out the time
after Bert's appointment. She would have plodded ahead, but an inner
prompting had directed her to take the afternoon off. Ellen was in town
running errands, leaving Libby alone.

She lay on her bed and propped a pillow behind her head. The moment she opened the novel she had been longing to read, the doorbell

rang and rang again. She wondered if Ellen had locked herself out, but the time indicated it was too soon for Ellen's return.

Annoyed by the interruption, she marched into the living room, prepared to fend off a solicitor. She swung the door open, and Kipp greeted her with a scowl that could have knocked her flat. His energy was that intense.

"We need to talk," he said.

He'd surprised her, and the only thought that came to mind was the last thing he'd mentioned when he dropped her off from the airport. "About dinner?"

"This is not about dinner. Can I come in?"

He grabbed hold of the screen handle, but Libby stood her ground. "Normally, people are considerate enough to make an appointment."

"I was going to call, but... I didn't." He rubbed the stubble on his chin. "This is important. We have to talk."

Libby read the confusion behind the anger and stepped away from the door. He declined any refreshment, and they went straight to her office. She wished she'd had time to change into something less revealing because he seemed preoccupied with her appearance, eyeballing her without saying a word.

"Well... did you have something to say to me?"

"Right." His eyes pierced hers with a showdown stare. "I don't know what kind of witchcraft you subscribe to, but whatever it is, I wish you'd back off."

Libby's head lurched backward. "What are you talking about?"

"You're making things happen. Strange things. Things are appearing in my bedroom, and I want it stopped."

"What things?"

"Things," he said. "Ghosts."

"Why don't you sit down and explain to me what's been going on, so I can help you."

"You don't know?"

"I have an idea. I suspect you're opening up."

"Opening up? What the hell does that mean?"

"Please sit down and give me the details."

"I'd rather stand."

"Suit yourself."

Kipp described the experience of the last two nights, including waking up in cold sweats and seeing what he thought were ghosts, glimpses of a little girl. When he finished talking, Libby reached out to touch his arm, but he withdrew.

"Kipp, this is happening to you because you are opening to it. It's the right time. Messages need to come through. I have a feeling about this, but I need your permission to tune in to your energy field."

"Like you did last time I was here? I don't think so."

"Please, I just need to get a picture of what's going on. I won't scare you. I'll only relay what your guides want you to know. I think it will help."

"What guides? What kind of garbage are you feeding me now?"

"Listen to me," she said. "We all have guidance from the other side. Sometimes it's from people we know, perhaps a grandparent. And you're familiar with guardian angels, beings that watch over us?"

"That's all hocus-pocus."

"Angels are with us all the time. They protect us. They serve as messengers of Spirit. They're here to keep us safe on our path."

"That's crap."

"It's the truth," she said. "Haven't you ever had the experience of getting a strong feeling you should avoid something, like going down a certain road, but when you don't heed that feeling, you either get in an accident or there's a long delay? Or the opposite. You do avoid the road, and you hear later that something bad happened there."

"Maybe."

"We all get strong feelings, and we don't know where they come from. Coincidences happen that we can't explain. We have help, otherworldly help."

Kipp dropped his gaze and picked at his nails.

"I can't make you believe it. You'll have to trust me. I can help you."

With everything that had transpired in the last few weeks—the visions, the strong feelings associated with Kipp, his appearances on her doorstep—the reason for all this was close at hand. Determined to keep him here until she found out the truth of the matter, she laid a hand on his arm, calming him.

"What can you do?" His tone was softer, less hostile now.

"I'll ask your guides why this is happening and what you need to know. Trust me."

The silence between them could have been counted in hours, not minutes. Libby studied him. By the way his brows knitted together, his eyes searched the floor, and one hand was massaging the other, she could tell he was agonizing over letting her into his world again, a difficult decision for him.

Finally, his willing eyes met hers, and he sat in the recliner. "But I'm not convinced this will help."

Libby assured him it couldn't hurt and instructed him to lean back in the chair and take several deep breaths. She sat near her desk, synchronized her breathing with his, and prepared to enter a different reality. Her eyelids drifted shut.

Silently, she prayed for the love and protection to increase around them and asked to receive information about Kipp's experience. She waited for the information to come into her field, and in a matter of minutes opened her eyes and said, "These occurrences definitely have to do with the loss of a child. Your guides are trying to get your attention."

"But why?"

Knowing Kipp's reluctance to move ahead with this, she remained cautious. "Do I have your permission to delve deeper?"

"What do you mean?"

"I'd like to understand the circumstances surrounding the loss."

"I can tell you that."

"Would you?"

"I would, but it's painful."

"Can you tell me in general terms? The feeling I got last time you were here was that the child was taken away from you somehow and—"

"She was kidnapped. Is that what you wanted to know? Now you know." He brought his fist to his mouth to hold his emotions in check.

"I'm so sorry." For a moment she could feel his pain, as if it were her own, and her whole body ached with remorse. "Let me give you the information I feel needs to come through concerning this."

"You've already opened up the wound. Do you want to rub salt in it?" Kipp stood. "I don't need to be reminded she's gone. I live it every day."

"Kipp, listen to me. I want you to sit down and let me bring this information through. It needs to be said."

She was so emphatic Kipp eased into the chair.

She closed her eyes and took a deep breath, listening for the words and symbols to come through. "I feel you have been looking for this child a long time, but I see many paths and many roadblocks. You haven't been able to find her, but a new path is opening up to you."

Libby's eyelids fluttered open and she stared at Kipp. "These impressions are coming to you because your guides are trying to get your attention."

"They're doing a good job of it."

"They want you to try again. They want you to look for her again. What have you done so far?"

"This is ridiculous. I've done everything I can. The FBI. The police. I even hired a private investigator. She's on the registry for missing kids.

There are nothing but dead ends."

"How long has she been gone?"

"Two years."

"Well, I'm sensing you need to start again. Not the authorities. You."

"Me." He shook his head, looked down at his hands. "I can't do it." He paused, then met Libby's gaze. "I was finally coming to grips with the fact we'd never find her. I was beginning to accept it. I don't know if I can go through the pain of rehashing everything and not finding her." He raised a hand, shielding his eyes.

Libby didn't know why he was being prodded to retrace his steps, but she trusted the source of these urgings. "All I can tell you is that having those impressions and being led to me wouldn't have happened unless it was important. You are being led to do this."

Kipp looked up, his eyes tearful. "I don't want to get my hopes up. It's too risky."

"Everything good in life is risky. Don't let this opportunity go." She handed him a tissue.

He paused, deep in thought. "I don't know if I can go through this again."

"I understand, and I wouldn't want to push you. Why don't you go home and sleep on it. If you decide to come back, you can ask me whatever you want, and we'll see where it leads."

Kipp struggled to his feet. Libby led him down the hallway to the front door. In the sunlight he looked worse than when he'd arrived—dark circles around his eyes, his face pale and strained.

Her heart went out to him, and she wrapped him in a caring embrace. He lowered his head on her shoulder, his arms limp at his sides. She sensed a heaviness deep within.

She patted his back and told him to think about everything that had been said. He gave her a drooping smile and turned to leave. She watched his car lumber down the road.

TEN

KIPP BLINKED his eyes to stop the burning. He was beyond exhaustion and in no condition to drive all the way to Port Anderson. If he were lucky, he might catch Charlie at home. He could never remember Charlie's ever-changing schedule.

Charlie lived across town from Libby, in the southwest part of town, in a small cul-de-sac of ramblers. In twenty minutes Kipp turned onto Charlie's street and into his driveway and parked next to the Chevy pickup. Kipp dragged his tired body to the front door, was about to knock, when the buzz of a chainsaw revved up from the backyard.

He wandered around the beige house, following the smell of freshly cut wood, and opened the back gate. Inside the yard he had to protect his eyes from flying wood chips. Charlie switched off the saw and pulled off his safety glasses.

"Isn't it a little early to be cutting up wood for the winter?"

"You look like you've been dragged over gravel."

"Yeah, well, I just had a conversation with Libby."

"Come on inside. I'll get us something to eat. I'd offer you a beer, but it might not be a good idea, especially if you're driving home."

"I really shouldn't drink anything."

"I'm going to the station in a little while. I'll make us a sandwich, and you can catch a nap if you want to. You look like you could use one."

Kipp couldn't argue with that.

From the fridge Charlie took out the mustard and a package of ham. "So what did she tell you this time?" He stood at the counter making sandwiches while Kipp told him about the unsettling events leading up to his meeting with Libby, including seeing images of a little girl.

Charlie blew out a whistled breath. "That would be enough to send me packing. Now that you've got my attention, what did our local voodoo gal tell you? Did she say you were going to grow scales?"

"You were the one who encouraged me to see her, if I remember right."

"Well, what did she say?"

"She said a bunch of psychic mumbo jumbo, but the bottom line was she told me I should start looking for Kelly again."

"And are you?"

"I don't know if I have the stomach for it. I don't want to get my hopes up."

Charlie brought the sandwiches to the table. "Listen to her, Kipp. Do it."

"Why do you defend the woman, the 'voodoo gal,' in your own words? You're a black-and-white, by-the-book cop."

"All I know is she helped the police up north find some kids. I think it's worth a try."

When they'd finished their meal, Kipp followed Charlie past a sink of dirty dishes into the living room.

"If you can find the couch, it's yours."

"It's been a year, Charlie. I thought you'd learn to keep a house by now." Kipp removed a pile of wrinkled shirts, a crumpled beer can, and an opened newspaper from the sofa. "Have you heard from Patty and the kids lately?"

"The kids call once in a while. I guess their mom is moving on. She's dating again."

"Too bad."

"I'll get over it. Make yourself comfortable. I'm going out to finish up."

Charlie banged the kitchen door on his way outside to finish his project, and Kipp slipped off his shoes and lay on the couch. He heard the chainsaw start up, then drifted into sleep. Later on, he vaguely heard the clicking sound of the front door, then silence again.

Libby populated his inner space—on her porch, at the airport, in his car. But what he remembered last before he was stirred awake were the eyes of his daughter.

He sat up alarmed. "What the…" Disoriented, he scanned the room and glanced at the window—Charlie's house, still daylight. He checked his watch. It was four in the afternoon. He'd only slept three hours, but it seemed like days. He ran his hand over his jaw and realized it had been a while since he'd shaved.

Maybe it was the rest, maybe it was his talk with Charlie, or maybe it was Kelly's pleading eyes, but something had shifted in Kipp. He remembered the dream he'd had just before waking up: Kelly was on his lap, and he was reading her a story about a princess lost in a meadow. Kelly begged him to find her.

The confusion had cleared. Kipp knew what he had to do. He used Charlie's phone and punched in Libby's number. No one answered.

When he returned from the bathroom, he grabbed the phone to call her again, but thought better of it. He remembered his reflection in the bathroom mirror. His hair was greasy, his face unshaven to the point of looking dirty. He looked like a bear coming out of a winter's cave. First things first.

❧

Every table was taken at the Harbor Restaurant, Harbordale's premier eating establishment. Libby and Ellen were dining near a window that provided them with a view of the inlet at sunset. Wispy clouds were bathed in pink, and the pinks and deep blues of the sunset mirrored the colors of the restaurant's décor.

The waitress, a young woman dressed in uniform black, brought Ellen a glass of the house wine, a dry Chardonnay, and Libby a glass of water with a lemon wedge. Before taking her first sip, Libby clinked glasses with Ellen.

"To two gorgeous women out on the town," Ellen said.

"I'm glad I took a nap after Kipp left, or I wouldn't look so great."

"He really affects you, doesn't he? Did you ever wonder why that is?"

"He's going through a difficult time, and he's a client. That's nothing new."

"But I've never seen you this frazzled with any other client. I mean, you have to take a shower and nap after he leaves."

Libby sipped her water without commenting.

"He's getting under your skin, isn't he?"

"I'm just being empathetic. That's my job."

Ellen leaned back and folded her arms. "Libby McGraw, it's more than that. Some of your clients wait weeks to talk to you. Not Kipp, and you don't even charge him." She straightened her posture, her attention suddenly drawn away from Libby. "There's Charlie Bender at the hostess station."

Libby twisted around to get a better look. When she turned back, Ellen was waving Charlie over. "What are you doing?"

"I want to see him up close and personal. Doesn't he look like that hunky Randy Quaid?"

"You and your obsession with movie stars."

Charlie sauntered up to their table.

"You shaking down this place?" Ellen said.

"Just picking up an order."

"Why don't you join us?" Ellen offered and was the recipient of a scorching look from Libby.

"No can do. I've got to get back to the station."

"You're eating pretty high and mighty tonight," Ellen said.

"Expensive burgers. So, what are you doing in town?"

"I'm staying with Libby for a while. Marital problems."

"I know all about that."

"Oh?"

"Patty and I split about a year ago."

"I didn't see her at the reunion, but I didn't want to pry. I'm sorry to hear that," Ellen said.

"Just one of those things. Happens to the best of us."

"You know Libby, don't you?"

Charlie turned to Libby. "You're the gal that's got my buddy all tied up in knots."

"Your buddy?"

"Kipp Reed."

Libby was at a loss for words but was saved by the hostess calling Charlie's name.

"Got to go. Nice to see you ladies." Charlie focused his full attention on Libby. "Take good care of my friend. He needs your help."

Ellen followed his every movement as he strolled past the other tables back to the hostess. "God, he's sexy."

"You never quit, do you?"

"If I weren't married… Charlie was always the guy you could count on in high school. Mr. Responsible. I had to marry Mr. Life-of-the-Party."

The waitress brought a salmon dinner for Libby and seafood fettuccine for Ellen.

Ellen placed a napkin in her lap. "How come Charlie gets to know Kipp's problems, and I, your best friend, am kept in the dark?"

"That's Kipp's choice. It's not up to me to say anything. You know that."

"I was just kidding," Ellen said. "You're always so serious, Libby.

Where's your sense of humor? I know you've had a difficult time these last few years, but I, on the other hand, am always cracking jokes. I wonder why that is? I guess for me it's easier to hide behind all the laughs."

Libby studied Ellen's eyes. "You're not happy here, are you?"

"Of course I am."

"I mean, away from Mel."

"It shows, huh?" Ellen laid her fork down. "Stupid, aren't I?"

"Not stupid. Lonesome."

"I have a confession to make."

By the glimmer of hope in Ellen's eyes, Libby didn't have to be psychic to know what was coming next.

"I'm thinking about trying again."

"So soon?"

"I miss the bastard."

A sad feeling lodged in Libby's chest. She hated to think Ellen might fall into the same old trap of accepting a life filled with betrayals.

"I've just decided. I'm going to surprise him." Ellen's eyes lit up even more, as if she were thinking of Christmas to come and anticipating all the gifts. "I'm going to go home on Thursday afternoon, cook him a sexy meal, bring out the candles and wine. When he gets home from work, who knows? Maybe we won't even need dinner."

"I thought you never knew from one day to the next when he was coming home."

"He always comes home on Thursdays to rest up for his Friday night poker game. But if I get him into bed, maybe he'll forget about cards."

"Do you really think that's wise?"

"I know it's a long shot. But I have to do something."

❧

Kipp rinsed the flecks of hair down the drain and returned the electric shaver to the top drawer next to the sink. He knew Charlie wouldn't mind him borrowing the shaver. After all, he had made a disparaging remark about Kipp's appearance and any improvement would justify its use.

He ran his fingers through his shaggy mane. He needed a haircut. He'd needed one a month ago, but lately it hadn't been a priority.

Charlie's mouthwash tasted as sharp as vinegar. He gargled and gladly spit out the bitter liquid.

He towel-dried his hair, threw the towel in the hamper, and straightened up the bathroom, putting it in better order than he'd found it. Corners of the bathtub were growing dark mold, but he would leave the deeper cleaning for Charlie.

He checked his appearance in the mirror one last time. He looked better than he had in the last two days.

He slipped on his jeans and tee shirt and tried pressing out the wrinkles with both hands. If it weren't for Charlie's large size, he would have borrowed a clean shirt. What he had on would have to do.

In the living room he strapped on his watch. It was getting late, and he considered going home and calling in the morning. But changing his mind by morning was a real possibility, and he had to reach out now or forget about it altogether. He punched in Libby's number. This time she answered.

"Is this a bad time?"

"Kipp? What can I do for you?"

"I've made a decision. I'd like to see you tonight. Am I too late?"

"No, but it will be too late by the time you drive down here, plus I have a full day tomorrow."

"I'm in Harbordale, and I can be there in fifteen minutes. Please, Libby. I'm not sure how I'll feel by tomorrow."

"All right."

Kipp picked up his wallet and keys and locked Charlie's door on his way out. He took a shortcut to Libby's, avoiding the main part of town, cutting off five minutes, but the shadows of the forest were deepening by the time he knocked on her door.

Ellen answered, grinning. "As the world turns... Hello, Kipp."

As he entered the house, he forced a smile and hoped his face didn't register the disappointment he felt that Libby was not alone. "I didn't know Libby had company," he said.

Then Libby came into the room, decked out in a casual cotton skirt and blouse.

"Don't mind me," Ellen said. "You two go have your talk."

Kipp frowned at Libby, but she seemed to take him and Ellen being there at the same time in stride and motioned him toward her office. After she closed the door, he couldn't hide his irritation. "How much does Ellen know?"

"Don't worry. She knows people who come to see me are dealing with personal problems, but that's the extent of it. She doesn't know any details, so you can rest easy. Sit down and tell me what you've decided."

They took their respective chairs, and Kipp opened the conversation. "I've given it a lot of thought. In fact, I had another dream about her. I'll do it. I want to look for my daughter. I'm willing to try again. Just tell me what to do, where to start. You must think she's alive."

"I can't say that for sure. I don't know what you'll find. All I know is your guides want you to keep looking."

"I have to admit I'm not buying everything you're telling me about these so-called guides. But I want my daughter back, and I'll do anything to make that happen."

"You have to be prepared for any outcome. Are you willing to take that chance?"

Kipp's face slackened, as if he hadn't thought of the outcome being anything but positive. "I have to find her, Libby, no matter what. I have to have closure in whatever form that takes. Right now I have nothing."

"Then why don't you sit back and we'll have a look."

Kipp ignored her, instead sitting forward on the edge of his seat with his arms resting on his thighs, and waited for her to finish her prayer.

"I'll ask your guides directly what you need to know to begin your search." Libby's eyes moved from side to side behind closed lids and remained closed as she issued a response. "They're saying to start from the beginning, from where she was taken."

"She was taken from my home in Connecticut. I don't own it anymore."

"Not your house. The town where you lived."

"Where? Where in the town?"

"There was something left behind. A toy of some sort."

"Something left behind?"

"Something was missed."

"What something?"

"The police missed it."

"They looked at everything of hers."

"Who's the older woman with your daughter? Did she have a grand-mother nearby?"

"Tanya doesn't have anyone. My mother lives in Florida."

"An older woman close to your daughter. I see the calendar changing from month to month. That indicates to me she was with your daughter frequently."

"Mrs. Crowley. The woman who helped me take care of Kelly after Tanya and I divorced."

"Ask Mrs. Crowley."

"The police questioned her extensively."

Libby opened her eyes and stared at Kipp.

"Do you think she's involved?" he said.

"I don't sense that, but it's not clear at this point. Just talk to her."

The heat in Kipp's body rose along with his frustration. "What the hell does this have to do with anything? I don't know why I even came."

"Kipp." Libby's eyes bore into him.

"All right. All right. I'll call her tomorrow."

"No. It's important that you talk to her face to face."

"Jesus, Libby, what's the point of all this?"

Libby stood abruptly. "You asked for my help. You'll have to trust what's coming through."

Kipp shot up from the chair. "You mean, trust this mumbo jumbo?"

Libby strode from the room. "You can do what you want."

Kipp shadowed her. "What do I pay you for your time?"

Libby spun around, causing him to stop short. "I don't take money from skeptics." Her remark silenced him.

Before he walked through the doorway, Libby grabbed hold of his arm. Instead of the eyes of a stone-cold businesswoman, he saw the eyes of a woman, soft and loving. "Follow your heart," she said.

The change in her manner stunned him, but in that moment, with her hand touching him, he longed to embrace her and to be comforted by her. She let go, and he snapped out of the dream. When he reached his car, he glanced back for reassurance, but she'd already disappeared inside.

On the drive back to Port Anderson, he considered her advice. Though he hardly comprehended her crazy symbols and psychic messages, in his heart he knew she was right. When he arrived home, he made arrangements to fly to New York the next day.

ELEVEN

On a last-minute whim Kipp booked a room at the Marriott Hotel for one night. By the time his plane landed at LaGuardia and he'd rented a car, it was close to midnight. He checked in and took the elevator to the third floor. Though the room was just another standard hotel room, it was decorated in cheery yellows and reds, and its cushy mattress and down pillows gave him hope for a restful night's sleep.

Traveling had always been an adventure, but planes, hotels, and meals in every country of the world held none of the excitement it had in the past. Now, even a trip across the states was an imposition, and he wanted to be done with his mission and back in Port Anderson as soon as possible.

He lay on the bed, but fatigue couldn't counteract an active mind. For help in falling asleep, he turned on the TV and concentrated on the drone of the news anchor. Sometime during the night he woke to the spattering of machine gun fire on the twenty-four-hour news channel, but closed his eyes again and drifted in and out of sleep.

The next morning he was tired, but hyped at the same time. He made it a point to leave the hotel early, so he could be on the Hutchinson River Parkway by nine o'clock. Within two hours he'd turned off I-95 in Connecticut and traveled over secondary roads until he came to the sign for

Old Town, population 2,039.

He turned left toward the town he'd lived in two years ago and soon neared the old four-bedroom farmhouse where he and Tanya had fled after their daughter was born. Oak and birch trees lined the long, meandering driveway to the house, and he couldn't tell if she was there. When they'd split up, she wanted the property, even though most of the year she occupied their New York City apartment.

Farther ahead was the two-story house he and their daughter had moved into. After the divorce, Kipp quit his reporting job to care for Kelly, a heartfelt decision and the logical one, considering Tanya's love of the high life and her lack of maternal instincts. A mother who'd deserted her when she was young was no role model for Tanya.

He and Kelly lived comfortably on his income as a freelance writer and a small trust fund that had been set up by his parents when he was younger. Tanya made considerably more money than he did, and when he agreed to care for Kelly, she agreed to pay child support. He bought his house with the money he received for his share of the farmhouse. He rarely traveled beyond the picket fence, save for that fateful day.

As the car passed by, his throat caught with barely a swallow. There, in the shadows, someone had abducted Kelly.

The current owner's rosy-faced boy darted across the yard, and for a split second Kipp conjured up a scene from the past: an image of Kelly waddling across the grass, arms outstretched. The twisting in his gut was overwhelming, and he turned his gaze toward the road.

He wiped away the tears. How many times had he been racked with guilt, wondering if he should have kept the house in case whoever took her brought her back? Or what if one day she returned only to find strangers where her father once lived? Such thoughts were irrational. The police assured him he would be contacted, so he left the house with the painful memories, knowing that Tanya had the old farmhouse and still had ties to the community.

Just seeing the yellow house with the white shutters brought up all the guilt and anguish. He cursed Libby for sending him on this agonizing and, more than likely, fruitless journey. Nevertheless, he continued on.

In front of Harvey's Grocery Store he got out of the car, stretched his legs, and breathed in the fresh country air. He sidestepped around a woman in the doorway and looked up to see a man with a rounded belly, gray crew cut, narrow hawk-like eyes, and a broad thin-lipped smile.

The man came around the counter and grasped Kipp's shoulder. "Kipp Reed. If it isn't Kipp Reed. Never thought you'd come back to this old place."

"Hello, Harvey. Glad to see you're still here."

"Be here till I die." He scooted back around the corner. "Say, did they ever find your little girl?"

The pain in Kipp's gut was inching back. "No. Not yet."

"Sorry to hear that. I see the missus every once in a while. She picks up a few things now and then. Never says much. Pity you two couldn't work it out."

"Listen, Harvey, I'm looking for Mrs. Crowley. Is she still on Adams Street?"

"What business you got with her?"

"No business. I was just passing through, and I wanted to say hello."

"She hasn't been too well since you left. Still blames herself for everything. Not being watchful and all. Doesn't watch kids anymore."

"Maybe she'd feel better if I talked to her."

"Worth a try. You want me to close up and go with you?"

"I think I should go alone. But thanks for the offer."

Before leaving, Kipp rounded up bottled water and a newspaper. The air outside had a sticky feel to it; the day promised to be hot and muggy. He rolled down the car window to let the morning breeze cool the inside.

Main Street looked like a Norman Rockwell painting. Not much had changed over the years. Many of the businesses were still family-owned: Del's Hardware, Old Town Clothing, Harvey's Grocery Store. None of the superstores had found their way to Old Town yet. The pace was slower than in the larger New England towns, and that was what drew Kipp and Tanya here in the first place, although once the newness wore off, it hadn't suited Tanya.

He turned onto Adams Street and pulled up to the curb in front of Mrs. Crowley's house. Bare flower beds and the grass, tall and straw-like, gave the yard a neglected look. The curtains were drawn, and he considered turning around, but Libby's words rang out like a reminder: follow your heart. His heart had brought him this far, and he resolved to go through with the plan that she'd laid out.

Kipp straightened his glasses and knocked on the door several times. He was about to give up when a corner of the curtain rustled.

The door opened a slit, then swung wide. A plump woman in an apron-covered housedress, her graying hair matted in places, her pallid skin flecked with age spots, smiled at him in anticipation. "Did you find her?" When he shook his head, her smile faded to a frown.

"May I come in?"

"Of course, Mr. Reed, of course. Please come in." She opened the curtains and dusted a Queen Anne chair with her opened palm. "Please sit down. Would you like some coffee? I can make coffee."

"No thanks. I can't stay long."

She fussed with papers and magazines, trying to straighten them into neat piles, pushed two dirty cups and a glass to the end of the coffee table away from Kipp. The dark rug was dappled in light, showing numerous specks of lint. The room smelled of camphor. Except for the happy sounds of a caged bird, cheeping and gurgling in the adjoining room, the house felt weighty and lifeless.

When she finished her flurry of activity and settled on the end of the brown paisley couch, he noticed the tremor in her left hand. "How have you been, Mrs. Crowley?"

"I've had good days and bad days, but I'm all right." Her stab at optimism was brave, but her weary eyes told the honest truth.

He asked her about the weather and her family. After they'd chatted for a while, he decided to broach the subject of Kelly. "Harvey tells me you aren't taking care of children anymore. I know how much you liked to do that."

"I couldn't, you know. Not after…" She lowered her gaze.

She was in his house with Kelly, and not as vigilant as she should have been. But he should never have left Kelly with a sitter while he traipsed around Washington, D.C., hunting down leads for a story he was working on.

He leaned forward to look into her eyes. "It wasn't your fault."

"I lay down for just a minute. She was napping. I just don't understand."

"Mrs. Crowley, don't blame yourself."

"They must have come from the alley behind your house. They snuck up on me. I didn't see any cars, or I would have called the police." She was crumpling her apron, agitated and anxious.

"You don't have to convince me. I didn't come here to upset you or to question you about that day."

"I know, but—"

"I need your help."

She looked up, curious. "My help?"

Kipp hesitated, thinking about how to phrase the question without distressing her any further. "I wondered if Kelly left anything with you to keep for her while she's away, something you might have of hers."

She stared at Kipp, her eyes widening.

"Mrs. Crowley? Did she leave something with you?"

"What do you mean?"

"Did she leave any toys with you? Anything you might have forgotten to tell me?"

She twisted the corner of her apron into a wrinkled mass. "Well, I don't know, Mr. Reed. I mean, maybe."

Encouraged, Kipp put his hand on hers to stop her fidgeting. "Please. It's important. If you have something of Kelly's, I need to know. I promise I won't be angry."

She studied his face, perhaps measuring his sincerity. She abruptly left the room and returned holding a six-inch stuffed bear with a red ribbon around its neck. She laid the bear in Kipp's lap. He swallowed hard to suppress the surge of emotion that welled up in him. The tattered brown bear was a toy he'd won at a carnival.

The memories of walking on sawdust and carrying Kelly around with her lips blue from cotton candy, amidst the crowds and calliope music, began rolling in, swelling his already bursting heart. Mrs. Crowley's raspy voice stopped the flow of images.

"I'm sorry, Mr. Reed. I know I shouldn't have kept it. But it reminded me of Kelly. I wanted something to remind me of her. How did you know?" She squeezed her eyes shut, forcing back tears.

Kipp could have used the comfort himself, but he moved to the couch and held her hand. He would never get over the loss of his daughter, but this dear, sweet lady, the last person to see Kelly, would for the rest of her life always share the blame with him.

"I'm not angry with you," he said. "In fact, I think it was very thoughtful of you to hold onto this bear for her. I want you to know that I'm going to look for her myself, and hopefully this toy will help me find her. May I take it with me?"

"Oh, yes, you take it. You should have it."

Kipp rose to leave, and she walked him to the door.

"You know, Mrs. Crowley, I think you should take care of children again. You were a very good sitter, and what happened wasn't your fault." He gave her a warm hug. "When I find Kelly, we'll come back to visit you."

"Please find her, Mr. Reed," she said softly and hurried inside and closed the door.

Kipp set the bear on the passenger seat and glanced at it from time to time on the drive out of town. As he passed the two-story house, he had a renewed sense of hope because just as Libby predicted, he was led to Kelly's toy. In his enthusiasm he thought he might stop at the farmhouse to see if Tanya was there, but then he remembered she was in Paris.

He drove on to the main highway, anticipating getting on the plane and back to Libby, but traffic slowing to a crawl and flashing lights up ahead dashed his hopes of leaving early. He'd have to fly out the next day.

He returned his rental car and called the hotel. The clerk told him he was lucky it wasn't a Friday and booked him a room for the night. He rearranged his flight and hopped on the hotel's shuttle.

His room was on the sixth floor. It had the same layout as his former room but faced the courtyard.

He lay on the bed and held the bear to his cheek, hoping to catch a hint of his daughter, the sugary clean baby scent he remembered. He held the bear next to his heart. His eyes blurred with tears. The day had been emotionally draining, but touching the bear made him feel closer to Kelly than he had in a long time. He ached to find her.

He removed his glasses and dried his eyes. He felt the need to nap, but the neurons in his brain were clicking away like the gears in a clock.

He tucked his hands behind his head and skimmed the events of the last few weeks: being led to Libby, her uncanny way of knowing things about him, her pushing him to look for his daughter, his coming to Connecticut and finding the toy as she predicted.

What else was in store for him? Was he really being led to his daughter? He didn't want to get his hopes up, but how could he not after everything that had transpired so far.

For the first time in months an excitement surged in him, and he wished he had someone to share his enthusiasm. Libby was his first choice, but then he thought of Tanya and wondered if the time was right to let her know he was active again in his search for their daughter; but Tanya was in Paris.

He'd leave a message for Tanya, and because of the time difference he'd wait to call Libby in the evening.

His gurgling stomach reminded him he hadn't eaten since morning. He'd take a short nap and then get some food and make the calls.

T W E L V E

O N THE WAY up I-5 Ellen sang along with the radio and glanced at herself in the rearview mirror. She'd taken considerable time primping and getting ready for the evening, and she considered herself especially foxy today.

Heavy clouds obstructed her view of the Cascade foothills from the highway. Sunshine would have made the day perfect, but the lack of sun and the blocked view of the mountains did nothing to dampen her spirits.

She exited the freeway and drove through the valley. She'd be home in fifteen minutes. She stopped at the market and bought wine and two sirloin steaks.

She loved the two-story house they'd lived in for the past fourteen years. Even though Mel traveled a lot, she'd made a comfortable nest for herself and the children. The neighborhood had held up over the years, nothing upscale, but a good solid community of homes, each unique from one another.

As she neared the suburban community, she experienced the same giddy feeling she'd had in the first years of her marriage before the children came, before Mel fell into his destructive habits. Back then he never brought her gifts or flowers, no show of affection on his part, but their bedroom always glowed with the aftermath of sex.

Mel's Taurus was in the driveway, and she wondered if he had come home for a late lunch or if he had taken ill. She thought better of parking behind his car, in the event he had to go back to work, and pulled up behind the old beater Jason used whenever he graced them with his presence.

Mel's being home stirred her imagination of what might transpire in the next few minutes, and she walked toward the house as if she were floating on clouds.

Hoping to surprise him, she carefully opened the side door and set her purse and groceries on the kitchen counter. With one hand against the frame and the other on the doorknob, she latched the door without making a sound.

She listened for footsteps or water running. Except for his car parked outside and the unlocked door, she would have guessed no one was home. She assumed he was taking a sick day. She slipped off her shoes and tiptoed through the living room and up the stairs to the second floor, careful to avoid the creaky steps in case he was asleep.

Halfway down the hallway she heard thumping and moaning sounds. Her first thought was that poor sick Mel was writhing in pain, but then she heard a high-pitched squeal.

By the time she reached the master bedroom, her heart was racing ahead of her and blood pounded in her temples. In the doorway she froze, her mind desperately trying to catch up with her eyes.

Viewing the gyrating mass of covers, she shook herself conscious and threw the door wide open, crashing it into the wall. A woman screamed. Ellen screamed. And Mel toppled to the floor.

He scrambled to his feet and wheeled around, looking for his shorts. Once he found them, he hopped from one foot to the other, tugging them on, looking to Ellen like one big blob. "Ellen, wait!" She turned on her heels and stormed out with Mel carrying his shoes and clothes, puffing behind her.

In the living room she grabbed the first object she set her eyes on—a framed photo from the piano top—and hurled it at Mel, barely missing the side of his head as he ducked out of the way. The picture smashed into the wall, shattering the glass.

"You could have killed me," he bellowed.

"I wish I had!" Stationed in the middle of the room, she glared at him, her body tense with rage.

Mel huffed and grumbled while he dressed in his slacks and shirt and wrestled with his shoes and socks. His face was beet red. "It's not what it looks like."

"What is it, if it isn't you humping another woman in my bed?"

"She's a two-bit tramp."

"She's your secretary, Mel, and you had her in our bed. In my bed. You bastard!"

The woman, with velvet black hair and a dress that clung to her like spandex, slunk down the stairs. Ellen watched Mel follow her with his eyes as she glided through the room and out the door.

Draping his tie around his neck, he inched toward the foyer. "Listen, Ellen, I have to take her back to the office. I'll be home at six, and we'll go out to dinner and straighten things out."

In her numbed state, Ellen didn't even hear the door close. She stumbled into the kitchen and peeked out the window to watch Mel backing out. He had an arm draped over the woman's shoulder. In full view of the neighbors, he stopped the car and kissed her on the cheek.

Ellen bowed over the sink and wailed like a siren, her tears, black from mascara, pooling on the stainless steel surface. After she'd cried herself out, she soaked a dishtowel in cool water and wiped her face clean of the makeup she'd put on for Mel.

She took a ragged breath in. She knew what she had to do.

She tossed the steaks in the garbage and staggered upstairs to the bedroom. The mound of sheets and the unbearably cheap perfume made her want to wretch. She would not stay in this house, not when Mel had contaminated it with another woman.

She tracked down the extra suitcases in Jason's closet and filled them with clothes, shoes, and every memento she could squeeze in. She trekked out to the car twice, dragging the luggage with her and filling the trunk. Back inside, she took the latest photo of her kids off the wall, the one they'd surprised her with on her birthday, and made sure she had a credit card and some blank checks.

Driving down the freeway, she pictured Mel in bed with his secretary. All these years she'd made excuses for his horrible behavior: He wasn't loved as a child. He hated himself and acted out. He needed understanding.

Then there were her faults to consider: She wasn't the best wife. She was too fat and ugly for him. She was too involved with the children.

Whatever might be wrong with her, his secretary in their bed was the last straw. Forget the excuses. She was determined to make the break.

⌘

Ellen, her eyes red-rimmed and glassy, her dress splattered with mascara, slumped in Libby's arms. "Can I stay here?"

"Of course, you can."

"You were right, Libby. You warned me not to go. But no, I had to see for myself. I had to have my face rubbed in it." She followed Libby inside and told her everything about discovering Mel with his latest fling.

Hearing this most recent story of betrayal, Libby was unfazed. All day long, an ominous feeling had haunted her, keeping her in a state of agitation.

She ran a lavender bath, lit a candle, and left Ellen in a steaming tub with a Hawaiian CD for background music. By the time Ellen wandered into the kitchen, snug in her bathrobe, dinner was on the table and the delicious smell of garlic and basil hung in the air.

Ellen pushed her pasta around the plate and made a few twirls. "I can't say I didn't have a clue. I just feel so stupid."

"You're not stupid, Ellen. You're a wife who loves her husband and wants to believe in him."

Ellen shrugged and laid the fork aside. "You know what? I can't get that picture out of my mind. Mel's tank of a body humping that skin-and-bones woman. I kept thinking he was going to grind her into bonemeal. That's what a sick mind I have."

Libby burst into laughter.

Ellen joined in until tears streamed down her cheeks and she slumped over her plate. "I don't understand myself. It's not like he's a huge prize with his fat belly and bald head." She sniffled and wiped away the tears. "But he's *my* fat man."

Libby walked around the table and squeezed Ellen's shoulders. "I'm here for you, Ellen. I'm not going anywhere."

THIRTEEN

INSTEAD OF a quick nap, Kipp slept well into the evening; the jet lag had caught up with him. He called Tanya, expecting her message service to pick up, but he was surprised to hear the syrupy, Southern voice that used to melt him from the inside out.

"I thought you were in Paris," he said.

"Kipp, is that you, sweetie?"

"What are you doing in the city?"

"The shoot ended earlier than we thought. I got home late last night."

"I was going to leave you a message." Considering who he was dealing with, he had momentary thoughts about not confessing where he was. "I'm at LaGuardia."

"You're in town? Wonderful. I want to see you."

"We can talk on the phone. We really don't need to meet in person."

"Not when you're this close. Why are you here? Business?"

"Something like that."

"Where are you? At the airport? A hotel?"

"I'm at the Airport Marriott."

"I can catch a cab and be there in minutes."

"That's not a good idea. I just—"

"Wait for me." She ended the call.

As luck would have it, she had to be home. Since he was in the neighborhood, he supposed seeing her was the right thing to do. Determined to stay in control of the situation, he tucked the bear in his carry-on bag. If she saw it, she'd want it, even though she had all of Kelly's other toys.

Tanya had appeared to be so distraught after Kelly's disappearance he'd boxed up and given her everything. Keeping Kelly's belongings turned out to be Tanya's way of dealing with the guilt of being indifferent to her own child.

But he wanted the bear: his connection to his daughter and to Libby. When he explained everything to Tanya, he would skirt around the issue of the bear.

While he waited, he hung up his clothes and straightened the bedcovers. He hadn't eaten and could use going out to dinner as an excuse to talk to Tanya on neutral ground. After all this time, he still didn't trust himself with his incredibly sexy ex-wife.

Thirty minutes later he answered the door to her. He wasn't prepared for the blast of beauty that greeted him. He hadn't been this close to her in a very long time. Aging agreed with her, if judged by the modeling jobs that kept coming to her at a healthy pace. The world of fashion loved her.

She smiled the tempting smile that had captivated him the first time they met at a party given by one of his journalist friends. Her gold-spun hair, hugging porcelain skin, touched the top of her shoulders. Her hazel eyes, which changed to gray depending on the color of her mood, flashed behind lush black lashes.

He simply wasn't prepared for this.

She threw her arms around him, squeezing her body against his, and whispered in his ear, "Let's make love."

He felt a surge in his lower body, a rush he hadn't experienced since the car ride with Libby, but he peeled her arms away and backed into the room.

She took off a light jacket, revealing a form-fitting tank top tucked into tight white jeans. She kicked off her sandals, revealing her tiny narrow feet—the feet he so often rubbed warm on cold winter nights. Sitting on the edge of the bed, she patted the space next to her. Mesmerized, he sat down, his leg butting against hers.

"I've missed you, lover." She massaged his thigh, pressed the top of his knee and stopped at the crease in his slacks. "What did you want to talk about?"

Kipp lifted her hand off his leg and stood because it was the only way to break the spell of her touch. "I've decided to look for Kelly again. I mean, seriously looking."

"You're going to look for our daughter?" She stared at him, puzzled, letting the words sink in. "Where, how?"

Without thinking it through, he told her he'd gone to a psychic. "This person I went to has been successful in helping the police find missing children."

"A psychic? What a stupid thing to do."

"At first I didn't understand it myself."

"Then why would you even go to one?"

Tanya always had a way of making him question himself; she was good at it. The doubts started to creep in, but then he remembered the toy bear.

"What does that have to do with your being here?" she said.

"The psychic told me to go back to Old Town and see Mrs. Crowley."

"What for?"

"Just to talk to her."

"Did that make any difference?"

Not sure that it had and not wishing to reveal the part about the bear, he shook his head.

Tanya rose and embraced Kipp. "I love that you're going to look for

Kelly, but don't waste your time with people who just take your money to tell you things you want to hear. Isn't there anything else you can do?"

Deflated, Kipp sat slumped on the side of the bed with his hands cushioned between his legs and withdrew into himself. Tanya leaned over and put her arms around his neck, her breasts fully in front of him.

"I should call you a cab before it gets too late," he said.

She sat beside him and ran her fingers up and down his arm. "I can't go home. I loaned my apartment to a friend for the night. I'll have to stay here with you, if you don't mind."

"Don't expect anything from me," he said, although the lemony scent of her perfume flooded him with memories of all the times they'd made love with that scent filling his nostrils.

She crawled on top of the comforter and asked him to join her. "Just hold me."

Arguing with her was pointless; she knew how to wear him down. But for some inexplicable reason, the thought of her body next to his comforted him.

She moved his glasses to the nightstand and made room for him to snuggle. As soon as he put his arm around her, she reached up and began stroking his hair the way she used to do when they were together.

The hypnotic rhythm of her touch and the gentle, feathery strokes soothed and relaxed him to the point of nodding off, but he woke, startled and somewhat disoriented, to a pull and a tug and found her naked, loosening his belt, her irresistible eyes pleading with him. How was he going to resist her and did he even want to?

She took advantage of his hesitation and leaned over to kiss him, and every inch of him longed to return the kiss. He longed to massage her breasts and the small of her back and her tiny round bottom. He longed to let down his defenses and open up to her, but instead he blocked the kiss with a hand. He couldn't go there. The past still hurt.

Undaunted, she pushed up his shirt and ran her tongue through the reddish hairs on his chest down to the top of his slacks.

When she grasped his zipper, he gripped her wrists. "No, Tanya."

"I want to love you," she said. "Why can't I?" She sounded like the spoiled woman-child she was. She pulled free and made another attempt at the zipper.

"That's enough." He pushed her aside and swung his legs to the floor.

She draped her arms over his shoulders, pressed into his back, and nuzzled his ear. "I just want to love you."

"We're not going down that road again," he said. "I'll get you another room."

She let her arms fall away from him. "Never mind. I'll get a cab."

"Where will you go?"

"Home."

"What about your friend?"

"I lied." She climbed off the bed and picked up her clothes, her eyes clouded with tears.

He watched her dress, staring at the contours of her body. Because of her profession, she maintained slender hips and a tiny waist, but her breasts were full and round, bouncing with every movement. He ached to touch them. But he denied himself the pleasure.

She slipped on her jacket and found her purse on the floor. "Let me know what you find out about Kelly."

"I'm sorry, Tannie."

"I'm sorry, too. I just love you so much." She kissed him on the cheek and hurried from the room, her lemony fragrance lingering after her.

After so many betrayals those words meant nothing to him. He used to blame it on her age—twelve years younger than he—or their jobs. Being apart from one another had a definite impact on their relationship. There were too many temptations in a job like hers, too many photographers, too many admirers. He wouldn't go through it again.

He felt weak from dealing with her, but with the nap he'd taken, he feared another sleepless night. He dug through his bag and pulled out the bear. The reason he'd gone to Connecticut in the first place filtered back to him, and Libby came to mind. He reached for the phone and paused. Too drained for another conversation, he decided to wait and call her from home.

FOURTEEN

KIPP'S HOUSE had a heavy feel to it—hot and stuffy—and the smell of bacon lingered from two days ago. With his free hand he pushed open the kitchen window to let the air circulate.

He dropped his bag in the living room, opened the blinds. He'd had a layover in Denver, but due to the time change, it was relatively early. Exhausted from the long flight, he lay on the couch, and with the late afternoon sun flooding the windows and warming his body, he dozed off.

Upon waking, he thought of Libby. All the way across the country, he'd thought about her. He was anxious to call her, but first a soul-reviving shower was due.

Afterward, he slipped on a robe, rubbed his hair with a towel, and wandered into the kitchen to find Libby's number. He placed the call, but no one answered. He left a message.

He checked the messages on his answering machine and cringed when he heard his editor's voice because it reminded him of his lack of progress on the article. His distractions came out of the blue, and he'd have to beg for more time.

The second message was from Tanya. She told him she loved him and encouraged him to look for their daughter but with the caustic reminder that going to a psychic was as useless as seeking the answers from a magician.

Again, Tanya's remark brought up the doubts he'd had from the beginning about enlisting Libby's help, and he wondered if it was a stupid thing to do. Already his hopes were unrealistically high.

Annoyed and restless, he dressed and went to The Fish and Ale to get a bite to eat. The parking lot was full, normal for a Friday night. He tried to avoid the crowds by frequenting the establishment on weekdays, but being alone wasn't satisfying any longer, especially since he'd met Libby.

Even if the reasons for his attraction to this oddly unique individual were unclear, he was still drawn to her. Holding a woman, even if that woman was Tanya, had awakened the need for a woman's soft gentle touch. It brought back memories of the good times: snuggling by the fireplace, walking hand in hand in the park, making love on a rainy afternoon. Was he ready to begin anew with someone like Libby?

The last two years he'd had opportunities—a caterer he'd struck up a conversation with at The Fish and Ale, who slipped him her business card with her home phone number; a friend of his editor, a sleek-looking advertising executive, who reminded him too much of Tanya—but he never pursued them. The disappearance of his daughter had tied up his emotions. He'd had no room in his heart for anything, except the memory of his little girl.

Since he'd been around Libby, he was stirred up again in more ways than one. His emotions were somehow intertwined with both his daughter and Libby; he wanted his daughter back and he wanted Libby, the woman who held the keys to finding her. Maybe he needed to separate the two—keep to the business of finding Kelly—before he launched into something he might regret. It hit him then that even contemplating a relationship with Libby was a waste of time. She'd shown no interest in him.

Inside the pub, the Eagles thundered from the jukebox, all the pool tables were in use, and every table was filled. The cool, salty air drifted in from the opened door.

Kipp eyed an empty stool at the bar next to a brunette dressed in black jeans and a halter top. She smiled at him when he sat down. He waved Sam over and ordered a draft and a hamburger.

When Sam came back with the beer, he shouted over the music, "Didn't work out with that lady friend of yours?"

"Why do you assume that?"

"You're never here on Friday nights. I figured your coming here on a Friday night is serious. You either want to talk about it, or you want to get laid."

"You sure know how to dish it out." Kipp took a swig of beer.

"So, what's up?"

Being honest with Sam had always been easy because talking to him was like talking to a friend with nothing to lose. Sam had a good ear and never spread rumors. Kipp gave him a rundown of his trip to Connecticut—particularly the part about seeing his ex-wife, even embellishing on how hard it was to keep his hands off her.

"You want my opinion?" Before Sam could dish his advice, a man hollered from the other end of the bar, and he left to take the man's order.

Kipp drank more of his beer and reached for the pretzels in front of the brunette.

She shoved the basket his way. "I couldn't help overhearing you talk about some woman, like your ex-wife. Sounds interesting. I'm a good listener if you want to talk about it."

"I've probably talked enough, but thanks."

She swiveled her stool to face Kipp. "My name's Sherry. What's yours?"

"Kipp."

"Kim?" she yelled over the music.

"Kipp, with two p's."

"That's different. Would you like to play pool or something?"

"I just ordered a burger."

"After?"

"Maybe." Kipp noted how young and pretty she was. In the past that would have been an attractive combination, but now the temptation wasn't there.

Sam brought Kipp's meal. He'd just sunk his teeth into the first bite when a man in a cowboy hat and a plaid shirt stormed the bar and latched on to Sherry's wrist. "Come on, babe."

She wrenched free. "Forget it."

He grabbed for her again, but she leaned into Kipp, her hair grazing his face. He leaned away. The cowboy tossed Kipp a dirty look, his face aflame from anger and embarrassment. He tugged her hair hard. "I'll be back." He stomped out of the building.

She swiveled around and began chewing her nail.

"Can I help?" Kipp said.

Sam, who had witnessed the scene, came over to her. "You okay?"

She nodded, then shook her head, a tear finding its way down the side of her face.

"Guy's a jerk," Sam said. "If you want me to call you a cab, I will."

She shook her head again.

"Just let me know." Sam walked away to tend to another customer.

Kipp studied her profile. She couldn't have been more than twenty-two. She reminded him of Tanya in the beginning of their relationship: vulnerable, sweet, eliciting in him the need to protect. He felt the urge to reach out to this girl. "Can I give you a lift?"

She looked at him for the first time since the incident, her eyes brimmed with tears. Kipp paid the bill and told Sam he was taking her home. They walked out to the Jeep in the star-filled night.

"So, where's home?" Kipp said.

"I can't go there. He'll find me."

"Is there somewhere else I can take you? Your parents' house, a friend's?"

When she said no, the picture became very clear. He'd have to take her to his house, and he suddenly wished he hadn't offered to help. His life was complicated enough. All the way up the hill, he thought about what to do.

Once they were inside the house, she looked around the living room and ran a hand across the top of the TV. She seated herself on the couch, scanned the coffee table, and picked up one newsmagazine, then another, and tossed both aside, unsatisfied with the content. She said she was cold, so he gave her a blanket to wrap up in and made her a cup of hot chocolate.

He handed her the cup and stood nearby. "Is that guy your husband?"

"Boyfriend."

"Does he get rough with you often?"

"Yeah, I suppose. But he loves me. Even when he hits me, he always tells me he loves me."

Hearing her reply, Kipp knew what to do. He excused himself and thumbed through the community service pages of the phone book and dialed the local crisis clinic where he was given the number of a women's shelter. He made that call and returned to the living room.

She met him at the end of the couch. "Can I stay here with you?"

He wasn't sure how to interpret her meaning, but sleeping in the same bed with him was unacceptable, as was sleeping anywhere else in his house. Though he felt sorry for her, he wanted their involvement to end, as much as he'd wanted his and Tanya's to end. "I'm taking you to a shelter for the night. They'll help you figure things out."

"Please, let me stay here."

She looked frightened, but Kipp wasn't about to rescue her any further. He picked up his keys. "Let's go."

She followed him outside, quiet and sulky. On the way back to town, the only conversation they had was when she asked him to stop at The

Fish and Ale so she could retrieve the jacket she'd left behind.

He swung into the parking lot, and before the Jeep came to a complete halt, she had the passenger door open and ran toward a red pickup truck. She hopped in, and the truck burned rubber swinging onto the main road.

Kipp turned around and headed home. He could never understand why women like Sherry went back for more. He hoped one day she'd wake up before it was too late.

While he cleaned up the kitchen, he thought about his daughter and how he would never want her to grow up to be like Sherry with low self-esteem, cowering at the hands of a man. He yearned to be instrumental in shaping Kelly's life. If only he could have the chance.

He reached for the phone and dialed Libby's number. No one answered. He left another message for her to return his call.

FIFTEEN

Waves crashed over the rocks toward a row of weathered cabins. Libby's car was parked next to Cabin 1, The Starfish, at a rustic resort on the shores of the Straits, one of her favorite getaways. The cabin had a fully equipped kitchen, table and chairs, a sofa and a rocking chair—all in one large area—a bathroom with shower, and a bedroom with a captain's bed.

Libby hauled in the remaining items from the trunk of her car, including two sleeping bags. She set the bags on the sofa and watched Ellen in tee shirt and jeans teeter on jagged rocks, making her way up the narrow beach. The sun was beginning its descent, and the wind that had whipped wildly during the day was diminishing.

Twenty minutes later Ellen returned to the cabin, took off her sneakers, and smacked the soles together to release the accumulated sand. She came inside with a shiver. "It's cooling down out there." She warmed her hands over the propane heater. "I'm so glad you whisked me away for the weekend."

Libby smiled. "It's a good place to clear the mind. No outside distractions."

"You mean like Kipp?"

Libby ignored her by searching in the cupboard for a saucepan. "What do you want tonight, spaghetti or stew?"

"You didn't answer my question?"

"I was thinking of you."

"I can be depressed anywhere, distractions or no distractions."

Libby handed Ellen a bottle of spring water. "You had a nice long walk on the beach. Have you come to any decisions?"

Ellen's lips quivered, her smile turning into a frown.

Libby saw in Ellen's expression that her question was premature. Leaving Mel seemed so obvious a solution, but she had to be patient and let Ellen come to that decision in her own time. "I'm sorry. I shouldn't have asked you that."

"I still love the bastard. I hate him and I love him. Can you imagine that?"

"You've had quite a shock."

Ellen stared out the window. Libby wiped off the table and left her alone with her thoughts.

After a long interval of silence, Ellen turned to Libby. "You know, I'm really tired. I think I'll go on to bed. I wouldn't be good company tonight anyway." She took a sleeping bag into the bedroom without waiting for Libby's comments.

Libby made herself a peanut butter sandwich and sat in a rocking chair near the window to admire the view. Each time the waves receded, tiny stones rolled toward the sea, creating a hissing sound. Farther into the Straits a tanker, making its way toward Puget Sound, passed a cruise ship, decked in lights, on its way to Alaska. The sights and sounds from the cabin were ideal for contemplation, and Libby thought about Ellen.

She hated to see her best friend this depressed. It was so unlike her, although she realized Ellen had probably been stuffing the emotions for years—laughing on the outside, crying on the inside. She missed having Ellen to talk to, but sleep would help clear Ellen's mind.

The sun dipped deep into the western sky, the most brilliant colors, an array of pinks, toward the left of the cabin. Except for the wave action outside, the cabin was quiet.

Ellen had asked her about Kipp. If it hadn't been for Ellen's problems, Libby would probably be talking to him instead of spending a weekend away from civilization, but supporting her friend came first.

Whenever she had time to think about her own life these days, no matter where she was—in her office, downtown, making dinner, sitting in a cabin on the Straits—her thoughts strayed to Kipp.

With Ellen in bed Libby was free to let her mind wander. She wondered how Kipp had fared in Connecticut. Closing her eyes, centering herself, she had a strong feeling he was trying to contact her that very moment.

She wouldn't admit to Ellen that he was indeed getting under her skin, but she couldn't afford to let him burrow deep. Her life was ordered, her future set as far as she was concerned, and no man would change that.

After giving Kipp and Ellen enough thought for one night, she slipped out of her jeans and sweatshirt, rolled out her sleeping bag, and curled up on the lumpy sofa. She let the hissing sound of the waves lull her to sleep.

❧

In the morning Libby woke to seagulls screeching and crows squawking. She stretched her stiff muscles that had cramped from the confines of her makeshift bed. The sky was a dismal gray and the wind was whipping the water into whitecaps. Ellen was already roaming the beach.

She was tempted to join her, but remained inside to give Ellen more breathing room. She lit the stove under the coffee pot and tugged on her jeans and sweatshirt.

Ellen hurried in and emptied her hands of stones, smoothed and tumbled by the waves, and a few clam shells, adding to the pile she'd gathered yesterday. She washed her hands and poured herself a cup of coffee. She sucked in a shuddering breath. "It's chilly again this morning."

"Why didn't you wear a sweatshirt?"

"I don't know. I wasn't thinking. That's par for the course."

"I put some granola on the table if you want to get started on breakfast. The toast is almost ready. You must be starving. You didn't eat any dinner."

"I still don't have much of an appetite," she said. "Hey, maybe I'll lose weight. That's one good thing that might come from this."

Libby buttered the toast and brought it to the table. "So, how are you feeling this morning?"

"Like a truck hit me."

"No better, huh?"

"The only thing that's changed is I'm angry as hell. I woke up furious. I just wanted to scream."

"That's a good sign, Ellen. You should be angry as hell. Anger can spur you to do something about your situation."

"Well, right now I have enough anger inside me to move mountains. I could kill him."

"Are you angry enough to consider leaving him for good?"

"Like a divorce? God, I don't know." Ellen shoved her bowl of cereal aside and fled to the bathroom.

The pipes clanked as the hot water flowed into the shower. With a patient heart Libby cleared the table, washed dishes, and waited for Ellen to reappear.

When Ellen came out of the bathroom, her eyelids were swollen from crying. "I still love him, Libby. What's wrong with me? I hated seeing him with that woman."

"What you're going through is normal, Ellen. You are dealing with all kinds of emotions besides depression—anger, jealousy, low self-esteem. Just let your feelings out. Don't judge them." She handed Ellen a sweatshirt. "Come outside and help me chop wood. We'll have a fire on the beach tonight."

Libby picked up the ax. She didn't mind that Ellen wandered off down the beach. As a sensitive and a close friend, she had to work at keeping Ellen's energy from bleeding into her own field and causing her to take on Ellen's depression. Chopping wood helped.

The tide was too far in for heavy beachcombing. After splitting a few logs, Libby went inside to meditate and to make notes for another workshop. She let Ellen roam the thin strip of beach alone.

౼ఴఅ

Later that evening Libby built a fire in a sandy area surrounded by driftwood close to the cabin. She sat on a driftwood log and poked the fire with a stick to expose the glowing embers, the fiery reds matching the western sky. Ellen had gone inside for a jacket. Before Libby could drift into thinking about Kipp, Ellen returned with two cups of hot tea, a bag of marshmallows tucked under her arm, and then she combed the immediate area and returned with two twigs.

"We're so lucky the sun came out this afternoon to create this lovely sunset, and look at that huge freighter," Ellen said as she pointed out to sea. "I wish we didn't have to go home."

Libby stared at her friend, amazed. "Do you hear yourself, Ellen? This is the first time you've noticed the beauty of this place all weekend."

"Am I making progress?"

"I would say so. I'm happy you're feeling so good tonight."

"Me, too. Depression stinks."

"You'll probably have more times like these. The road toward separation, or wherever you're headed, isn't easy. Believe me, I know."

"I forgot. You've been through all this. And Dan was worse than Mel. A hundred times worse. How'd you get through it?"

"Just like you, Ellen, one day at a time. Even if you want a divorce, it isn't easy."

Ellen stabbed a marshmallow with a stick and held it over the fire.

"Have you given Kipp any thought this weekend?"

"Let's keep this weekend about you, Ellen."

"You're no fun."

⨳

On Sunday morning, after all their equipment was stored in the trunk, Libby encouraged Ellen to take one last stroll on the beach before leaving the resort.

A few miles down the road toward home, Libby checked in with her. "Now that the weekend is over, how are you feeling?"

"Numb."

"You can stay with me as long as you like. Don't feel pressured to do anything rash."

"Like go back to Mel? Don't worry. I'm not planning on it."

"I was hoping you'd say that." Libby thought about the weekend and the information she'd received when she asked about Ellen during meditation. She glanced at Ellen, sensing whether or not to share what she knew. "I'll give you my impressions if you want them."

"You know I do."

"This is what I get," Libby said. "I feel that when you get past the shock of it all, if you choose to move on, there will be a huge surprise waiting for you. One that right now you could never imagine."

"That sounds wonderful. But it's so vague."

"I can't tell you any more right now because you have to make some choices first." Libby squeezed Ellen's hand. "Trust me. It's a wonderful surprise."

SIXTEEN

LIBBY JIGGLED the key in the lock, hurrying to open the door. She could hear a man's voice on her answering machine, but by the time she made it inside and emptied her arms of a suitcase and sleeping bag, the machine clicked off, and she missed the call.

Ellen rushed in after her. "Was that the phone? Maybe it was Mel."

Libby pressed the missed call button and discovered two messages from Kipp. Each time he'd asked her to call him as soon as possible.

Ellen slumped in a dining room chair.

"I'm sorry, Ellen. I need to make this call."

"I'll be all right. Do you want coffee or tea?"

"Tea," Libby said, then went to her office and closed the door. She'd sensed excitement in Kipp's voice and hoped the reading she'd given him proved accurate, or at least close to it.

Kipp acknowledged her after the second ring. "Where have you been? I've been calling all weekend."

Libby explained she'd taken Ellen out of town to ponder her marital problems.

"Is she okay?"

"She'll survive."

"I didn't have your cell phone number, or I would have tried that."

"I had it off most of the time. Reception was bad. Plus, cell phones and cabins don't exactly mix. So, what happened in Connecticut?"

"That's why I called," he said. "It happened just as you told me it would. Mrs. Crowley did have something of Kelly's."

"What was it?"

"A stuffed animal, a teddy bear, something I won for her at a carnival. Kelly used to carry it around all the time. I brought it back with me."

"Are you willing to let me use psychometry on it?"

"What the hell's psychometry?"

"You said Kelly carried that bear around all the time, right? Well, her energy is probably all over that object. If you let me hold the bear, I may get information about her. It might give me a clue to her disappearance."

There was a long pause, and Libby knew Kipp was digesting this latest bit of information. She could practically see the wheels turning in his analytical brain. She knew he'd agree, but not without the usual push and pull.

"You're stretching me again, Libby. You know my first reaction is to write this whole thing off. If I weren't so desperate for answers…Why didn't you tell me before I went to Connecticut what you wanted the bear for? I can't say it would have made sense, but—"

"If I'd told you that, you wouldn't have gone. I know the whole idea of the paranormal is foreign to you. Let's just say your guides needed to ease you into it."

"There you go again with that business about guides. I don't see—"

"Kipp. Don't spoil it. Try to accept the fact that something good may come of this."

"You mean the end justifies the means?"

"That's exactly what I'm saying. Let me look at my schedule for tomorrow." Libby thumbed through her appointment book. "I could see you tomorrow at three."

"I'll be there."

"Don't forget the bear."

On Monday afternoon on his way out the door, Kipp remembered he hadn't returned his editor's call. Not wanting to be late to Libby's house, he wrote a note to remind himself to touch base with Jerry first thing Tuesday morning. That article was a thorn in his side, but right now he had more important things on his mind.

The traffic, slower than usual because of a summer downpour, delayed him, and he knocked on Libby's door ten minutes late. The trees around Libby's house wept with moisture.

When she greeted Kipp, he had a difficult time keeping his eyes focused on her face. She wore a ruby-red blouse tucked into a pair of tight blue jeans. Her sandals and the shade of her toenail polish matched the color of her blouse. Stunning was too mild a word for her. Charismatic. Isn't that what he and Charlie had decided?

He apologized for being late, but she was smiling and didn't seem to mind. She poured him a cup of coffee, and they went straight to her office.

Anxious to proceed, he produced the bear from his jacket pocket. "Do you want this now?"

She took it from him and had him sit down. "I want to see what impressions I get before I ask you anything."

Immediately upon sitting, she closed her eyes. Water, dripping from the downspouts, filled the silent void. After what seemed to Kipp like an insufferable amount of time, she said, "I'm just going to launch into this."

"Go ahead."

She paused for a second. "I see a light-haired girl, curly-haired, about three years old or maybe four, round face, big eyes, not unlike her mother's."

"She was four when she was taken."

Libby rolled the toy around in her hands. "Yes. I see her in a room with wooden floors and colorful scatter rugs. She's sleeping, but then she wakes up. The screen is unlocked, and she slips outside, unnoticed. They take her from the backyard."

"They? More than one?"

"I see two people. A man and a woman. It's easy. They saw an opportunity. They coax her with candy from the back gate. No one stops them."

"Mrs. Crowley was asleep in the living room," he said. "Do you know who they are? Is she alive?"

Libby turned silent for a few minutes, her eyes darting from side to side behind closed eyelids. By now Kipp was poised on the edge of his seat, desperate for her response.

She opened her eyes and scooted her chair toward Kipp. "I do. I sense she's alive."

"My God, she's alive?" Kipp's voice wavered a little, and he kissed Libby's hand.

"But it's important you find her soon. I don't know why yet, but when I get this information, I feel like someone is pushing me from behind, pushing me to hurry."

"Where is she?"

Libby's eyes narrowed in concentration. "When I sense her vibration, I sense others around her."

"The man and woman who took her?"

"I'm not sure." Her eyelids closed again.

"What else do you see?"

"I feel she's with others. That's all I can tell about that."

Kipp's chest constricted. He felt as though he couldn't breathe. "Can you tell me where she is?"

"East of here."

"Connecticut?"

"I see mountain peaks, golden hills. I get the letter I."

"Indiana? No, that can't be right. That's not a mountainous state. Where else?"

"I'm sensing Idaho."

"Idaho? Of course, but where in Idaho?"

Libby quieted, then said, "The east. I get you need to look somewhere in the east or southeastern part of the state." Her eyes shot open, and she searched Kipp's face. "Are you okay? You look pale."

"Are you sure she's there?"

"All I can tell you is what I'm told, that you should search that area."

"I should notify the police."

"No!"

The sharpness in her tone alarmed him.

"I'm sorry if I sounded blunt, but that answer just came through me. I don't think you should get the authorities involved at this point."

"Why not?"

"You need to do this on your own. I can't say why. You'll have to trust me on this. That's just what's coming through."

Libby's remarks were sinking in, that his daughter might be alive, the first hope he'd had in two years. The tears welled up. He lifted his glasses and wiped his eyes. "I don't know if what you're telling me is true, but if there is even a remote chance she's alive, I've got to find her. I'll comb the area. But I don't understand why you can't give me more details."

"I can't tell you any more than I'm told. At least for me, it's easier if I'm in the vicinity of the person. The energy comes through stronger."

"Then come with me. Help me look for her."

"I can't."

"Is it your work? I'll pay you double for your time. You won't lose money."

"No, it's not that."

"Please, Libby."

"It's not the money."

"Then what?"

"Ellen needs me."

"She'll understand." He squeezed Libby's hand. "Please. I need you, too."

"I can't, and it's not just Ellen."

"What is it?"

"I used to help the police."

"I know that. That's how I got your card."

"But it was too hard on me," she said. "You never know what condition… I mean, I've had cases where they've not been found or if they were, they weren't alive. It's too draining emotionally. I had to stop."

"But you said my daughter is alive."

"I sense she is, but when you go there, I can't guarantee anything."

"You don't have to. You said once that you aren't always accurate. I understand that. Please come with me. I need closure. That's all I'm asking."

Libby glanced at her appointment book. "I have other clients, and Ellen. I'll help you by phone as best I can. That's all I can do."

Frustration was building because he didn't know how to convince her to come with him, but he settled his thoughts on Kelly and lifted the bear from Libby's hands. "I guess I'll leave in a day or two after I map out where I'm going."

"When you get there, call me. I may be able to get impressions through you."

"Are you sure you won't go with me?"

"I really can't."

Kipp paused in the doorway, hoping she'd change her mind, but she turned her attention to the papers on her desk. He let himself out and drove to the two-lane highway.

The thrill he'd experienced at the possibility of finding Kelly was tempered by Libby's outright refusal to accompany him. He could be stubborn, but for whatever reasons Libby held back, she was stubborn, too.

He continued down the highway over rain-soaked pavement, his chest bursting with the likelihood of seeing his daughter again. He called Charlie. In light of the new information Libby had given him, he counted on Charlie's perspective.

Inside the police station Kipp waited with the desk sergeant for Charlie to come out of the secured area. He didn't have to wait long. On the way back to Charlie's office, in an area that smelled musty from desks afloat with paper, several police officers were huddled together, having a lively conversation.

"What's all the commotion about?" Kipp said.

"A teenager, booze, and a gun. You put it together."

"Was anyone hurt?"

"Just some pride. What can I do for you, pal?"

"Maybe I shouldn't bother you."

"I can take a minute." Charlie closed his door for privacy. "What's up?"

With hardly a breath taken, Kipp relayed all the messages that had come through Libby. "Can you believe Kelly may be in Idaho? She could be this close to me. I knew there was a reason I moved west."

Charlie beamed. "When are you going to leave?"

"So, you think I should pursue this, considering the source?"

Charlie slapped a hand on Kipp's shoulder. "You can't *not* do this."

"I'm not exactly sure where to look first. I've got to figure that out. I'm not familiar with the state."

Charlie left the room, came back with a map, and laid it out across his desk. Together they scanned the southeast section of Idaho.

"Not too populated there," Charlie said. "If I were you, I'd start in the Falls area, ask around, branch out from there. I'll alert the police."

"Libby said not to involve them."

"Why not? They have resources."

"I'm not sure. She said it was important I do this by myself, without the authorities."

Charlie's eyes narrowed. "I don't know if that's a good idea."

"So, now you think I shouldn't go?"

"I didn't say that, but you might want to contact the FBI and clue them in to what's going on. They can help."

"I know you're coming from a cop's point of view, but I have to follow Libby's instructions."

Charlie whistled. "How the tide turns. I thought you didn't believe in this psychic crap."

"I don't know if I do, but she led me to Kelly's toy bear. She knew what Kelly looked like. I can't deny the things she knows about me. Maybe I want to find my daughter so badly I'll believe anything, but I've got to try."

"You don't have to convince me," Charlie said. "I'm the one who gave you her card in the first place. But I think you're making a mistake not contacting the authorities. Usually, these psychics give the police information and they let the police do the investigative work, not the family members, but if you're determined to go that route, I want you to promise me you'll call me if you need any help. I'll be on the next plane."

"I appreciate that, but I can assure you, I won't do anything stupid. If I find out where she is, I'll get the FBI involved right away."

"What about your appearance?"

"What about it?"

"Aren't you worried that people will recognize you from your TV days? They'll think you're doing a story."

"Look at me. I wear glasses now, my hair is longer. I used to have a mustache. I don't look the same," he said, though he gave a fleeting thought to the autograph incident at the airport.

"You look the same to me, mustache or no mustache, but I guess you could fool most people."

"That's good enough for me."

Charlie walked outside with Kipp into the sunshine that had broken through the clouds and shook his hand. "Be careful, buddy."

When Kipp got to the bottom of the steps, Charlie called out to him. "I ran into Libby at a restaurant last week. I don't have to tell you what a class act she is. If I were you, I'd escort her right to the bedroom."

Kipp continued walking without looking back, holding his middle finger in midair.

Later, he made arrangements to leave for Idaho on Wednesday afternoon, giving him ample time to call his editor and to research via the Internet the southeastern part of the state.

SEVENTEEN

Libby showered, but before turning in for the night, she peeked into Ellen's room, which she found dark and quiet and smelling of peaches from Ellen's shampoo. As she prepared to close the door, Ellen called for her to come inside. She followed the shaft of light from the hallway to Ellen's bed.

"I hope I didn't wake you."

Ellen switched on the lamp and scooted up against the headboard. "I was just lying here. I've been tossing and turning. Did Kipp leave?"

"A while ago. Did you get yourself something to eat?"

"I wasn't hungry."

"Can I make you something? A snack?"

"No, thanks."

Libby sat and stroked Ellen's hand. "It will get better. I promise."

Ellen shrugged. "So, what happened with Kipp? I know you can't tell me the details, but did he bat those beautiful emerald eyes at you? Make your heart skip just a little?"

Libby squinted at Ellen. "You're incorrigible. Even in your misery, you find a way to tease."

"You haven't answered me. Doesn't he get to you?"

"He's a client."

"Quit answering like a counselor and tell me how you really feel. What does Libby the woman think of him?"

"Ellen…"

"Libby…"

"Oh, all right. I like him."

"Is that all? What else?"

"He seems sensitive and caring. He's attractive."

"Attractive. Is that all you can say?"

"He's very good looking."

"He's a hunk. Admit it."

"Ellen…"

"Why are you fighting this?"

"Fighting what?"

"Your attraction to him. This guy is available, Libby. You should be jumping in and swimming after him."

"He wants me to go to Idaho with him," Libby said and immediately wished she hadn't.

Ellen sat up straighter. "Why didn't you say so?"

"He wants me to go for business reasons. Nothing more."

"Business, shmizness. It could be more than that."

"I told him I couldn't."

"Somehow I knew that was coming."

"I have commitments here. My clients. You."

"Me?"

"I promised I'd be here for you. And I will."

Ellen let out a sigh. "Oh, Libby. I love you for that, but I'll be all right. Don't give up this opportunity to be with Kipp."

"I wouldn't be with him that way. It's business."

"I know what your kind of business is, and if Kipp wants you to go with him, he needs you, too."

"Nope. You come first."

"Libby…"

Libby held her finger to Ellen's lips. "This subject is not open for discussion. I'm going to bed."

Libby turned off the lamp, but before she made it across the room, Ellen said, "How'd you get so stubborn?"

"Good night, Ellen." Libby closed the door and crossed the hall to her bedroom. Since the nights were still warm, she pulled back the quilt, crawled into bed, and nestled under one sheet.

Kipp's sudden appearance in her life would have seemed extraordinary, but she knew from working with the energy, events always happened for a reason. More than likely, all it meant was she had to help him find his child. Anything other than that would have to play itself out. She certainly wouldn't encourage it, although if a relationship were meant to be, other than a business relationship, she wouldn't be able to stop that either.

She hadn't realized how tired she was until she lay down. The last thing she saw before sliding into a deep sleep was Kipp's face.

Deep into the night a quivering sensation spread throughout her body, feeling like the tremor of a train passing by. She woke, thinking earthquake. She grasped the mattress, but the bed was stock-still.

A cold breeze swept through the room, fluttering the sheet. The hairs on Libby's skin bristled from the room's electrical charge. Chills ran up and down her spine. She strained to see in the dark.

Rising from the corner of the room was the same glowing light she'd experienced before. Looking closer, she noticed the light shifting. This time a blue mist materialized inside, along with the shimmering form of an older woman, short and rounded with silvery hair.

Libby swallowed hard and forced herself to speak. "Who are you?"

From the mist, a faint voice answered, "Help them."

"Who? Who do you want me to help?"

The image began to fade with the words trailing after, "Help them."

"Who?" Libby cried out.

The woman disappeared into the blue mist and the glowing light evaporated as quickly as it had appeared.

Seeking more information, Libby closed her eyes and deepened her breath. She pictured the old woman in the mist and silently asked her questions, then drifted into a sound sleep. The answers came in a dream.

The next morning Libby, recalling the dream, lay in bed and put the pieces of the puzzle together. The woman in the mist was someone Kipp knew who had passed over, someone who cared about him and wanted Libby to help him find his child. But something else came through that disturbed her: in finding the child, an element of time was involved.

She stayed in bed, pondering the situation, until the robins announced the morning light. On her way to the kitchen she grabbed a robe and sneaked into her office to retrieve her appointment book. She brewed a fresh pot of coffee, opened the kitchen curtains, and watched the birds flitting about the backyard. A rabbit scurried into the bushes. The sky was a pale blue with tinges of yellow around the edges.

With her coffee cup nearby, she sat at the table and tried to calculate how many clients she'd have to reschedule but realized it depended on how long she'd be gone, and that bit of information was unknown. The feeling that came to her was it would take as long as it takes.

She looked ahead a month and noticed she'd scheduled a two-day workshop in Minneapolis for a group of businessmen looking to improve their intuitive skills. That event had been booked three months in advance and would be difficult to cancel.

She recalled the night before: the apparition, the dream, and the answers she was given. It sent shivers all through her body. She had no doubt at all that her instincts were correct. She had to go with Kipp.

Ellen wandered into the room, yawning. "What are you doing up so early?"

"I have to talk to you."

Ellen poured a mug of coffee, sat beside Libby, and scrutinized her face. "This is serious."

"I can't tell you why right now, but I have to go with him."

"What changed your mind?"

"I had the vision again, and this time a woman appeared. She told me to help him."

"And you listen to a ghost before you listen to your old friend?"

"Ellen…"

"This is so unlike you, Libby. Don't get me wrong, I'm glad you're going, but normally you wouldn't up and leave without planning ahead. You said yourself you have clients."

"I know what I told you, but now I'm feeling this strong, powerful urge to go with him, and I have to follow my intuition. But I'm worried about you. I don't like leaving you alone right now."

"Don't give it a thought, kiddo. I'll be just fine."

"I don't want you getting lonely and running back to Mel."

Ellen reared back. "Are you kidding? I wouldn't walk back to him."

"Are you sure?"

"I've done a lot of thinking these last few days, and I'm through with him. I swear. So, go, already."

"Okay, but I'll keep in touch. Hopefully, we won't be gone long. I have to call Kipp and the airlines. I'll have to call clients to reschedule or cancel."

"Let me do that," Ellen said. "Let me give back for all you've done for me. I can be your official secretary while you're gone."

"You'd do that for me?"

"It'll give me something to do."

"Thank you, Ellen. For now, reschedule my appointments two weeks out. If it doesn't take that long, I'll readjust things when I get back." Libby sipped her coffee. "What else will you do while I'm gone?"

"Oh, let's see. The gym wouldn't be a bad idea."

"You can use my membership. I'll leave my card for you. Just tell them you're trying it out." Libby got up and deposited her cup in the sink. "I better call Kipp."

"Can you give me a little bitty hint about why you and Kipp are going to Idaho? I am your best friend."

"If this wasn't confidential, Ellen, I would, you know that. But it will have to come from Kipp."

Ellen walked over to Libby. "Whatever you're doing, I'll be rooting for you."

Libby embraced Ellen, and for a long moment they held onto one another. Libby gave Ellen a peck on the cheek, then headed for her office.

❧

Kipp grabbed his cell phone and punched in Libby's number, then clicked the off button. Wrestling with his need to convince her, he questioned what he could say that hadn't already been said. She'd made it perfectly clear the day before; she wouldn't go with him. But this was important. How could she turn her back on him? He knew her reasons, but it still hurt. He needed her help, and having her with him would strengthen his resolve. Hell, he wanted her with him, plain and simple.

The ring of the phone startled him, as did the voice on the other end. "I was just thinking about you," he said.

"I'm glad I caught you. I was afraid you'd left already."

"I've got a few loose ends to tie up, then I'm gone."

"I'm going with you," Libby said, pointblank, "if that's all right."

He felt the tension in his chest ease. "It's more than all right. I was just going to call you. What changed your mind?"

"I'll explain later. I assume you're driving."

"I want my own car."

"I can't leave until Thursday at the earliest. I called the airlines, and the only flight I could get was to Salt Lake City. That's three hours from the border."

"Do you want me to wait for you? I could pick you up Thursday. We could drive together."

"That would waste time. If you are going to drive, you need to leave as soon as possible."

He paused, letting the words sink in. "Is there something you're not telling me?"

"I've been getting strong feelings about the time involved. You'll have to trust me on this."

"What is it, Libby?"

"We can talk about it when I see you. My flight on Alaska Airlines arrives at four-thirty in the afternoon. Will that give you enough time to drive there?"

"Plenty."

"Good. I'll see you then."

"Libby?"

"Yes?"

"Remember what I said about the money. I'll pay expenses, everything, even your airline ticket, plus any income you would lose by coming with me, so keep track."

"We can figure all that out when we get back."

"Did you tell anyone else the reason for our trip?"

"If you mean Ellen, that's your call."

"You can tell her, as long as she and Charlie are the only ones who know." He gave Libby Charlie's cell phone number. "If she has any problems while you're gone, I'm sure he'll be glad to help out."

"That's thoughtful of you."

"I know how hard it is for you to leave her right now."

"Yes, it is, but she assures me she'll be okay. You have a long drive ahead of you. I better let you go."

"Libby?"

"Yes?"

"Thank you."

On completing the call, he wondered why she had changed her mind and if it had anything to do with the statement she made about the time involved. She said leaving soon was imperative. What did that mean? Thinking about that was more than he could handle at the moment. He had to stay positive, and the idea of making the journey with her helped ease his mind. Who knew for sure what the outcome would be? To have Libby along for support gave him an added boost. Besides, he liked her company.

He filled a suitcase with a week's worth of clothes but hoped they wouldn't be gone that long. He shoved his bag in the Jeep and returned to the kitchen to give Jerry a call. After connecting with him, Kipp expected the first question.

"How's the article coming?"

"That's why I'm calling. I need more time."

"Jesus, Kipp, I gave you a wide berth."

"Something's come up regarding Kelly."

"Your daughter? Did they find her?"

"Let's just say I've got a good lead, and I'm going to need time to follow up on it."

"You're putting me in a tough spot, but what kind of a friend would I be if I thought this article was more important than your daughter. I'll have to put something else in its place."

"I'm sorry to do this to you."

"I just hope you don't get your hopes dashed."

"When this is over, I owe you big time."

"Yeah, yeah."

"I mean it, Jer. If this works out, I'll deliver a story that will be mind-boggling."

"I didn't want a story about finding missing kids."

"I promise, you'll be amazed. It'll be worth the wait."

Jerry wished him good luck and grumbled a goodbye.

The freeway was unusually light—no bumper-to-bumper traffic—and Kipp had time to focus his thoughts on the journey. A shimmer of doubt raced through him. What if it was a farce? What if everything Libby told him was a sham? What if Tanya was right and Libby would tell him whatever he wanted to hear? If that were true, why would she agree to go with him? Unless she *was* delusional. That notion brought him back to his early-on assessment, that Libby was a nutcase.

Even though his inner critic nagged at him to turn around and forget the whole business, something deeper kept the Jeep moving in an easterly direction.

He shook off the doubts and latched on to the possibility of finding Kelly. If nothing else, he could say he'd tried every avenue, turned over every stone, as Charlie had encouraged him to do. Plus, he'd gained a friendship with Libby, a woman he never would have considered in a million years.

EIGHTEEN

Late Wednesday evening Kipp arrived in Salt Lake City into the arms of a brilliant sunset. Clouds laced with deep magenta flushed the heavens from the Wasatch to the Oquirrh mountains.

Weary from the long day's drive, he gladly pulled into the parking lot of the Airport Hilton. The air was thin and dry compared to moisture-driven western Washington. He wasn't used to the drying effects of the low humidity. Thirstier than usual, he bought an extra bottle of spring water before turning in for the night.

Due to a last-minute cancellation of one of the eighteen thousand attendees of the Outdoor Retailers Convention, he was lucky to have a room for the night. The hotel was only ten minutes from the heart of the city, and the next day he planned to stop at the police station to ask around.

He got up early, ate breakfast, and checked out at nine. The clouds had dissipated overnight, and the sky capped the city in an indigo blue. Situated between mountain ranges, the Salt Lake City area sprawled for miles. He vowed to come back in the winter to take advantage of the ski season. Skiing had been a passion of his until his daughter disappeared.

Libby hadn't told him to check with the police, but he thought it wouldn't hurt, so after he found a parking spot, he went into the building on South and asked to speak to a detective in the Special Victims unit.

Detective Manning, a husky bald man with a crooked scar under his right eye, came to the counter. "What can I do for you?"

"My name is Kipp Reed. I'm here from Washington State, looking for information about my daughter, Kelly."

"A runaway?"

Kipp removed a picture from his wallet and handed it to the detective. "She was kidnapped."

The detective slipped on his reading glasses and examined the photo. "How many years?"

"Two."

"That's a pretty cold case. Do you have reason to believe she was brought here?"

"Well, no."

"The FBI involved?"

"Yes, but they haven't found a trace."

The detective studied the picture and repeated Kipp's last name, then looked at Kipp above the rim of his glasses. "Are you that reporter on TV?"

"I'm a freelancer now."

He returned the picture to Kipp. "You know, if the authorities can't find her, no one can. If she's in the system—"

"You've had your share of abduction cases in the last two years."

"There have been kids missing. The usual." Detective Manning eyed Kipp, his eyebrows coming together. "Just because we had that one high profile case, doesn't mean we have any more abductions than the rest of the country. This is a pretty family-oriented place. We pull together. Of course, there are some fanatical groups in the area, but they don't abduct kids. I'd say your best bet is to let the system do its work."

Kipp realized this was leading him nowhere. "If it's all the same to you, Detective, I'll keep looking." He turned to leave.

"Good luck, and sorry about your little girl."

Kipp strode out of the building and sucked in a few deep breaths to shake off the detective's callous attitude. Two years might be a long time to the detective, but for Kipp, who spent every waking moment thinking about Kelly, the kidnapping was as fresh as if it had happened yesterday.

In this sea of doubt, Libby would be a welcome contrast, but he had several hours to kill before her arrival, so he spent the time exploring Temple Square, including the Tabernacle with its grand pipe organ, and the Great Salt Lake with its vast waters and salt flats.

By the time he'd parked the car in the airport parking lot, he was more than anxious to greet Libby. Two long days had increased his expectations about both the trip and his traveling companion.

When he saw her from a distance, he wished he hadn't shown up in khakis and sandals, ragged from a day of sightseeing in the sweltering heat. Dressed in baby blue slacks, a matching jacket, and beige pumps, she looked as though she were about to step into a room full of business associates.

Her smile threw him, and he was suddenly gripped by that giddy teenage feeling, accompanied by stomach flutters and the need to use his fingers as a comb to brush his windblown hair into place. Before he left, a haircut would have been wise.

Libby was a jewel, glittering in the light. He couldn't help but return her smile. "I'm glad you're here." He kissed her cheek and hoped he hadn't overstepped the boundaries of their relationship, but she seemed to take the kiss in stride. "How was your flight?"

"Too long for such a short distance. We had a stop in Portland. How was your drive?"

"This has been the longest two days, waiting for you." Instantly, Kipp felt the flush of embarrassment. Every time he was in her presence, the words seemed to bypass his brain and rush out of his mouth. "Let's get your suitcase and head out."

When they were seated in the car, Kipp slid the key into the ignition but held it steady. "I don't even know where to drive from here. We haven't discussed it. It's after five. Are you hungry?"

"Not yet."

"Do you want to get a hotel room?" He cringed. That question sounded too much like a proposition. Again, his brain was malfunctioning. "I mean, do you want to stay in the city tonight? I couldn't keep my room because of the convention in town, but it was only one room with one bed, and well, if I'd been thinking ahead…"

"Let's head north. There are still a couple of hours of daylight left. Maybe we can find a place to eat on the way. And a motel."

"Sounds good." Relieved she'd pulled him out of his miserable attempt at decision making, he started the car and drove from the parking terrace.

He was about to turn north when Libby placed her hand on his arm. "Take me into the city."

"Now? May I ask why?"

Libby didn't reply.

Great. No answer. He wondered why she'd want to waste the time. He begged for patience. "Anywhere in particular?"

"Show me the sights."

He felt the heat of frustration rise, since they were now in the midst of the commuter traffic, but then he remembered who he was dealing with—a woman who knew more about life than he could ever fathom. He took a deep breath.

As they approached Temple Square, she asked him to stop the car, and it took all the patience he could muster just to satisfy her request. He pulled over into a no-parking strip, at which time she closed her eyes. Meanwhile, Kipp scanned the streets for roving police cruisers. After what seemed like five minutes, she opened her eyes and directed him to drive north.

He wanted to quiz her, but she was like a homing pigeon with her eyes alert to the streets ahead and her mouth pinched tight. He stayed quiet until they were well on their way northward. "What happened back there?"

"I wanted to see if I could get any impressions around the Mormon temples. I felt drawn there."

Wondering what he'd gotten himself into, Kipp prepared for an unpredictable ride.

The sun, descending in the west, deepened the blue in the eastern sky and left traces of pink on wispy clouds.

The traffic thinned out as he drove farther on, allowing him time to fiddle with the radio, but he found nothing of interest. He waited for Libby to make conversation. When none was forthcoming, he said, "Are you getting more vibes, or can we talk?"

"Go ahead."

"Can you tell me where we're going?"

"I'm not exactly sure yet."

Kipp gritted his teeth to stop from launching into a tirade about the trip being a stupid mistake. Libby was so organized, normally so sure of everything, and now she sounded as if she were lost at sea, and that did nothing for his confidence.

Nearing the next small town, he exited the freeway and parked in front of the first restaurant he spotted. The building was badly in need of paint, had wooden steps and a red neon sign that buzzed on and off from an electrical short. He marched toward the entrance, leaving Libby to hurry after him.

The room, cluttered and smelling of warmed-over cabbage, echoed with loud conversation and the twang of country coming from the jukebox. Kipp found a booth on the far wall. Libby scooted across from him. A middle-aged waitress, dressed in jeans and wearing an auburn wig slightly askew, slapped two menus on the table and walked off.

Kipp gave Libby an apologetic look. "This is a dive. Do you want to go someplace else?"

She studied the menu without answering him. When the waitress returned, she ordered a French dip sandwich and decaf. He ordered the same.

Kipp shouted over the music. "I'm sorry I didn't ask you where you wanted to eat. I got a little impatient."

"I could tell."

"It's just that you're so quiet and mysterious about everything."

"Maybe I'm a little—"

The waitress shoved two cups of coffee in front of them and asked if they wanted cream or sugar. They both declined.

Kipp watched her move on to the next table, then turned to Libby. "What were you saying?"

"I said, maybe I'm—"

A man stumbled by their booth, singing to the music. When Libby opened her mouth again, the music swelled to a crescendo.

Kipp took out his wallet and left enough money to cover the tab. "Let's get out of here."

In the car he asked her to finish what she was saying.

"I said maybe I'm a little nervous about being in this situation with you."

"That makes two of us," he said. "But you surprise me."

"How so?"

"You always come across like you have everything all together in your life."

"Not in a situation like this."

"I thought you had experience looking for missing persons."

"Yes, but I don't have experience driving around the country with a man I barely know."

Kipp laughed.

"What's so funny?"

"I'm glad that's out in the open because I'm just as nervous as you are. I mean, I don't know what I'm doing following you to who-knows-where. I feel like I've somehow lost my mind."

"You might feel that way when I tell you how this came to be, my being here with you."

"Tell me."

"Later. Let's find a place to eat and sleep for the night."

Along the highway Kipp spotted a red motel sign and took the appropriate turn. The closer he came to the one-story motel, he realized it was a place to park for the night on the way to someplace else, second-rate at best. He glanced at the clock on the dashboard and decided not to be choosey. He pulled into one of the two empty parking spaces. "Doesn't look too promising. I'll run in and see what they've got."

He returned with a desperate look on his face. "They have one room left, two beds." Libby didn't respond, and he took the initiative. "It's the end of the summer. People are traveling, and I doubt if we'll find anything else." She wasn't smiling, and he hoped she didn't think he was trying to force her into a compromising position. "You take the room, and I'll sleep in the car."

"There's no need to do that," she blurted. "We can manage."

Kipp checked them in and carried their bags to a room in the middle of the complex. Libby unlocked the door.

The two beds took up the better part of the room. The full impact of spending the night in the same space with a woman like Libby gave him a start, and he wondered how the hell they were going to manage. At least the room was clean.

"I saw a coffee shop across the street," he said. "How about something to eat?" That should delay the inevitable.

"I could use a sandwich, but could we order out?"

"Sure. I'll go. What would you like?"

"Turkey or tuna. And decaf."

Kipp left the musty-smelling room, happy to get some fresh air and to clear his head. How the hell were they going to manage, the two of them in one room? The dry, unrelenting wind nearly swept him across the street to the little cafe.

Back at the motel, he heard sharp, angry voices coming from the room two doors down from them and people laughing from the room next door. He searched for the key with one hand and juggled the sacks with the other, trying to keep from spilling the coffee.

The door burst open with Libby standing there like a vision. He must have stared at her for a full minute, thinking how attractive she was, before he managed to tame his thoughts and pay attention to getting the food to the tiny round table in the middle of the room.

He sorted the sandwiches and presented her with a Styrofoam cup. "No cream or sugar, right?"

"You remembered."

A feeling of pride washed over him, like a boy impressing his first date.

She unwrapped her sandwich and announced, "This is a BLT."

Pride turned to embarrassment. "It was turkey, wasn't it? I'll go back and get you another one."

"No, no. This is fine." She opened the sandwich and set the bacon aside.

"I'll go back."

"Sit down. There's something I want to tell you."

The razor-edge of her voice turned Kipp's attention to why they were here. "Is it about Kelly?"

"Indirectly. I want to explain why I changed my mind and decided to come with you."

He held his coffee cup and sat down.

"Do you remember the visions you had?"

"How could I forget?"

"Well, I've had visions, too. I had them two months before I met you. I didn't know what they were trying to tell me until a few nights ago. It wasn't clear before. Someone was trying to come through the veil to give me a message. A woman finally appeared to me. The message was about you."

Kipp leaned back and gazed at Libby. He knew she was waiting for a reaction, but all he could think of was what a bizarre situation he'd found himself in.

Libby continued, "After you left my home, the last time I saw you, I woke up in the middle of the night and saw the form of a woman, an older woman with silver hair and glasses with large, round rims. Her nose was crooked, as if it had been broken at one time."

"Wait a minute."

"In a car accident."

"Just hold on, okay?"

"She told me to help you. She's—"

Kipp slammed his palm on the table to get her attention. "Now, Libby, just hold on, will you? How much of this do you think I can take?"

"She's your grandmother, isn't she?"

"I don't know. I suppose."

"I told you in the beginning we all have guides, sometimes people who have passed over."

"Yes, you told me all that, but if that's true, why didn't she come to me?"

"I was the one who needed convincing. It was urgent that I come with you."

"What do you mean urgent? You said over the phone we couldn't waste time. What does that mean?"

"I don't know yet, but I'm sure we'll find out."

"I don't like that answer."

"You have to trust me on this."

"That's not my forte. I like to know what I'm getting into."

"Sometimes you have to go out on a limb, step into the unknown, take a risk to find the answers."

"You don't have to tell me about taking risks. I've done that all my life. I've been all over the world."

"And haven't you ever felt like you were out on a limb?"

"All the time."

"Well, why not this time? What's the difference?"

"You. I've never been with anyone like you." His voice caught, and he felt compelled to clarify the words that just stumbled out of his mouth. "I mean, it's the way you are. One minute you know so much, and the next minute you trust some unknown, I don't know what you call it, to lead you on. Does anything I'm saying make sense?"

"That unknown force is called intuition, guidance, and there is always timing involved."

"What do you mean?"

"It's called being in the flow of life. You let your feelings or instincts lead you from one moment to the next."

Kipp shifted in his chair.

"If an opportunity comes up, and it feels right, you go for it. If it doesn't, something else will come along when the time is right. You trust it."

"What does this have to do with finding my daughter?"

"There are some things that might confuse us or panic us if we knew them too soon. So, we relax and let the information come through in its own time."

Kipp threw up his hands. "I don't have a clue what you're talking about."

"You will. Trust me."

Kipp worked over his sandwich while pondering Libby's words. Afterward, he crumpled the paper bags and tossed them in the waste can.

Libby finished her sandwich and slipped into the bathroom. When she returned, she placed her hands on Kipp's slumped shoulders. "Don't think so hard. It'll come in its own time."

Totally confused, his head reeling, Kipp turned his attention to something more tangible. He took his turn in the bathroom and began to stew over how the sleeping arrangements would work. She would certainly want privacy, and he wasn't too keen on parading around in his shorts. If he left the room for a while, she would be all tucked in by the time he returned. Or, maybe she would want him to get into bed first. Prepared to give her the option, he came out of the bathroom only to discover she was still in her street clothes and already curled up on the bed nearest the window.

He sneaked close enough to see if she was asleep. Her eyes were closed, and she didn't move. He couldn't resist smiling. As much as this woman with the weird talent and strange explanations frustrated him, she also intrigued him.

The room held a chill from the air conditioning, and he took a blanket from the closet shelf and laid it over her. Her familiar rose scent aroused his senses. Kissing her cheek right now would have been so natural. Instead, he switched off the lamp, slipped off his trousers, and climbed into the adjoining bed.

NINETEEN

I N THE MORNING Libby woke to the sound of water running. During the night she had shifted positions and was now facing Kipp's bed. The clock was turned away from her, but by the heightened color of the walls reflecting light from the windows, the sun had risen.

The door latch clicked, and artificial light flooded the closet area. She pulled the blanket up around her face and peered over the edge. Kipp came out of the bathroom with a towel wrapped around his waist, exposing part of his thigh. He rummaged through his suitcase and slipped back into the bathroom with a piece of clothing in his hand.

It had been a long time since Libby had seen a man's partially nude body, and she experienced a stirring long suppressed. She willed the feeling away.

Thankful she'd been spared the uncomfortable position of parading around in a nightgown, she got up and smoothed out her wrinkled clothes as best she could and retrieved the brush from her purse to tame her hair.

While waiting for Kipp, she opened the curtains and viewed the brown arid foothills, tinged with a greenish blue, abutting the town they were in. When she turned back, Kipp, dressed in jeans and a tee shirt, his wet hair slicked back, was staring at her. She hugged her arms to her body and glanced at the clock. "I guess I slept in."

"I couldn't sleep. I guess I'm anticipating."

"That's understandable."

"I thought I'd go out for a walk and let you have some privacy. Is thirty minutes enough time?" When she nodded her assent, he stuffed his wallet in his pocket and left Libby to herself.

Sleeping in street clothes brought back memories of traveling by bus or train in her youth. But they also brought back memories of the excruciating times she lay on the couch, waiting for her ex-husband to come home. She shivered with dread and drove that thought away.

Kipp was giving her a half hour, but one look in the bathroom mirror and she decided an hour wouldn't be enough time to fix the problem.

While in the shower, she recalled glimpsing Kipp's body and experienced a rush of heat. She thought about his sincerity, his kind and respectful manner. But one glance at her own body reminded her she would rather keep their relationship platonic than to suffer the humiliation of seeing him repulsed by her deformity.

Once she was out of the shower, she hastened to style her hair, and by the time she heard the main door open, she was putting the finishing touches on her makeup. She dressed in capris and a blouse, nothing too clingy, and joined Kipp in the outer room.

He glanced up from opening paper bags. "You look terrific."

Her face warmed from the comment. She hadn't had this much attention in a lifetime. Kipp was a gentleman, something she was definitely unaccustomed to.

He set a Styrofoam cup on the table in front of her, and she picked out a banana nut muffin.

"I thought we might drive up to Idaho Falls this morning. Then go east from there," he said. "What do you think?"

She stared off into the distance.

"Libby, you're not going to get quiet again, are you? We need to keep talking."

She focused back on him. "I guess you haven't been around me enough to know that sometimes I'm tuning in. Like when you mentioned Idaho Falls, I was getting information."

"Did you get something?"

"I think your instincts are good. I sense Idaho Falls is going to be pivotal."

Kipp laid his hand over Libby's. "Are we that close?"

"We need to get up there."

Kipp leapt up, collected the paper bags, and threw them in the trash. Libby hurried to grab her cup to keep it from being confiscated.

"I'd like to call Ellen before we go," she said.

An irritated look crossed Kipp's face, the same expression she was beginning to recognize whenever he was impatient. "Can't you call on the way?"

She snatched her purse from the bed and hastened from the room. Kipp followed with the luggage.

While she waited in the car for him to check out, she called her home number. No one answered. She tried Ellen's cell phone.

TWENTY

"WHERE ARE YOU?" Ellen yelled into her cell phone, rock music blaring in the background.

"We're on our way to Idaho Falls."

"Can you speak louder? I can hardly hear you. I'm on the treadmill, sweating like a gorilla in heat. Can you hear the machines?"

"Yes, and the music. How are you doing?"

Ellen slowed the treadmill to a stop and rested her sweaty palm on the handle. "I'm A-okay. I wasn't last night. Mel called. He wanted me to come home. He says he loves me, the fool. I told him to stuff it where the sun don't shine. Aren't you proud of me?"

"I guess the workouts are doing you good. You sound great."

"Where did you stay last night?"

"In a little town north of Salt Lake City."

"I mean, is there anything to report in the snuggle department?"

"The what?"

"Did you sleep together?"

"Of course not."

When Ellen scanned the room, her jaw dropped. Charlie Bender had come around the corner.

"Ellen?"

"Oh my gosh, it's Randy Quaid."

"Who?"

"You know. Charlie Bender. He just came out of the weight room. I'm a wreck, and he's coming my way." Ellen turned to the side to avoid eye contact.

"Ellen. I'll call you in a day or two and let you know what's happening."

"Okay, hon, you two take care." Ellen crammed her cell phone in her bag and held a towel in front of her legs just as Charlie approached in faded shorts and a wrinkled tee shirt.

"Didn't know you came here," he said.

She plastered a smile on her face and batted her eyelashes, all the while feeling like a two-ton whale. "I'm using Libby's membership while she's gone. What are you doing? Keeping that boyish figure in shape?"

Charlie patted his belly. "Too many dinners out. I put in my time and lift a few weights."

"I bet you come in here to ogle the women with their tiny little figures, like all the rest of the men here," she said, nodding toward the thin young woman who had stepped onto the elliptical machine across the room.

He gave the woman a sweeping look. "Naw. I like to have something to cuddle."

"That's refreshing."

"Are you about done here?"

"As done as I'll ever be."

"How about some juice? I'll buy. We can go sit in the park and talk if you want to. I have a little time before I have to get back to work."

"I'd be delighted. I'll just clean up first and meet you there." She watched him walk away and give her a little salute from the top of the staircase. The man definitely made her heart skip a beat.

Wishing she'd been better prepared, she left the gym, dressed in a faded oversized sundress, the only outfit she'd brought with her. She crossed the street, smearing on extra coral lipstick.

Scanning the grassy area of the park, she spied Charlie on one of the benches near the river. A few geese were pecking the grass near the water's edge, their backs glistening gray in the sunlight. Downstream, water gushed over the falls.

Charlie stood and handed her a paper carton. "Hope orange is okay."

"You bet." She pulled the tab and took a long swallow of the cold sweet liquid, and he waited for her to sit first, which she happily took note of. "I just talked to Libby. They're on their way to Idaho Falls."

"You know their plans?"

"Kipp said it was okay if I knew. Actually, we're the only ones they told. God, I hope they find that little girl."

"Are they running into any problems?"

"Not as far as I know."

Charlie rested his arms on his thighs. "Kipp's a driven man when it comes to Kelly. I hope this deal works out."

"You mean finding his daughter, or Kipp and Libby?" Ellen shifted to see Charlie's reaction and wasn't disappointed.

"Wouldn't that be something? The guy deserves a good woman."

"She deserves a good man."

"You ever meet his ex?"

"No, but I saw her once on a magazine cover. The perfect woman," she said with mild disdain.

"She's a real…" He waved the comment away. "Let's just say they weren't compatible. What about Libby? She ever marry?"

"Yeah, if you could call it a marriage." She huffed in disgust. "The man defined the word abuse."

"I don't remember any police action concerning her."

"They lived in a different county when they were married."

"What happened to him?"

"He spent a week in jail. Then he left her when she got cancer."

Charlie's eyes widened. "Libby had cancer?"

"Breast cancer." Ellen told him all about the two surgeries, one of which Ellen considered to be a botched job, and the agony of the chemotherapy and after that the radiation treatments. "Her ex couldn't handle it."

"Nice guy."

"I always told her there was a gift in having the cancer. At least she got rid of him."

"She ever hear from him?"

"He calls once in a while when he's drunk or needs money, and he visited her once. He did remarry, so we've heard, and now he has another woman to kick around."

"I don't know how those assholes live with themselves. The department gets sick of having to deal with them." He took a large gulp of juice. "How'd she get mixed up with the guy?"

"That's the kicker," Ellen said. "He's an ex-cop. She met him when she was working with the police on a missing person case."

"Abuse knows no bounds."

"And Libby is a capable, intelligent businesswoman. You'd think she would know better than to stay with a man like that. Of course, I'm a good one to talk."

"Your husband ever hurt you?"

Ellen had never been asked that question and had to think how to answer it. "Mel? Hell, he barely ever touched me." She sucked in a breath. "God, I can't believe I told you that."

"Don't feel bad. I had the same problem. My wife would never put a hand on me. Not even a hug."

"Is that why you divorced?"

"That and a million other reasons. She said my belly disgusted her, but hey, this baby's all muscle." Chuckling, he pounded his midsection like a drummer.

Ellen laughed. "You're so funny. I like that."

Charlie emptied his juice carton. "I hate to run, but I have to get back to work. I'll walk you to your car."

They strolled along the sidewalk, talking about the unusual heat wave that had gripped the town. His holding the car door open for her was another courtesy that didn't go unnoticed. She tossed her bag in the backseat, climbed in, and rolled down the window to say goodbye.

He stooped near the opening. "You free to go out to dinner sometime?"

Her pulse quickened, hurling her depression into oblivion. "You better believe it. Mel doesn't have a claim on me anymore."

"I'll call you tomorrow." He winked and sauntered toward his vehicle.

Ellen yelled after him, "Did anyone ever tell you, you look like Randy Quaid?"

He yelled back, "All the time."

TWENTY-ONE

Wild grasses, parched by the late summer's sun, blanketed the eastern hills in a golden hue. Puffy clouds dotted the midday sky, and the air was pleasantly warm.

The trip north was uneventful, but the closer they came to the exit for Idaho Falls, the anxious feelings Libby picked up from Kipp were overwhelming. She tried deep breathing or counting the number of passing vehicles to focus her mind elsewhere, but little helped. Kipp remained quiet, except for the incessant tapping of his thumbs on the steering wheel.

Kipp veered to the right off the interstate. Traveling down one of the city streets, he finally spoke up. "Are you sure we shouldn't go to the police and ask around?"

Libby shifted away from the window where she had been staring at storefronts and looked at Kipp. "I feel we should do our own investigation first. We should turn east."

"But we don't even know where we're going."

She noticed a hint of frustration in his voice and wondered if he would ever trust her instincts.

At the next intersection she told him to turn left into the lot of the visitor's center. Kipp found a parking spot, and without a word he strode toward the red brick building as if he were grateful to have something concrete to do. She could almost see the nerves popping out of his skin. He'd escaped inside before she even got out of the car. Considering the gravity of the situation with all the unknowns, she shrugged off his lack of civility.

She entered the center and found him engaged in a dialogue with the attendant. The older gentleman, wearing a flannel shirt over his stooped shoulders, even though it was a summer day, spread out a map of the eastern counties.

"I want to get some good shots for a magazine," Kipp said, then turned to Libby. "I was just telling Ted here that I want those mountain shots. I said you'd been there before but didn't remember how to get there. Do you want to describe what you saw?"

Nice cover, she thought, as she advanced to the counter. "I was here a while back, and all I remember are three peaks grouped together. You can see them atop a long sloping meadow with lots of golden grass. They seem to rise out of nowhere."

The man ran his palm across the map and stopped near an area of green. "Wyoming or Idaho?"

"Idaho," Kipp said.

"Do you mind?" Libby slid her hand over the map's surface down the eastern part of the state and pointed at a spot on the border of Idaho and Wyoming.

"That's pretty close to the Tetons, but there are more than three peaks in that range. I guess you'll just have to have a look see." The man pressed a finger along the map. "If you follow this road, you'll get back on the highway, then take that road east. It'll take you to the town of Grand. You can see the mountains pretty close from there. You'll get an eyeful."

"What's Grand like?" Kipp said.

"Nice little town. Potato country. Farms all around. I'll warn you, though. There's a different breed of people living up in those hills. It's like going back in time."

"What do you mean by that?"

"You'll see for yourself."

A middle-aged couple came through the doorway, arguing about where they were going to eat lunch. Kipp folded the map and moved aside.

In the car he studied the map one last time before passing it to Libby. He started the engine and drove off. Asking him about lunch was pointless. He seemed intent on finding the highway out of town.

As they drove farther into farm country, Libby's feelings drew her strongly to the east. She kept prompting Kipp to find a path in that direction, and Kipp exited on the easterly road Ted had marked on the map. Motoring over rolling hills, they were deep into acres and acres of wheat.

They'd been traveling well over an hour. Rounding a final curve, they perched on the crest of a hill. By now the sun was behind them, and when Libby looked up from studying the map, she braced herself with both hands on the dashboard. "Oh my gosh, Kipp. I think this is what I pictured. Pull over, quick."

He had witnessed the same sunlit scene and swerved to the side of the road. Libby jumped out first and stood trembling with excitement. With an arm over her shoulders, Kipp steadied her.

In the far distance several craggy granite peaks jutted out of the tree line. Opposite, where Kipp and Libby were, golden fields sloped to meet the town nestled in between. Libby's impression was dead-on.

She leaned into Kipp, thankful for his support. Maybe now she would be vindicated. She hated having to constantly prove her gift. Only when a car whizzed by, did she make an attempt to change positions, but his arm stayed snug.

He drew her closer and gave her a tender kiss on the cheek. "Thank you, Libby."

His spontaneity was contagious, given the circumstances, and she returned the kiss.

He lifted her chin, forcing her to look into his intense green eyes. "When this is over..."

His eyes led her deeply into his soul, and she sensed a longing, but also a connection between them, far more than a passing friendship. Her breath caught. "We've only just begun. We don't even know for sure where the exact location is. We won't know until we feel it out. There is so much more to discover." She loosened his hold and hurried into the car.

Kipp slid into the driver's seat and held up his palm to her. It took her a second to understand his meaning, and then she laid her hand limply in his.

"I'm sorry if I've been a jerk," he said. "I've just been edgy."

She smiled briefly and withdrew her hand. He'd given her that tender look again, the one she'd observed now and then throughout their business relationship or friendship, or whatever their relationship was morphing into. Yet, for her, things hadn't changed. She couldn't allow any feelings she might have for him influence her. She had to stay strong and centered with a heart full of compassion and love, but not the kind of love she sensed he wanted. If he saw her body, the disappointment in his face would kill her. She shuddered to think about it.

Descending into the valley gave her a chance to concentrate on the task at hand. At the bottom of the hill, the highway branched—one arm turning south and continuing on, and the other arm reaching into the town. Kipp followed the sign to Grand.

They passed a café, a gas station, a grocery store, and a few older buildings until the road veered left out of town. They traveled down this long country road with nothing on either side except wheat-colored fields and a spectacular view of the mountain peaks. The farther they drove, more aspens highlighted the landscape. The only signs along the way were mileage signs.

Kipp tried to follow along with the map between them, glancing from time to time, until Libby snatched it away just to be safe. "This is leading nowhere, Libby."

"I know," she said. "In my mind, all I saw were the mountain peaks, but I have to sense my way from here. This way doesn't feel right. Turn around and go back."

With no cars coming toward them, Kipp made a U-turn in the middle of the road. He motored through Grand again and found the gas station. "I'm going to fill up and talk to the attendant."

Libby stayed in the Jeep. She was thinking about the symbols she saw in Kipp's reading and wondering if she'd made a mistake in her interpretation when she spotted two women in identical dresses going into the grocery store. Without warning, Kelly's face flashed before her, signaling a connection. She started shivering—another positive sign.

If she told Kipp, knowing his state of mind, he would rush headlong into the store and start bullying them with his questions. That would be the worst thing he could do. She sensed this matter had to be handled with delicacy.

When Kipp got back in the Jeep, she put her plan in motion. "I need something at the store."

"Okay. I'll drive over and go with you."

"I thought maybe you could stay here and ask the station attendant about motels in the area."

"Let me go for you," he insisted. "I'll buy you whatever you want." He put the key in the ignition.

Libby rested her hand on his. "I don't think you'll want to buy what I need." She waited for him to make the connection.

He responded with a perplexed look, then his face turned a healthy pink. He opened the door to get out. She swung her purse strap over her shoulder and scurried across the street, chuckling over Kipp's reaction.

The store, in mild disrepair, was old and battered from the wind. The white paint on the screen door was chipped and peeling. It creaked as she entered.

She nodded to the clerk, a stocky woman with rough skin and thick muddy hair. Straight ahead, she saw the two look-alikes. From the back, they mirrored each other: drab ankle-length dresses, dark shoes, hair tied back in a bun. She instantly felt drawn to them.

The shelves were stocked full of canned goods, the aisles narrow. Libby pressed forward, and when she squeezed by one of the women, gently bumping her arm, a swirl of images bombarded her: clapboard buildings, golden meadows, people in strange, colorless clothing gathered around a table.

Dizzy, she braced herself against a shelf post. Though nothing made sense, the images were strong and clear and reinforced her feeling that she and Kipp were on the right track.

The two women had advanced to the front of the store, and Libby strained to hear their conversation over the hum of the freezer compartment next to her. The only words spoken came from the gravelly voice of the clerk.

Libby grabbed a box of tampons for Kipp's benefit and waited for the women to leave the store. She walked up to the counter to investigate. "It's unusual to see someone dressed like that in the middle of summer."

"You mean those women?"

Libby nodded.

"They're just unusual, period."

Libby laid her money on the counter. "So, are they twins?"

"You're not from these parts, are you?"

"No, just passing through."

"See those hills?" She pointed at the window behind her over a Coca

Cola sign. "There's a religious group up there. They make up half this town now."

"What kind of religious group?"

"Sort of like the Mormons used to be. They're polygamists."

"Isn't that illegal?"

"They don't bother nobody, and nobody bothers them. You know what I mean? We're all peaceful around here."

As she counted out Libby's change, the screen door rattled open and a bearded, gruff-looking man in black pants, gray jacket, and work boots—heavily dressed for the time of the year—entered the store. Curious, Libby watched the man disappear down one of the aisles. When she turned back, the clerk gave her a challenging look. Libby deemed no more questions were allowed. She left the store.

Before crossing the road, she looked westward toward the hills the clerk spoke of, but the sun, at a glaring angle, prevented her from seeing very far. When she climbed into the Jeep, she could feel her heart thumping.

Kipp glanced at the package in her hand and started the engine. "Did you get what you needed?"

"Yes. Thanks for waiting."

"I found out there are no motels in the area. We're going to have to drive back to Idaho Falls tonight."

Libby pondered whether or not to tell Kipp about the women and what she'd sensed in the store. Something inside kept harping at her to go slow, but as anxious as she was to share the information, she ignored the warning. She heard him say her name, and she blurted, "I have something to tell you."

"What is it?"

"There's a community of polygamists living up in the hills."

"That's interesting," he said. "That must have been what Ted at the visitor's center was talking about."

"It's more than interesting," she said. "When you were talking to the attendant, I noticed two women who were dressed identically in long dresses, had hair done up in buns. They belong to that community."

"Must be what Ted meant when he said it was like going back in time."

"That's not all. When I was near them in the store, I had some strong feelings, Kipp. I think there might be a connection."

"To Kelly?"

"I think so. The feelings were so strong."

"But it's a polygamist community. What would that have to do with Kelly?"

"I don't know right now. I got a powerful feeling. I saw her face. I just know what I'm feeling."

"Okay, if you feel that strongly about it, let's go up there and have a look for ourselves."

"Not yet."

"What if she's up there?"

"I'm not positive."

"But you said there's a connection."

"A connection, maybe, but we have to take this slow."

"Why?"

"Please trust me."

Kipp gunned the engine and swung onto the road west.

"Where are you going now?"

"To have a look."

"Kipp, don't." Why hadn't she listened to her inner voice?

Trying to convince Kipp to back off was like trying to persuade a boxer to stay out of the ring. She only prayed he would not get them into a precarious situation.

Across the highway was a gravelly road leading deeper into the hills.

She hoped he wouldn't see it, but her hopes were dashed when he crossed the highway and made the turn. He slowed way down to avoid spraying the car with pebbles. Tall yellow grasses lined both sides of the roadway that appeared to end in a grove of aspens.

As they drove farther on, the gravel thinned to dirt. The road wove through the trees, but it was blocked by a locked gate. Tacked to one of the end posts in bright orange letters was a sign that read No Trespassing.

Kipp got out and inspected the gate. He yanked on the padlock, but it held tight.

Libby's stomach fluttered and churned. This had to be the place because the forward feeling was overwhelming.

She sprang from the car. By the time she reached Kipp's side, her sandals were covered with dust.

She placed her hand on one of the posts, and a jolt of energy passed through her, so strong it was painful. Sucking a breath in, she turned away from Kipp to mask her reaction, because instinctively she knew it was the wrong time to probe.

Back in the Jeep, Kipp slammed his hands on the steering wheel. "Damn."

"We better go back," Libby said, "and think about what we're doing."

"I'm tired of thinking." Kipp backed the Jeep around, flipping rocks, and drove onto the highway.

"Where are you going now?"

"I saw the sheriff's office on our way through."

"No." She clutched his arm.

"Libby," he said, "this time you'll have to trust me."

Desperate to keep him from dynamiting their best chance, she said, "Whatever you do, Kipp, don't mention Kelly. Please."

When they pulled up to the sheriff's office, Libby begged him once again to remain silent about his daughter, but he wouldn't acknowledge her and seemed intent on doing things his way. Exasperated, she trailed him up the steps of the square wooden building, uncertain what he planned to do.

Inside, two metal desks faced the entrance, the room empty of life. Toward the rear, a partition blocked the view to an extended area. A fan whirred in the background. The clock on the far wall ticked off the seconds, yet it seemed like minutes went by before a lean uniformed deputy with hair as wiry as a bristle brush came out from the back, picking between his lower front teeth with a thumbnail. He looked up, surprised. "Didn't know anyone was here. What can I do for you?"

Libby stared at Kipp, pleading with her eyes to be cautious, but he kept his gaze on the young man. "I'm a photographer, and I was hoping to get some shots of the mountains."

"Be our guest."

"It looks to me like the best view would be from the hills across the highway, but the road is blocked with a locked gate."

"You've been up that road?"

"I was looking for a way up the hill."

The sheriff, a puffy-faced, plain-looking man in jeans and cowboy boots, came out of the back room and stood next to the deputy. His deep penetrating eyes spurred Libby to take a step closer to Kipp and latch on to his arm.

"These people want to take pictures of the peaks from up on the hills. They've already been up the road."

The way the cowboy sheriff squinted at them, bunching the creases around his eyes, made Libby squeeze Kipp's arm in a warning attempt to get him to give up his foolish plan.

"That's private property."

"Maybe if I could talk to the owner, he'd let me—"

"Mister, we don't like people messing around where they don't belong.

You understand what I'm saying?"

The muscles in Kipp's arm tensed. Libby dug her nails into his flesh, and he glanced at her for the first time since they'd entered the building.

"We don't need those pictures, dear," she said to Kipp, then turned to the man. "My husband gets so carried away when he sees beauty like this. He likes to keep scrapbooks of pretty pictures when we go on trips. But we'll just get some postcards after all. By the way, does that restaurant in town have good food?"

The deputy cracked a smile. "Yes, ma'am. Best in the county."

"We'll be on our way then. Come on, honey." She pinched Kipp's bicep, but she couldn't help notice him and the sheriff exchanging stares like rams ready for combat. Once they were outside, she put her finger to her lips to warn Kipp not to say anything.

Once they were in the Jeep, Kipp's face turned into a flaming torch. "Did you hear that S.O.B.? 'We don't like people messing around here.' What have they got to hide? I'm going to go up there and break the god-damned lock."

Libby took his hand and held it to her face.

Kipp's arm twitched, revealing his urge to draw it back, but her warmth calmed him. His muscles relaxed, and his anger subsided. He said in a much softer tone, "What are you doing?"

"Getting your attention."

"Now that you have it…"

She lowered his hand into her lap. "Will you listen to me? Will you trust my judgment?"

He stared at her, calmed but concerned.

"We should leave and go back to Idaho Falls now."

"Idaho Falls? We need to figure out what's going on here."

"No one is going to let you do anything here," she said. "They know we're outsiders. They'll be watching us. We need to go back and regroup.

Eat, sleep. We'll figure out something in the morning."

"What if she's here? I can't leave her."

"Please, Kipp. If you'll just take a breath and ask yourself what's the best thing to do, you'll know I'm right."

Kipp sat silent, and she knew he was working her words through his logical mind. She was becoming accustomed to his behavior: react first, think later.

He started the motor and pulled away from the building. "I guess we'll head out like you said." He turned right, toward their destination, finally giving Libby a reason to breathe easier.

The sun had set behind the hills. Dusk was settling in.

When they reached the highway, Kipp lingered at the stop sign longer than needed, glancing in the direction of the gravel road. Libby held her breath, hoping he wouldn't do anything rash. He turned in the right direction, but drove slowly at first, and she wondered if he might turn around and go back. But then he pressed on the gas.

As soon as the Jeep began to accelerate, a car screamed up behind them, practically ramming their bumper, its high beams blasting the Jeep's interior. Just as Libby jerked around to have a look, the car with the anonymous driver swung into the oncoming lane and passed them at full speed, cutting in front of them, nearly clipping their front bumper and forcing them off the road. Kipp swerved onto the shoulder and came to an abrupt halt. Libby braced herself from smashing into the dashboard.

"Sonova… We could have been hit."

Libby leaned back with a heavy sigh.

He reached over and touched her cheek. "Are you all right?" She nodded, and he said, "Did you get a look at the driver?"

"It happened too fast, and I think the windows were tinted."

Kipp checked the road behind them before pulling onto the highway and continuing up the hill at a slower pace. At the top of the incline he glanced over at Libby. "That wasn't a random shot, was it?"

She knew the answer but wouldn't indulge in talking about it for fear of adding fuel to Kipp's burgeoning anger. He was spring-loaded for action. For the time being, she was just happy to be leaving the town with the mysterious, and incensed, residents.

Following a sober drive back to Idaho Falls, she called Ellen. No one answered.

TWENTY-TWO

AFTER ELLEN LEFT Charlie at the park, she treated herself to a movie, got a bite to eat, and shopped for a new dress. She felt like a young woman looking for a prom outfit. She hadn't been to dinner with a man, other than Mel, ever.

She left the mall around eight-thirty and drove toward Libby's house with emotions ranging from giddiness to terror. Happy-go-lucky Ellen was having her first date in twenty years. By the time she parked the car, she settled on the fact that Charlie was easy to be with. If any guilt popped into her head, guilt because of her marital status, all she had to do was picture Mel with the scarecrow woman in her bed and the guilt just scuttled away.

She stepped onto the porch, thinking about her date with Charlie and rummaging for her keys, then glanced up and froze. The door was halfway open. Trees hovered over the property, darkening Libby's area earlier than in town, and the house was dark inside.

Ellen's first thought was she had forgotten to latch the door all the way, but she'd always been careful to make sure doors were latched shut. Her next thought was a burglar had entered, but there was no sign of a break in, no scrapes or splintered wood around the door jamb. She shuddered at the thought that followed.

The subject of Libby's ex-husband had just surfaced in her conversation with Charlie. Libby's ex had not been seen in a while, but he used to be a cop and could be knowledgeable and resourceful when it came to such things as breaking and entering. She would not put it past him to come slinking around. Plus, a little way down the road she had seen an abandoned car.

She began to hyperventilate. Afraid to proceed, she rushed to her car and locked the doors. She thought of Charlie.

Libby said she could call him if she had any problems. She hated to bother him, but he was a law enforcement officer, after all. From her purse she retrieved her cell phone and address book and with a flashlight from the glove compartment she skimmed down and located his number.

Within ten minutes a sheriff's cruiser, followed by a pick-up, drove up Libby's driveway. Ellen opened her door, but Charlie told to her to stay put, and he and the deputy disappeared inside. Soon the house was illuminated. She chewed at her nails until Charlie emerged and motioned for her to join them on the porch.

"Everything looks okay," Charlie said. "Let's walk through, and you can tell us if everything is in place." He held on to her arm.

His touch made her realize how unsteady she was, but she made a futile attempt at a smile. She led the way through each room. There were no signs of anything disturbed or taken, no signs of forced entry. When they returned to the front door, Charlie nodded to the deputy, and he left in the cruiser.

"You could have forgotten to lock the door," Charlie said. "It's an easy mistake, especially when the house isn't yours and you aren't used to the feel of things."

"I thought I did. I'm sorry I bothered you. I feel like an idiot, making you come all the way out here for nothing."

"It's my job. And, hey, it's not nothing if it means you're safe."

"You're quite a guy, Charlie. You called it in, didn't you?"

"It's the county's jurisdiction, and I figured a deputy might get here before I could. Are you going to be okay here?"

"Yeah, but it might take me a while to calm down."

"I could stop by after a while. I need to do a few things first. I could check up on you, unless it's too late."

"I'd like that."

"I'll stop by in a couple of hours. Now, go in and lock the door. I'll wait."

She relished taking orders from a man like Charlie. She locked the door and flicked the porch light on and off as a sign everything was secure. His car started up, and she heard the tap of his horn.

Although the deputy had searched the house and all the lights were on, and despite what she told Charlie, Ellen was still spooked. She double-checked every room before she padded into the bathroom and drew a hot bath. She locked the door for security, though any man could battle his way through if he wanted to. She recalled Libby telling her how Dan had busted through a secured bathroom door. But that was Dan and Dan wasn't here.

She studied her naked body in the mirror, admitting to herself it was going to take years at the gym to improve the image she saw. She shrugged with indifference.

As she lowered her body into the tub, her pale skin reddened, and she welcomed the soothing heat. She sank deeper into the water and let her feet rest against the smooth porcelain surface. Her thoughts coasted from Kipp and Libby to Charlie's recent visit, and to other less-defined reflections until she drifted toward sleep.

A banging noise catapulted her into consciousness, and she struggled to sit up without sinking any deeper. A rattling sound, followed by several short rings, had her grasping for a towel. The ringing persisted, along with several pounding sounds.

She wrapped her robe around her on the way to Libby's room, her heart bursting through her chest with every breath. She was thankful Libby kept a pistol in her nightstand drawer—insurance against an impromptu visit from Dan. Without giving a thought to what she would do with it, she dug out the gun and strode toward the front door.

By now the banging and pounding had increased. Ellen held the pistol with both hands, lengthened her arms, and pointed at the door. Shaking uncontrollably, she screamed out, "Who's there?" The rattling ceased. "Who's out there?"

"It's me. Charlie. Are you okay?"

Energy rippled down her body as her muscles relaxed. She lowered the gun and opened the door. "What are you doing here? You scared the pants off me."

"I didn't mean to. When you didn't answer, I thought something might have happened to you."

"I was in the bathtub. I must have dozed off. Is it that late already? I didn't think I was in there that long."

"I decided to come back early. I was worried about you."

"What a sweet thing." She melted at the concern in his eyes. "Come in. Come in." When he didn't move, she woke up to the fact that the screen door was still locked. She let him in.

The first thing he did when he entered the house was stare at the gun in Ellen's hand. "You know how to use that?"

Ellen glanced at the gun, then grinned. "It's Libby's. I got scared. I wasn't really going to use it, I don't think."

He relieved her of the gun and checked the chambers. "It's empty. Why don't you put it back where it belongs, in a safe place?"

"She keeps it by her bed in case her ex decides to make a grand entrance. When I heard the noise, I thought it was him."

"I doubt if a gun would deter a guy like that. They can get crazy."

Ellen returned the gun to Libby's drawer and came back to the living room. "I'm sorry for the mistake, but I'm glad you're here. Would you like some coffee, a beer?"

"A beer sounds good. I've had a long day."

Ellen went into the kitchen. When she leaned over at the refrigerator, her robe flared, reminding her she was naked underneath. In all the commotion, she'd forgotten about her lack of clothing. She secured the robe's ties.

She handed him a can of beer, and he moved over on the couch. He had changed from the slacks he had on earlier to well-worn jeans, but he wore a short-sleeved shirt that looked as if he had recently run an iron over it, a wrinkle here and there. He rested his arms on his thighs and rolled the can around in his hands.

Ellen waited for him to say something, then decided to break the ice. "I didn't see much of you at the reunion."

"I had to finish a report. I've been swamped at work."

"If I didn't know that, I'd think you weren't too fond of high school. You live in town and don't even go to your reunion."

"I could take it or leave it."

"I guess."

"Seems to me you had a great time in high school. Even when you had to practice that cheerleader stuff after school every afternoon, you looked like you were enjoying it. You were always laughing and carrying on."

Ellen cocked her head. "How did you know that?"

"I used to hide near the bleachers and watch every day."

"What for?"

"So I could see you."

Ellen's mouth dropped open. "Me?"

"I had the biggest crush on you."

"Charlie Bender, why didn't I know that?"

He hitched a shoulder. "Oh, you know how dumb boys can be in high school. By the time I figured out how I was going to ask you out, you'd taken up with Mel."

"Oh, Charlie, you could have saved me years of heartache. So, do you miss being married?"

"Not with Patty, but I like the concept. I miss having someone there. How about you?"

"Me? I would just like the experience of having someone there."

"Wasn't Mel home much?"

Ellen huffed, shook her head.

"Was it his job, or was he tomcatting around?"

She raised two fingers. "I'll take door number two."

"Did he have a lot of women?"

"Yeah, I suppose. I never really added them up, though."

"Is that why you're leaving him?"

She thought she could handle the questions. Attempting an answer, she burst into tears.

Charlie draped his arm over her shoulders and pressed her toward him. As she scooted his way and leaned her head against his shoulder, her robe fell to the side, revealing a naked thigh. Charlie reached across and covered it with her robe.

That one sweet act from the boy who had had a crush on her sparked something in Ellen. She lifted her head and planted a kiss on Charlie's lips. He responded in kind.

She hungered for the attention of the man who seemed to care about her, and she could have smothered him with the passion of a woman deprived, but she suppressed her feelings, thinking more about her hideous body. She leaned back instead. "You're a good kisser."

"So are you." He leaned around and kissed her cheek. He ran his tongue around her lips.

Her heartbeat quickened, and the sexual feelings, long suppressed, wiggled to the surface. She pushed him back and flapped her hand in the air. "Whoa."

He grinned. "Am I moving too fast?"

Her head, captured by two voices, was spinning in different directions; she craved more, but the critical voice reminded her over and over she was too fat to pursue this. "I need to think."

He kept her close with his arm still locked in place. His fingers stroked the flesh on her upper arm, his touch gentle, yet insistent. Being honest with herself, Ellen wanted him to touch her whole body, not just her arm. Squashing the critical voice—the one that paraded all her faults into the open—she turned toward Charlie and kissed him again. He held her with both arms and returned the kiss with a passion that was so very foreign to her.

Sensual feelings were bubbling up, overpowering the need to hide her body, and she allowed him to slip his hand inside her robe and massage the thigh that had once been thoughtfully covered. She was anxious to run her hand over his bare chest, and everywhere else for that matter, but in an unlit room. She whispered, "The bedroom?"

Charlie responded with a huge grin. They held hands all the way to her room. Ellen crawled into bed, struggled under the covers to remove her robe, and waited for Charlie to undress. Neither of them turned on a light.

When Charlie climbed in next to Ellen, the bedsprings groaned. Immediately, his hands began to explore her body, breezing over her breasts, her belly, her thighs. For a second she tensed up at the realization that he could feel the bulges that defined her, but it had been so long since she had been touched this way, she let go of her angst and anticipated what was to come. "This feels so good. You don't know." She began tearing up.

"I don't want you to feel bad in the morning," he said.

"Sweetie," she said, sniffling, "if Libby were here, she'd predict we'll both feel good in the morning."

Once she opened her arms to him, the passion returned full force, and their hands were all over each other. For a while she worried he would be turned off by her weight, but once she was overcome by one sensation after another, she completely forgot about her appearance and gave in to the pleasure.

He stopped in the middle of a caress, and she froze, worried he was repulsed by her body. "What's wrong?" she said.

"I need to get a condom."

She released an audible sigh. "If you haven't been with anyone besides Patty and I haven't had sex with Mel for I don't know how long, then you're one lucky boy. I had a hysterectomy."

"In that case…"

"Come here, big boy."

Charlie rolled back to her and kissed her again and again, deepening the passion for both of them, Ellen breathing hard and moaning with delight, when he let out a muffled groan. "Jeez, I'm sorry. It's been a long time."

Panting, she hugged him close. "It's okay. I understand."

"You women have it easy."

"Oh, sure. Like you miss having to shave your legs or having a period."

He chuckled. "Are you always this clever?"

"That's me, Miss Funny Ha-Ha."

He ran his hand over her breasts. "You're funny and beautiful, Ellen."

"Every inch of me, right?"

"Every inch of you."

❧

In the morning Ellen woke to Charlie's staggered snores. She rose on an elbow and watched his lips move with each breath. His hair was straight in the slept-on places.

This had been the best night she could ever remember, even though she was a little sore from all the love-making. He had surprised her in the night by kissing her awake and making up for the overeagerness he'd experienced hours earlier.

She gave Mel a quick thought. Feelings for Charlie, the man who treated her with more respect and tenderness than Mel ever had in their whole marriage, washed away any guilt she may have felt by being with Charlie. He stirred, and she kissed his cheek. "How ya doin, big boy?"

He opened his eyes and smiled. "I think I died and went to heaven. How about you?"

"You have to ask? I'm glowing. You're such a good lover."

He slid his arm under her neck, and she nestled against him. "Want to have another go at it?"

"Let me slip into the bathroom first. Now, close your eyes."

"Why?"

"Come on, sweetie. In the dark is one thing."

He threw the covers to the foot of the bed.

"Charlie." She scrambled to catch hold, but he secured the sheets with his feet.

"Look, Ellen. Look at me." He patted his belly. "I'm not a model of slimness. You're beautiful just the way you are." He pulled her next to him.

As her gaze slid down his body, her eyes lit up. "My, oh my, Charlie. There's one part of you I like nice and plump." Just as she reached for the object of her affection, the phone rang. "Oh shoot. I better get that. It might be Libby."

TWENTY-THREE

K IPP LINGERED at the door of Libby's motel room, suitcase in hand, his mind crowded with yesterday's events. Libby did not have to tell him they were getting close to something. He could feel it, like a person sensing bad weather; his muscles ached with it. Ready to convince her to go back down that gravel road, he rapped at the door with fierce determination.

She answered with her cell phone to her ear and motioned him in. He watched her move around the room, chatting and laughing. Dressed in an aqua blouse, tucked into lightweight, cream-colored jeans that hugged her hips, she was picture-perfect. His pinched lips broadened into a grin. He'd lost his edge.

She finished her phone call, her smile widening. "I just called Ellen. You'll never believe who was there."

"Am I supposed to guess?"

"Charlie."

"Oh no, did she have a problem?"

"If you could call needing some affection a problem."

Kipp gave her a questioning look.

"He stayed the night."

"Charlie? Charlie and Ellen?"

"Isn't that fantastic?"

"How'd that come about?"

Libby told Kipp about Charlie investigating a possible break-in, how he checked on her later and never left. She also told him about Ellen holding a gun on him.

"I hope it works out between those two," Kipp said.

"I knew something good was going to happen to her."

"You seem to know everything."

"I just had a feeling." Libby brushed by Kipp. "Let me get something out of the bathroom."

"Why do you have a gun in your house?"

She returned with her makeup case and tucked it into her bag. "You don't want to know."

"But I do. Tell me."

She looked up at Kipp. "To keep the big bad wolf away."

"The what?"

"Ex-husband. It's a long, boring story, and I'm sure you'd rather get on the road."

"Will you tell me someday?"

"Maybe. Did you get a good night's sleep?"

"I wanted to get going hours ago."

"I guess that's a no."

"How could I?"

Libby zipped up her bag and set it next to Kipp's.

"We should go to the Idaho Falls police and ask about the group living in those hills, like we talked about last night," he said.

Libby was silent.

"This town wouldn't have an invested interest in that group," he said. "The people in Grand are too enmeshed."

Libby didn't say a word but was focused elsewhere. Kipp knew by now not to press her for answers, but it was beyond him where her mind wandered when she got quiet. She seemed to reach someplace deep inside. She was a well of information.

She made eye contact again. "I think you're right. Hopefully, there will be someone we can talk to on a Saturday. We need to find out if they're in trouble with the authorities, find out what they're about."

Kipp made a move to pick up the luggage, but she shook her head. "Now what?"

"It might be wise to keep our rooms here. Who knows where our search will lead. At least we'd have rooms to come back to later."

Kipp acquiesced and called the lobby, then covered the phone's mouthpiece. "We can only have one room. They're full up tonight."

The expression on Libby's face told him she was not too pleased. "Have them hold it for two nights. Maybe another room will open up tomorrow night."

On the way, Kipp wondered about Libby's ex-husband and why she felt so compelled to have a gun in the house. He could only speculate how dangerous the man was. A thousand questions haunted him, but when the police station came into view, he let the questions slide.

By the number of cars in the parking lot, Kipp guessed the place would not be teeming with activity. Libby followed him inside to a counter where the officer on duty, a stocky, barrel-faced sergeant with the name Dubing on his lapel, stood up from his desk.

"What can I do for you?" Sergeant Dubing said.

"We want to know more about the people who live in the hills around Grand," Kipp said.

"Why do you want to know?"

"I'm a photojournalist, and I want to do a story about them, but I can't seem to get any cooperation from the locals there."

"That doesn't surprise me. They're pretty private. I doubt if you'll be able to do anything with them."

"We know they're a polygamist group."

"A religious cult, to be more specific."

"Are they Mormons?"

"The Mormons don't want anything to do with them. Some guy just made up his own rules."

"So, how does it work in this day and age? Do they really have multiple wives?"

"Yeah, and it's all in the family. Cousins marry cousins, and Grandpa marries nieces. From what I understand, the brides are awfully young."

"Do they ever take women or children from outside their community?"

"Not that I know of. I think it's strictly an internal operation."

Kipp glanced at Libby for support.

"Sergeant Dubing," Libby said, "has there been any attempt to stop them from existing like this? I mean, if these women are young."

"I've heard some of them are fourteen, fifteen, maybe." He scratched his chin, shuffled some papers in front of him. "They did have some internal problems a while back, some deaths due to illness, more than usual. I know there have been complaints against them, but those folks are so entrenched there. Plus, it's a religious organization, and nobody wants to deal with that, especially the authorities. And it's out of our jurisdiction."

"Do you know of any way we can contact the head of the community?"

"Not really, but I can give you the name of a lady in town here who has helped some of the girls leave. She has a safe place where they can go. I don't think she'd mind talking to you. She knows a lot more than we do." He went back to a desk and scribbled on a scrap of paper. He handed it to Kipp.

In the car Kipp handed the note to Libby. "What good is this going to do? He said they don't take kids from outside their families. Is this going to be another dead end?" He stared out the side window and wondered, for the millionth time, what in the world he was doing on this wild ride.

Without answering him, Libby exited the car and went inside the station. When she returned, she ordered him to follow her directions.

They drove along the Snake River through the central part of the city, past a stately LDS temple. Up ahead, a grouping of brick houses lined the street, but the direction she pointed in veered to the right. Halfway down the block on one of the side streets, Libby had him pull up to the curb in front of an older two-story house.

She was out the door before Kipp had a chance to turn off the motor. Reluctant to go any further with this, he stayed put.

She came around to his side and opened the door. "You need to come with me. This is important."

"What's the point?"

She crouched and came face to face with him, her eyes lasering into his. With no questions asked, he immediately got out of the car.

On both sides of the sidewalk, the grass was matted and dried from the summer's heat. They climbed the three concrete steps to the front porch, and Libby knocked. A gray kitten ran up the steps and rubbed against Libby's leg until a woman who appeared to be in her forties answered the door, and the kitten darted inside.

By the woman's looks and demeanor, she'd had her own struggles in life: Her hair was unkempt. She had dark circles under her eyes. She was too hunched over for her age. They introduced themselves. She introduced herself as Grace and asked them in.

A table that had been moved into one corner of the kitchen took up most of the floor space. She asked them to sit at the table while she made an effort to neaten up a stack of papers and push them aside, out of the way. She offered them coffee, which they declined. She dragged a stool over from a corner of the room and addressed Libby. "You said on the phone you wanted to talk to me about the group living in Grand."

"As I mentioned, Sergeant Dubing at the police station gave us your number," Libby said. "He told us you were helping some of the girls leave there."

"Can I ask why you need to know?"

"We're trying to find a missing girl," Libby said.

Kipp wondered why Libby was being so forthcoming with this stranger, but he remained silent and let the dialogue continue.

"I doubt if you'll find her there."

"Can you tell us something about the group?" Libby said. "Why are you trying to help these girls?"

Grace reached across the table, snatched up a pack of cigarettes and a lighter, and pulled an ashtray close. "Do you mind if I smoke?"

Kipp wasn't thrilled about it, but said no, as did Libby.

Grace opened the door a crack, returned to her stool, and lit up. She took a drag and blew out toward the door. "Have you ever heard of sister wives?"

"No, but from what the sergeant said, we can guess."

"My sister and I were given to a fifty-eight-year-old man for marriage when she turned fourteen and I turned fifteen," Grace said. "We belonged to a polygamist group south of here. I escaped my situation, but my sister remained behind. She's still there. She has ten kids."

"Are these two groups related?"

"The one in Grand is an offshoot of the one I came from. Same principles. The men need at least three wives to secure a place in heaven. It's nothing but child abuse. There's another offshoot in Canada."

"So, you came here to help these girls escape their fate?"

"I've helped at least twenty so far."

"How do they get away?"

"It's tricky," Grace said. "The men watch over them like vultures. The girls sneak out at night, and we pick them up on the road. It doesn't always work. There's hell to pay if they get caught."

"What do you mean?"

"Retribution. Beatings."

"Why can't the women just leave?" Kipp said.

"Some have." Grace sucked a drag on her cigarette and sloughed off the ashes in the ashtray. "But you've got to realize these women have been brainwashed into believing the men have sole authority. They aren't given education after the age of thirteen. They just follow along like sheep and bear as many children as they're told. It's slavery to the max. Plus, they have nothing if they leave. Where are they going to go? They don't want to leave their children behind. That's why it's important to get them out when they're young before they're given to the older men."

"Jesus," Kipp said. "What about the authorities?"

"They have a live-and-let-live attitude. Some of them even belong to the group. It's all kind of incestuous."

"That sounds about right," Kipp said. "We were in Grand yesterday and practically got run off the road."

"We've been pushing for an investigation, forcing the state to put pressure on them. We want convictions for child abuse, something to break up that cult. That's why they're a little edgy right now."

There was a patter of little feet above them, then a clomping down a flight of stairs. A toddler came around the corner, squealing. He ran into Grace and grasped onto her legs. A young woman in braids wearing jeans marched into the room, disentangled the boy, and hoisted him onto her hip. After glancing at Kipp and Libby, she backed against the wall and lowered her gaze.

"This is Rebecca and her boy Samuel," Grace said. "She left the community a week ago. She was lucky to get out with her boy before the transfer."

"What's a transfer?"

"Every once in a while they move some of the younger women to one of the other communities to be given to the men there."

"You weren't already married?" Libby said to the girl.

Rebecca kept her head lowered, nodded, and let Grace answer for her. "Her mother died three years ago, and her husband died last year. She was going to be transferred south and given to a man down there."

"What about the younger kids? Do they ever get transferred?"

"Not usually." Grace snuffed out her cigarette, her index finger yellowed with nicotine. "They stay with their mothers. But because of the pressure coming from the state, Rebecca told me some of the younger men are taking their wives and children to parts unknown. That's to happen next week."

"You don't hear about this on the national news," Kipp said.

"No one wants to touch this because of the religious aspects," Grace said. "We've tried to get the word out, but I'll be honest with you, when it comes to the plight of women, there's no real interest. So, we keep working behind the scenes, and do what we can do to save these girls amidst the threats."

"Threats?"

"I've been threatened many times. These men don't want people to mess with the good thing they've got going."

"That's unbelievable."

"But these people don't take kids. They have enough of their own. So, I don't think you'll find the girl you're looking for there. How long has she been gone?"

"Two years."

"How old was she?"

"Four. She'd be just over six now."

Grace let out a sigh. "That's sad. Where'd you say you were from?"

"Washington State, but she was abducted in Connecticut."

Libby nudged Kipp's arm. "Show her Kelly's picture."

Kipp pulled the photo from his wallet and handed it to Grace. Rebecca leaned in to get a look, then left the room with the toddler.

Grace handed the picture back to Kipp. "Your daughter? That's a sorry shame. Have there been any leads at all?"

"It's like she vanished into thin air."

Rebecca returned without Samuel.

"Did you put him down for his nap?" Grace said.

Rebecca gave a sharp nod and asked Kipp if she could see the photo again. She studied the picture as if she were trying to fit the pieces of a puzzle together. She met Grace's gaze. "That looks like Sarah."

Kipp and Libby exchanged questioning looks. Kipp opened his mouth to speak, but Libby beat him to it. "Tell us about Sarah."

"Sarah is one of Jed's little girls."

"Are you related to Jed?"

"No. But he got this new little girl."

"What do you mean 'new'?"

"He got her from someplace else because a car came one day that had New York license plates. I remember everyone looking because they was different."

Kipp felt a sinking in his chest, and he could not muster enough breath to utter a word. Libby seemed to read his anguish and grasped his hand.

Grace glanced at Kelly's picture again. "Why do you think Sarah looks like the girl in this picture?"

"That's what Sarah looked like when she came here, except…"

"Except what?"

"Her hair was cut off and she had a dark brown wig on. The people who brought her said she had lice, and they had to cut off her hair. But underneath the wig it was blond."

Kipp's hands were shaking, and he bowed his head to hide his emotions. Libby knelt by his side.

"It has to be Kelly," he said. "You were right all along."

Grace brought him a glass of water. "Right about what?"

"I had a hunch she'd be somewhere around here," Libby explained. "That's all."

Kipp wiped the corners of his eyes. "Why wouldn't they question the people who brought her there? Wouldn't they want to find out if she was a missing child?"

"They don't care to have any contact with the outside world. They don't watch TV. They don't read newspapers. If it was in the media, they wouldn't have seen it," Grace said. "It's unlikely they questioned where she came from."

"What about the locals? Wouldn't they have seen her and questioned them?"

"They don't let the children out of the complex," Grace said. "Once they got her there, that would be it. She'd be sheltered from everyone. A great place to hide a kid. Besides, I doubt they want to draw attention to their own illegal world."

"I thought they didn't take kids from outside," Kipp said.

Grace glanced at Rebecca, her face clouded with concern. "You know what I'm thinking? Two years ago a flu epidemic hit that community pretty hard, and it was rumored they lost several members, especially women and children. They could have been trying to increase their numbers. I'm just guessing."

Kipp addressed Rebecca. "Is that true?"

She shrugged. "Another girl came later, then the sheriff came out one day. He seemed to know one of those people who brought her and Sarah. I saw him give them money and tell them they had to leave."

"What are they doing, offering money for kids?"

Rebecca looked to Grace, uneasy, and Grace said, "She wouldn't have known that. That would have been a man's business."

"Do you know?"

"I have no idea. All I know is several members may have died of flu."

"Why would they condone something as atrocious as kidnapping?"

"Why would they have relations with children?" Grace countered. "None of it makes sense, except that once a child is in their compound, no one would ever locate her. It's a religious cult, and that means hands off."

"We need to find a way to see if the girl is really Kelly," Libby said.

"They're leaving soon."

"Who's leaving, Rebecca?"

"Jed and his wives and their children and Sarah. To Canada or somewhere else with the others."

Kipp lowered his fist to the table. Libby jumped, and the others fixed their gaze on him. "They're not taking her. We've got to find a way to get her out of there."

"That won't be easy," Grace said. "The Falls police won't overstep the authorities in another jurisdiction. Forget Grand. They're in cahoots. By the time we convince the FBI to get involved, and that's even if we can, they'll be long gone."

"Then we'll go there ourselves," Kipp said.

"Those people won't let you or anyone else in the place."

"I'm not talking about asking them," Kipp said. "I'll break the goddamned gate down if I have to."

"You don't know where she is or if she's really your daughter." Grace reached for another cigarette. "They'll be all over you. They have guns, and don't be fooled. They'll use them to protect their own."

Rebecca stepped forward and said in a gentle voice, "I'll help you."

Kipp and Grace continued their discussion, unaware of Rebecca's offer until Libby said, "Did you hear Rebecca?"

When all eyes were on the dark-haired girl, her face reddened. "I can help you."

"How can you help, dear?" Grace said.

"I know a way in off a back road through some trees."

"They'll have that road watched like everything else."

"Not on Sunday night." She turned to Kipp. "They have the Sunday night meeting where everyone over ten years old has to go. The little kids stay in another building near the edge of the trees. I could take you there."

"Aren't they being watched?"

"Usually by one of the younger girls."

"You'd have to go in and try to find her," Grace said. "That could take time. In the meantime, the older girl could warn the others."

"I could go in and get her and bring her to you," Rebecca said. "I could make up a story. The girls know me."

"I don't know," Grace said. "That might be too dangerous for you, Rebecca. What if they caught you? You'd never get out again."

No one spoke.

Finally, Kipp said, "I can't ask you to put yourself in harm's way."

"You have to think of your own boy," Grace said.

"I know, but Sarah don't belong there."

"Why are you so sure about that?"

"I knew something was strange when she came here. She kept crying and asking Jed where her daddy was."

The thought of his daughter crying out for him pierced Kipp's heart. Covering his mouth, he hunched over to stifle an anguished moan.

Grace handed him a Kleenex. "What can we do to help?"

"I need to get in there," he said and Libby nodded in agreement.

Grace turned to Rebecca. "Do you think you can get them into the complex?"

"I can try."

"When does the meeting start?"

"At seven and lasts till ten."

"If you leave here at seven, it'll get you down there by eight. Should be dark enough by then. How long does it take through the trees to get to the building?"

"Fifteen minutes or so."

"That should give you enough time to get her out before their meeting breaks up."

"Are you sure you want to do this, Rebecca?" Libby said. "What if they catch you and make you stay?"

"It don't matter," she said, shrugging a shoulder. "I can get my boy back, but he should have his little girl."

Kipp thanked them, and he and Libby departed for the hotel with the promise of picking up Rebecca on Sunday.

TWENTY-FOUR

Still reeling from Charlie's visit, Ellen waltzed into the laundry room with a load of sheets spilling over each arm. Even though he'd only been gone an hour, she awaited his call with anticipation. He had errands to run and promised to call later in the afternoon.

Who would have guessed this would happen to her after all these years of sexual starvation? And who would have put Charlie in the picture? Thinking back to high school, she remembered the boy in her English class being shy and quiet, nothing like the confident lover he'd grown up to be.

Her mind drifted back to the bedroom when the phone rang. She dropped the sheets on the couch and hurried to answer the phone, anticipating Charlie's earlier-than-expected call. "Hello, big boy."

"Ellen?"

Her heart sank. "Mel?"

"Who were you calling big—"

"Oh, well, you know, we've been having a lot of crank calls here lately, and I decided to give them a dose of their own medicine."

"Do you think that's wise, honey?"

She held the receiver away from her ear. That term of endearment, or any other for that matter, had not been a part of his vocabulary in a very long time. When she held the phone to her ear again, Mel was saying her name. "I'm here. What do you want?"

"I want to take you out to dinner tonight."

"Dinner? Why?"

"Whatever happens between us, we need to talk. Don't you agree?"

"I guess."

"Fine. I can be down there by five-thirty."

"Mel…" Before she could voice her objection, he hung up. He was always in command of the situation.

She settled in the chair, dumbfounded. Confusion began to seep in, confusion about Mel's surprise call and Charlie's surprise visit. She had no time to clear her head because the phone rang again. It was Charlie.

"How're you feeling, babe?"

"Fine."

"Are you all right?"

"I'm fine."

There was a pause long enough to fit in another conversation.

"Ellen, what's wrong?"

"I don't know. I just got a call from Mel. He's taking me out to dinner tonight."

"Dinner? What for?"

"He wants to talk to me."

"Couldn't he talk to you on the phone?"

"I don't know."

"I thought we were going to get together tonight. Why are you seeing Mel?"

"We need to talk. We need to straighten things out."

"I thought you knew what you wanted to do. Get a divorce."

"I'm just having dinner with him. After all, he is the father of my children. We need to discuss the family and what we're going to do."

"What *are* you going to do?"

"I don't know."

"You don't know? Christ, Ellen. Didn't last night mean anything to you?"

"Of course it did. We're just going to talk."

"He wouldn't come all this way if he just wanted to talk."

"You're just saying that because you're a man."

"Damn right. I know what he wants."

"What's done is done. He's coming at five-thirty."

"Do what you want."

"I'll call you."

"Go ahead. I won't be home."

"Charlie…"

There was another long pause, and she wasn't sure if he was still on the line until he said, "I'm sorry, Ellen. That was childish. It's just that I care about you."

"I care about you, too."

"But not enough to tell Mel to take a hike."

She was silent.

"Later." He hung up.

Ellen rubbed her cheeks dry. She thought about calling him back but decided against it. Everything was too mixed up.

❦

Mel seated Ellen at the Bayview Restaurant with a gentlemanly push of her chair—another act that amazed her. It was unlike him to be so attentive. He ordered steak dinners and wine for both of them. Immaculate in his suit and tie, he looked as if he were about to make a presentation. The waitress pulled the blinds partway down to shield them from the angle of the late afternoon sun reflecting off the water.

Ellen smoothed the wrinkles of her black sheath. She chose to leave her new dress home.

"Did I tell you how good you look?"

"You never do, so why start now?" She expected him to hurl a sarcastic remark back to her, but his smile remained tacked to his face. When the waitress brought the two glasses of wine, Ellen drained half her glass.

Mel brought up the subject of the children, and they spent most of the meal discussing their education and their future.

When the conversation waned, with two glasses of wine under her belt, Ellen decided to steer the subject in a more pointed direction. "So, why are you really here, Mel?"

"If you're going to be that blunt about it, I miss you, and I want you to come home."

Ellen scrutinized his expression, watching for down-turned eyes, hoping to catch him in a lie, but he met her gaze straight on. "You want me back? What about your secretary?"

"Jackie? She's history. She never meant anything to me."

"Just like the others?"

"Come on, Ellen. Why spoil our evening by rehashing the past."

"Because the past could be the future," she said. "Unless you've changed, I can't trust you'll never do it again."

"Now, honey, I have changed. Since you've been gone, I've been miserable without you. Let me prove it to you."

"I don't know if I want to go through that again," she said. "I'll always be wondering if you're going to come home at night. And what about the traveling you do? How can I trust you'll be faithful when you're away?"

He reached into his coat pocket, pulled out a small, black box with a gold bow on top. "Here, open it."

A flurry of feelings bombarded her. He never bought her gifts. She hesitated, as if opening the box would somehow decide her fate. She gasped at the sight of a pair of diamond earrings. "What's this for?"

"Can't a husband buy his wife a gift?"

"One gift in twenty years of marriage?"

"I've given you gifts."

"Yeah, like the time you brought home a frozen turkey you won in a raffle?"

"Oh, now, Ellen, let's just say this is how serious I am about having you home."

The waitress brought the check, and when she came back to deliver his credit card, he winked at the woman—a gesture not lost on Ellen.

He talked about his job all the way to the house, and she listened with the thrill of being with Charlie sneaking into her thoughts now and then.

Mel walked her to the door and embraced her, filling her with the musky scent of his aftershave. In the glare of the porch light, she noticed the spidery veins around his nose, an indication of too many martini lunches.

He kissed her harder than she expected, and she instinctively ducked her head back and away. He seemed bent on bringing her around to his satisfaction by putting his hand behind her head and drawing her into another kiss. Taken aback by her unexpected feelings for him, she didn't resist.

He stroked the back of her neck. "That's my girl. Now, why don't you let me stay the night?"

"I don't know, Mel. You're getting me all confused."

"We can talk about it in bed. Come on, open the door." He patted her rear, nudging her forward.

"Wait a minute. I need to think about this."

"What's to think about? I'm your husband. Come on now, open up."

While she was searching for her keys, he was running his hand over her breasts and nuzzling and kissing her neck. Flustered, she dropped her purse. When she bent over, he gave her rear a hard squeeze.

She jolted upright and aimed her purse at his midsection. "I think you better go home."

"I was just having a little fun. I won't do it again." He saluted like a boy scout. "Promise. Now, are you going to open the door?"

Ellen froze, unable to decide what to do.

"Look, Ellen, you don't want to be responsible for breaking up the family, do you? The kids will hate you down the road."

She despised it when he brought up the kids that way. Here he was, making her feel guilty, but about what, breaking up the family or not wanting to have sex? Confusion reigned again. She found her keys and shook her head no. "I need more time. You better go home."

"Come on, Ellen. I'm sorry."

"I said no."

He took a step forward, hesitated, took a step back. "Just think about what you're doing."

When he was off the porch, she rustled her keys and opened the door. Safely inside, she waited until she heard the rumble of his car fade away. She sat in Libby's rocking chair under the light she'd left on and prepared for a long, confusing night.

She opened the gift box and stared at the earrings. Maybe she had been too hard on him. After all, he was the children's father. She had discovered tonight the attraction was still there, God only knew why. But what about Charlie? She certainly had feelings for him. It was just that she and Mel had a history, and she wondered whether or not that history could ever be erased.

The phone startled her. She picked up and heard Charlie asking her if this was a bad time.

"If you call interrupting a confused woman a bad time, I guess it is. But maybe I need some help."

"Do you want me to come over?"

Having his arms around her was a welcome thought, but she didn't voice it. "I don't think that would be a good idea right now. I'm worn out."

"Should I hang up, or do you want to talk?"

"I'll talk, but I might sound like a babbling idiot. It's been a long night."

"How'd it go?"

"He wants me to come home."

"What are you going to do?"

"I don't know. He gave me diamond earrings."

"That's a good reason to go back."

"It's just that he never did that before. He told me I look good, too."

"What else did he do?"

"He promised not to fool around anymore."

"And…"

"And, what?"

"What else did he do?"

"I don't know. He kissed me. He hasn't done that in a while."

"Anything else?"

"You're sounding like a cop giving me the third degree."

"Did he want to jump your bones?"

"Charlie…"

"You want to know what I think?"

"Yeah, I want to know what the judge and jury have to say about it."

"I think he's schmoozing you. I think he'll say and do anything to make you go back, and once you're there, all the old habits will return. He'll be tomcatting around."

"Well, aren't you a know-it-all cop; how do you know that?"

"Did he tell you he loved you?"

That one question hit her in the gut like a wrecking ball, and she had to shift her weight to steady herself.

"He didn't, did he?"

There was a long pause.

"Ellen, don't go back to someone who doesn't love you. I've been there, and it's not worth it."

Another pause.

"I'm going to hang up and let you get some rest."

She cleared her throat. "Maybe you could come over."

"Naw. I think you should take the rest of the weekend to think things over."

"Can I call you?"

"I'm going to be in and out. I've got a lot of work to do."

"Will I hear from you again?"

"Think things over for a while, Ellen," he said. "Think about your family, and Mel. You need to clear your head. Think about what you want in life. Then think about us and what a good thing we could have. I'll be around. Bye, darlin."

Didn't he have a way with words? Everything was so simple to him. That's what being a year away from divorce could do for a person.

She toyed with the idea of calling Libby. If ever there was a time she could use Libby's advice, it was now, but Kipp and Libby had their own challenges, and Ellen was determined to figure this out on her own.

TWENTY-FIVE

UNTIL NOW, Kipp believed he would never see his daughter again, but having an inkling of hope stirred up all the old feelings, all those teeter-totter emotions that had been narrowed into numbness.

They had stayed up late the night before, planning the next day, until Libby finally lay down and pulled the bedspread over her body. He offered to leave the room and allow her to dress for bed, but she refused. He was at a loss over her stubbornness, but he went along with her modesty.

He had turned the TV on low and pretended to show interest, but his eyes glazed over and his thoughts drifted to Kelly. If only they could go to the authorities and demand assistance, but not knowing for sure if the little girl in question was his daughter presented a problem. All they had to go on was Libby's hunch and the statement of a sixteen-year-old runaway with her own grudges against the community. Then there was the matter of time; it would take too long to get to the right people. Going it alone seemed the only possibility. Besides, he preferred being in control of the situation.

He longed to have his daughter in his arms. When he imagined it, he could almost feel the weight of her tiny body against the crook of his elbow. It had to be her. It had to be.

The Jeep's tires hit a rough spot in the road, and the jolt brought Kipp into the present. He blinked his eyes to hold back the tears. They had picked up Rebecca and were on their way to Grand.

The clock on the dashboard read 7:30. Libby and Rebecca were engaged in conversation. Libby had turned so she could see Rebecca from the front seat. It was beginning to be hard for him to keep his eyes off Libby. If she was right and Kelly was in that community, he owed her everything. When he heard a voice, directed at him, he snapped out of his rambling thoughts.

"When we get there," Libby said, "are you sure I shouldn't go with you?"

"I'd rather you stay in the car," he said. "If something happens… say, we don't get back by nine-thirty, you can get help." He glanced at her sandals. "Besides you don't have the right shoes to be traipsing over this terrain."

They crested the hill that reached down into the valley, and Kipp pulled over on the shoulder to get his bearings. The mountains were shrouded in darkness. Lights from the town below littered the landscape.

Rebecca indicated the side road was about halfway down the hill. He waited for a car he saw in the rearview mirror to pass by, then swung back onto the highway. Rebecca scooted forward in her seat. Libby asked her if she was afraid, but she stared ahead without answering.

At Rebecca's insistence Kipp slowed down, pulled off the main arterial, and inched along the shoulder. He stopped to inspect the area with a flashlight, so he would know where to turn. In the dim light the road was hardly visible to the naked eye. He got back in the car, veered right, and followed the narrow dirt road until it ended near a clump of aspens. He backed the Jeep around, pointed it toward the highway, and killed the engine and headlights.

Libby stopped him from springing from the Jeep. "Kipp, please be careful and don't do anything to endanger yourself or Rebecca."

He knew Libby well enough to understand a warning from her was serious. "What are you feeling, Libby?"

She placed a hand over his heart. "You'll need to be swift in your decisions. I sense there won't be time to waste. I can't help but feel danger around you. Please be careful."

Kipp and Rebecca got out of the Jeep. Except for the sound of an occasional car speeding by on the highway, the night was still. The wind had died down to a breeze.

The sun was already behind the hills, and the temperature had dipped lower. Kipp grabbed a light jacket from the backseat, but with the moon lighting up the inside of the car, he noticed Libby hugging her arms to her body. He handed her his jacket and keys. In return, she gave him the flashlight that he had set on the dashboard.

She held out her hand to him, and for a moment they stayed connected. "Good luck," she said. "I sense you'll find your fulfillment." He squeezed her hand once again and closed the car door.

Rebecca waited for him near the trees and directed him through a small opening, undetectable to anyone who didn't know it was there. To be cautious, they had decided beforehand not to converse with each other. He would have been distracted anyway.

As soon as they started down the narrow dirt path, Kipp shined the flashlight in front of them. Its beam was less than adequate, and they had to rely on the moon to fill the gaps. Shadows, cast by the tree limbs, gave the impression there were rocks and twigs where there were none. Then Rebecca took the lead, her movements swift, and twice she tripped over branches in her path. Kipp dodged the shadows and followed close behind.

Somewhere in the brush was a rustling sound. Kipp grabbed Rebecca's arm, put a finger to his lips. They waited, listened. The rustling started up again, but nothing darted out of the shadows. Rebecca whispered, "A critter." Kipp nodded. Rebecca moved on, keeping the lead down the snake-like path through a maze of aspens.

The air was cool on Kipp's exposed skin, but his forehead and armpits were littered with moisture, his nerves on edge.

Farther along, Rebecca stumbled over a rock and fell forward. As Kipp helped her to her feet, he heard sounds coming from the rear. He nudged Rebecca off the trail. She stood so close to him her fear was palpable and contagious. He worked at containing his quickening breath.

The wind had picked up, sending a whistling through the thicket and the creaking of tree branches rubbing together. The air calmed. The unsettling sounds subsided.

They moved on, but Kipp, plagued by having second thoughts about abandoning Libby, kept his senses attuned to the woods behind him.

Edging closer to their target, Rebecca stopped and pointed ahead through the trees to the lights flickering. Kipp's thoughts shifted forward to the task at hand.

As they approached the end of the path, they slowed their pace. One hundred feet ahead, the light from the nearest building stood out like a beacon.

A strange feeling crept over Kipp. He didn't know how he knew it, but he would have bet everything he owned that his daughter, the light of his life, was inside. Then, with the prospect of what or whom they might be confronted with, he experienced a sharp jab in his gut.

The building was long and concealed the other buildings in the complex. After scouting the area, Rebecca, as planned, sneaked up to the back entrance, climbed the steps, and peeked in the side window. She waved at Kipp, then rapped on the door.

The door opened a crack and a shaft of light from inside illuminated Rebecca's body. Her hair, tied in a ponytail, hung down her back. She spoke to the person at the door and was allowed entry.

Out of sight among the trees, Kipp kept watch on the door, his body tensed with adrenalin, his teeth grinding, his fists clenched. The minutes hounded him like a nagging ache. He thought he could stand to wait for

Rebecca to bring out the girl they called Sarah, but the longer he waited, the more agitated he became, and his body screamed for action. All it took was the faint sound of children's voices to spur him across the field. He charged his way inside.

Upon seeing Kipp, the young attendant, in long dress and braids, trembled all over. She started to squeal and Kipp panicked. He grabbed her around the waist, put a hand over her mouth, and assured her he wouldn't harm her. Out of pure fear, she stayed perfectly still.

From what he could tell, he was in some kind of waiting area. Wooden chairs were lined up along the bare white walls. Tiny voices drifted in from the next room.

He was holding the girl, wondering what his next move would be, when Rebecca appeared, holding the hand of a six-year-old child with blond braids in an ankle-length dress. Rebecca froze, eyes wide. Kipp's entering the building was not in the plan.

He ignored her and studied the face of the small child with the flaxen hair. Childhood pictures of Tanya crowded his memory; this little girl was the spitting image of his ex-wife.

His arms went limp. His only thought was to embrace his daughter. He rushed to her side and fell to his knees. She scurried behind Rebecca. He wanted to reach for her, but her withdrawal had stunned him into realizing he'd frightened her. He had expected her to run into his arms, but the reality of the situation was she did not know him.

Rebecca jabbed his shoulder with her finger and pointed to the open door. The teenager had vanished.

Peering out a window into the complex, he saw light streaming out of another building and outlines of people swarming into the night. By now the children in the adjoining area were flooding into the room.

Kipp glanced from the window to the children and quickly handed the flashlight to Rebecca, scooped up the little girl, who began to cry, and ran out the back door. He charged across the field and into the woods with Rebecca trailing behind.

With only the moon to light his way, he prayed he would stay upright. The child whimpered in his ear, and it pained him to have to frighten her this way, but he had no choice. He held her close and took long strides, his breathing labored.

Halfway to the car, he stopped and turned around to check on Rebecca. Panic swelled inside. He couldn't see her, but then he heard crackling sounds, as if sticks and twigs were being trampled on. He scanned the area behind him and saw her shadowed form scrambling to get up off the ground. He ran back to give her a hand and heard muffled voices from the direction of the complex. He took off running again, but not for long.

Rebecca caught up to him and tugged his arm. They both stopped cold. In the distance was the dark form of someone coming toward them. Voices loomed behind them. They were trapped.

The little girl wept. He held her close, but his lungs were tight and raw from gulping the cool air and running with the weight of the child.

Rebecca aimed the flashlight forward. Libby ran up to them, her mouth open, her chest heaving. "There's a man coming this way," she said between staggered breaths. "I saw his flashlight. He came from the highway. He's following me. He's not far behind."

The adrenalin in Kipp's body shot through him like speed. He handed off the child to Libby. He grabbed the flashlight from Rebecca. He ordered them to hide in the shadowed thicket behind the trees. He leaped off the trail, clear of the moon's path, and hunkered down.

The thump of footsteps grew louder. The beam from the man's flashlight grew stronger. When the man was nearly upon him, Kipp lunged forward, knocking him off balance. He doubled over, and Kipp smacked his head with the flashlight. The man slumped to the ground.

Kipp took a labored breath but had no time to dwell on the pain.

The voices behind them were getting close enough for him to make out a word or two.

Libby and Rebecca tromped out of the thicket and rushed to his side. He scooped the child from Libby and barreled down the path. Within minutes they entered the clearing.

Libby and Rebecca hurried into the backseat, and he transferred the girl into Libby's arms. He searched his pocket for the keys. The voices coming from the woods were now loud and distinct. He remembered he had given the keys to Libby. When he got in the driver's seat, she thrust them into his hand.

He gunned the engine, and the Jeep lurched forward just as flashlight beams shot through the trees. In the rearview mirror Kipp saw bouncing lights coming toward them. To maneuver around a truck parked in their path, he had to swerve off the dirt into the tall grass. The Jeep swayed from side to side. He leaned on the gas pedal and turned the wheel onto the highway, spraying gravel and squealing the tires.

His heart shook in his chest. He drove as fast as possible, praying the long arm of the law didn't extend beyond Grand. Capturing his daughter from the people who stole her was his first and foremost priority. Their punishment would have to come later.

There was no time to tend to his little girl, even though he craved to hold her. He had to be satisfied with listening to Libby and Rebecca soothing her in the backseat.

By the time they got to Grace's house, the child had fallen asleep. Kipp walked Rebecca to the door and had a short talk with Grace. She agreed to testify on his behalf if the authorities questioned her about his daughter's rescue. She had plenty to say about that religious cult, and she welcomed any help from outside the area.

"If I were you, I'd take off tonight," Grace said. "Get your daughter as far away from here as you can. They won't go to the police outside the area because that would draw too much attention, but they may try to track you down themselves."

Kipp agreed and thanked Grace for her help. He gave Rebecca a hug and told her what a brave person she was and that he would be forever in her debt. He said he would contact them when he got home and promised to help them any way he could. For now his thoughts were on his daughter and getting her out of harm's way.

TWENTY-SIX

On the way back to the motel, Kipp told Libby his plans to drive straight home—a trip that normally would take a day and a half. He questioned whether or not it would be too hard on the child, but Libby assured him she would care for her, and like Grace, she felt leaving would be a wise idea.

Kipp retrieved their luggage. He stopped at a gas station to fill up and bought two coffees while Libby waited in the car. The child was still asleep with her head on Libby's lap. Kipp brought a blanket from the back and laid it over the girl.

Once they were on the interstate going west, Kipp's body relaxed for the first time in days, but he would not let his guard down until they were safely home. He had a good thirteen-hour drive ahead of him, and he needed to stay alert.

He glanced in the rearview mirror. His daughter was out of his view, and he couldn't touch her, even though he yearned to, but having someone like Libby in the backseat to comfort her reassured him. "She calmed so easily after I gave her to you. How do you do it?"

"She's responding to the energy that runs through my hands. It's warm and comforting."

"You're amazing," he said. "I don't understand what you do, but you're amazing."

"Are you going to be okay, doing all this driving?"

"I can do anything if it means getting her back home."

"Maybe if you talk to me, it will be easier."

"Don't you want to close your eyes and rest?"

"The caffeine wired me," she said. "Besides, this will give me a chance to know more about the details of Kelly's abduction. I didn't want to bring it up before. It was so painful for you."

"Talking about it now that I have Kelly won't be so hard. Where shall I start?"

"From the beginning. Where were you when you found out?"

"On my way home from Washington, D.C.," he said. "I had driven there to do an interview for an article I was writing. I'd stayed overnight. Mrs. Crowley agreed to stay at the house with Kelly. I got a call from the police on my cell phone."

"What a horrible way to find out."

"I didn't even remember the rest of the drive home. I was in a daze. The police were there. Mrs. Crowley got hysterical when she saw me."

"When did she realize Kelly was gone?"

"After she put Kelly down for a nap," he said, "she lay down on the couch and fell asleep. She'd been taking some new pain medication for her arthritis, and it made her drowsy. She slept longer than she intended. When she woke, she went upstairs to check on Kelly, but she wasn't in her bed. Mrs. Crowley searched everywhere for her. You filled in the rest of the story. As you told me in the reading, Kelly slipped outside by way of an unlocked screen door, and they took her from the backyard."

Kipp took a breath. "I think they had it planned because they left no evidence, not even a gum wrapper. They must have known my habits. I usually traveled on Thursdays or Fridays if I had to. Those two are the scum of the earth. I plan to unleash the FBI on them as soon as I get home."

"Where was Tanya when this happened?"

"She was on an assignment in California. She flew in on the first flight she could get."

"How did she react?"

"She seemed devastated. She went through all the right emotions, the crying, the questioning."

"I'm sure she felt something, Kipp. A mother would."

Kipp released a cynical laugh. "She never cared for her daughter. Kelly was always in the way of everything she had planned. They never bonded like mother and child. Tanya was out on assignment as soon as she got her figure back, which wasn't long at all. She practically starved them both while she was pregnant. She hardly gained any weight. I'd harp at her about eating, but it didn't do any good. She spent most of the pregnancy depressed about it. It's a wonder Kelly came out as healthy as she did. But sure, Tanya was upset, too."

A rest area sign loomed in the distance, and Kipp asked if Libby wanted to stop. She told him to keep going.

"So, what happened after Tanya got to the house?"

"The police searched the area. They combed the woods behind the house. They talked to all the neighbors. Finally, the FBI was called in, and the media got involved."

"I don't remember hearing anything about it."

"It was a strange time back then," Kipp said. "The country was still reeling from the terrorist attack. The media was too focused on that and the political climate at that time to give Kelly's story much publicity."

"I would have thought they'd pounce on a story like yours with Tanya being a top model and you being on TV."

"Tanya pretty much kept motherhood out of the picture. As for me, by that time I hadn't been on TV for four years. I was a has-been in media terms."

"So, they didn't find anything in their investigation?"

"Not a trace."

"You must have been torn in two."

"An understatement," he said. "It wasn't enough dealing with our own grief, but we were dragged through the dirt by the authorities, too."

"They accused you?"

"You've been on missing persons cases, you know how it works."

"I know they have to rule out the family members before they can move on with their investigation, but I didn't know if that was the case with you."

"Well, that's what they did," he said, "especially Tanya since she was the parent who didn't have custody. They thought she might have kidnapped Kelly out of revenge because she didn't get custody after the divorce. We both took lie detector tests. The whole procedure was demeaning and gut-wrenching."

"I can imagine." Libby, careful not to disturb the child, leaned forward a little and squeezed and massaged his shoulders.

"Boy does that feel good. You've got great hands."

"Do you need to stop and stretch?"

"The next rest area." He glanced back a second to check on the child, who'd made a moaning sound. "Is she all right?"

"She's fine. Don't worry."

Kipp drove through the darkness on long stretches of desolate highway, a handful of cars passing by, their headlights blasting his tired, burning eyes.

Libby had not said anything for a while, and he assumed she'd dozed off. Left alone with his thoughts, he wondered how he would ever make it up to her. She had given him back his life.

Once, he caught his chin sinking downward. He squeezed the steering wheel several times, exercising his arms, pumping life into the veins. He lifted and lowered his shoulders.

By the time the sky began to lighten, he was yawning and having difficulty keeping his eyes open. He pulled into a gas station to fill up and to stretch his extremities.

Libby rolled down the window a crack. "I'm sorry I fell asleep. I hope it wasn't too hard for you to stay awake."

"Just the last few miles. I'm going to get coffee and something for us to eat."

The child rubbed her eyes and pushed herself up to a sitting position. She looked up at Libby. "I'm thirsty. I want to go home."

Back in the driver's seat, Kipp turned and reached for her, but she recoiled. He snapped his arm back as if he'd touched fire.

"Give her time," Libby said.

She took the girl to the restroom and gave her a muffin and juice in the car. She answered the girl's questions about who Libby was and where they were going, but the girl never once asked about Kipp.

Back on the freeway, the child snuggled close to Libby and fell asleep again. Hurt, Kipp wanted to know why Libby thought it would take time for his daughter to warm up to him.

"I think it has to do with the way that community functions," Libby said. "The men are the authority figures, and the women probably take care of the small children all the time. She relates to women better."

"But I thought she'd know me."

"Be patient, Kipp. She's just been through something traumatic. You broke in there like a wild man, instead of waiting like you were supposed to."

"I know."

"She needs time to adjust. Besides, do you look the same as when she saw you last?"

"God, no. I didn't think of that. I had a mustache and my hair was shorter. But I thought she'd instinctively know her own daddy."

"For such a young child, she's been through so much change. Try not to take it to heart. She'll come around."

"It'll kill me if she doesn't."

"She will. I guarantee it."

For the moment Libby's reassurance calmed his fears. He drove on, lost in his own thoughts. Libby fell into silence, and he presumed she was asleep.

They were well into Washington now. The drive to Utah seemed a flash in the night compared to the trip home. It was as if the roads had stretched twice as long as they were in reality. He kept on and fought to stay awake.

On the final leg home Kipp stopped at a rest area, waking Libby. The child woke, too, and began to whine about wanting to go home. Libby took her to the restroom, and once she was settled back in the cocoon of Libby's arms, she quieted and slept. Kipp motored on, driving as fast as he dared.

"I'll try to stay awake this time," Libby said.

"Sleep if you need to."

"No, let's talk. Tell me what happened to you and Tanya after the kidnapping? I guess it didn't bring you together?"

"At first it did," he said. "We tried to comfort each other and do what we could to find our daughter. We hired a private investigator, but there were no new leads. I wouldn't go out of the house for weeks in case she somehow showed up. After a while Tanya got restless and wanted to go back to work. We began sniping at each other. She blamed me for leaving Kelly with an old woman. I blamed myself. I lived with that every day. I still do."

"You had no way of knowing."

"Then the anger set in," he said. "We were angry at the kidnapper, then we turned that anger on each other. I remember the yelling and the accusations and the blaming. She finally numbed out and returned to New York to her glamorous lifestyle. She left me to sit and wait for answers."

He shifted around to relieve the ache in his thighs. "I read everything I could about missing children. I read all the statistics. The police said a two-hour window gives anyone the opportunity to be out of the area, and they had at least a three-hour lead by the time Mrs. Crowley woke and searched the neighborhood on her own. Nothing was found in the first twenty-four hours, and they say that's critical. I read the chances of finding her alive after more than thirty days is two percent. All of these things added up to the fact I'd never see her again."

"How could you even function?"

"The worst part was not knowing. I'd go from hope to despair. After months had gone by with no word or clue, it just felt hopeless."

"Did you have anyone to help you through the grief, like your family or a counselor?"

"I thought I could handle it myself," he said. "And you know the old saying. If you don't have enough problems, you can always count on your family." He chuckled. "Well, my parents supported me by blaming me for divorcing Tanya in the first place. I guess that's how they coped with it."

"Why didn't you want to stay in Connecticut? I'd think you'd want to stay where you felt her presence."

"After a year I began to accept the fact she was never coming home. Every day I'd wake up paralyzed by fear, waiting for the police to knock on the door and tell me the news I couldn't bear to hear. God knows how many times I had to go to the morgue to make sure it wasn't her."

"Oh, Kipp."

"That's when I left town," he said. "I had it in my head that if I left, the police couldn't find me to give me the bad news. I guess moving helped me accept the fact she wasn't coming home. It forced me to work again, to fill the void, to get on with my life. Then I met you. You stirred up all those feelings and emotions I thought I'd buried. You made me relive everything."

"I'm sorry I brought you so much hurt."

"Don't be." He glanced over his shoulder. "Look at her. Having her with me again is worth every bit of agony I had to go through. I'll never be able to repay you."

"Just having you reunited with your daughter is enough for me."

"You know, Tanya tried to discourage me from using your services. She said you'd rip me off."

"As you know, I don't charge a fortune, only for my time and expenses, same as my other work. I do the best I can, but psychic work is not 100 percent accurate. There can be many misleads. There are so many variables."

"Well, why were you so accurate this time? I'm so in awe of how you got us to the right places."

"I'm sort of in awe myself."

"You? You always seem so sure of yourself."

"You don't know me that well, do you?"

He glanced at her in the rearview mirror. "No, but I'd like to."

After a long pause Libby said, "There was a special connection between us, something that made everything fall into place to make this happen."

"You mean, like it was pre-ordained?"

"Maybe."

"Before I met you, I would have debated you on that one."

"And now?"

"I'm beginning to come around." He hesitated, then made the decision to test the waters. "Do you think we were meant to come together for something besides Kelly?"

"That, I don't know."

"Why not? You're the psychic."

"I'm not good at seeing my own future."

"What if I could see it for you?"

"I think you should concentrate on finding my driveway. We're almost here."

She had a way of skirting personal issues, and Kipp vowed to get an answer to his question one day soon.

The sun was straight up in the sky, and the gray house with the aqua trim, partially shaded most hours of the day, was bathed in light. Kipp got out of the Jeep and stretched his arms and legs.

The child had woken and was still pinned to Libby's side. Libby made an attempt to slide out, but the girl gripped Libby's arm and pulled her back. Kipp tried to assure her everything was going to be all right, but she stared up at him with terror in her eyes. Libby spoke softly to the girl, thereby coaxing her out of the car.

Kipp went on ahead and stood next to Ellen, who waved to Libby from the porch. He watched his daughter come up the sidewalk holding Libby's hand. His heart burst with pride for bringing her home, but her detachment made the journey bittersweet.

"We have a little girl who's very hungry," Libby said.

"Hi. I'm Ellen. Why don't you come in, and we'll make you a toasted cheese sandwich. How's that?" The girl took Ellen's outstretched hand, and Ellen glanced from Kipp to Libby. "You two look like you could use a week's sleep. I'm so anxious to hear about everything."

"We'll talk later," Libby said. "I got some sleep, but Kipp has been driving for hours."

"Well, you've got to eat," Ellen said. "Let me fix you something."

During lunch Kipp sat across from his daughter and studied her face and every movement she made. She was chewing around the edges of the sandwich just like she used to do. Once, he caught her looking at him in a quizzical fashion. He took that as an encouraging sign.

After they finished eating, Ellen took the girl into the bedroom to pick out one of Libby's stuffed animals, so Kipp and Libby could talk.

Kipp watched her trail after Ellen. "You were right, Libby. She does respond to women better. She took to Ellen right away. But did you see her looking at me? I think she's beginning to recognize me."

"She'll come around. She just needs time to get adjusted." Libby grinned. "Did you look at yourself in a mirror lately? You look bad enough to scare anyone, let alone a child."

"Thanks a lot."

"You need sleep."

"I need to go home and get clean clothes," he said. "I need to get in touch with the authorities and Tanya. But I don't know what I should do. Kelly doesn't know me yet, and I don't want to upset her."

"Leave her with me, at least for a couple of days. I can work with her and talk to her about you, help her remember."

"I hate to leave her. We've been apart for so long."

"I know, but I have counseling experience. I can help her heal and remember. I can at least get her to the point of knowing who you are."

"I trust you. I know you're right. You've been right about everything so far."

Libby caressed his hand, and he put his other hand on top of hers and gave it a squeeze. Her eyes softened. A warmth spread though him. He was on the verge of kissing her when Ellen and the child returned to the table.

Kipp let go of Libby's hand and watched the child slide into the chair with a stuffed kitten. "What have you got there, Kelly?"

The child furrowed her brow, then resumed playing with the toy.

"You should go if you're going," Libby said. "Your eyelids are drooping. Or would you rather stay here and nap?"

"I better go. Once I lie down, I'll probably be out for hours."

He edged around the table, squatted beside the child, and held his hand out to her. With her head lowered, her eyes wary, she laid her hand in his palm. Kipp brightened. He glanced up at Libby, then at the child. "I'll see you soon, baby bear." Her head bobbed up, and he took it as a green light to give her a hug, but when he held out his arms, she scooted off the chair and dashed to Libby's side. His heart sank.

Libby rubbed the child's back. "Don't worry, Kipp. She'll come around. I promise."

Ellen went into the kitchen and returned with a small thermos of coffee for him. "Just in case." She took the girl's hand and led her into the kitchen for some chocolate milk.

Libby walked Kipp to the door. "Why don't you leave me the picture of you holding Kelly? I'll use it to help jog her memory."

Kipp took the photo from his wallet.

"Why did you call her that name?"

"Baby bear? That was my nickname for her when she was a baby. She loved her stuffed bear."

"Then bring the bear with you when you come back. It might help."

The ache of leaving his daughter barely overshadowed the ache of leaving Libby. The last several days had been intense and had increased his feelings for her. His heart overflowed with emotion, and he took her into his arms. She leaned into his embrace. He held her, and she accepted the closeness without drawing back. Her face was wet with tears. He smiled and kissed her cheek. "We need to talk."

"You better go," she said.

He looked past Libby toward the kitchen, listening to Ellen converse with the child. He was one step away from scooping his daughter into his arms, but he forced his attention back to Libby and hugged her one last time. "I'll be back Wednesday."

TWENTY-SEVEN

L IBBY WAVED goodbye to Kipp. As much as she tried to fight it, she knew she would miss him. He was impatient, he had a stubborn streak as wide as the Mississippi, and he could be curt at times, but under the circumstances, she couldn't judge him. His sensitive and loving side eclipsed anything negative.

She felt a tap on her shoulder.

"Earth to Libby. Are you going to stand there all day?"

"He's been through a lot."

"So have you," Ellen said. "Why don't you take a nice hot bath, and I'll watch baby bear."

Libby spent as much time as she dared away from the child, luxuriating in a soothing bubble bath. When she emerged from the bathroom, the girl ran to her and threw her arms around her.

"I guess we know who Mommy is," Ellen said.

Libby squatted and hugged the child. "Everything's going to be all right, little girl."

With Ellen's help Libby unbraided the girl's hair and bathed and cared for her. She rummaged through a bedroom drawer and found a tee shirt that could serve as a nightgown. "She's going to need clothes."

"I can shop for you, Libby, since I have more experience at it."

"I'll start working with her tomorrow, and you can go shopping," Libby said. "Right now, she needs to de-stress from the trip."

The girl stayed close to Libby's side.

"She doesn't talk much."

"Her speech may have been arrested when she was kidnapped. Kipp may have to have a speech therapist work with her. Or it could be, once we unlock her memory and she feels safe again, she'll speak freely."

Libby found paper and crayons, sat the child at the table, and encouraged her to play.

Ellen made jasmine tea, and they sat in the living room in close proximity to the girl.

Libby propped her feet on the coffee table. "Those were the longest days of my life. I'm glad I have the rest of the week off."

"Looks like you're going to need it."

"It worked out, didn't it?"

"I want to know all the details. Where did you find her?"

Careful to keep her voice down, Libby told Ellen how she led them to the polygamist community, how they were led to Grace and Rebecca, and how, with Rebecca's help, they were able to retrieve Kipp's daughter. Ellen wanted to discuss the strange community, but Libby thought it a bad idea.

"The whole thing gives me chills," Ellen said. "You are amazing."

"That's what Kipp said."

"Oh?" Ellen raised her eyebrows.

"Here we go again. I know what you're thinking."

"Since you brought it up, did anything of a romantic nature transpire?"

"There wasn't time for anything like that."

"Are you sure? The way you two were holding each other."

"Holding each other?"

"At the door before he left. I peeked around the corner and saw you two."

"That was just a friendly hug goodbye."

"Looked more like a sweltering embrace. When are you two going to quit pussyfooting around and admit your feelings for each other?"

"You know why I can't give in to my feelings."

"Aha! You admit you have feelings for him."

"Maybe I do, but I can't act on them."

"That's bullshit."

Libby nodded toward the girl and shushed Ellen.

"Oops." Ellen glanced toward the girl and back. "I thought she'd be hysterical when you brought her here."

"She was pretty upset when she came out of the woods, but I calmed her using my energy technique. She really responded."

"Is she going to be all right? I mean, will she ever warm up to Kipp?"

"I think deep down she knows Kipp is her daddy. It's just that her memory needs a little prompting," Libby said. "With a case like this, Kipp is going to be faced with a few challenges. My instinct tells me she'll eventually be all right. She's so special to him."

"Why don't you give Kipp a chance to be someone special to you?" Getting no response, Ellen said, "It's the cancer thing, isn't it?"

"It's not just that," Libby said. "He's going to have to spend time with his child, and his ex-wife will be in the picture. The timing is bad."

"And if it wasn't?"

"Ellen, I'm too tired to discuss it. Let's talk about you and Charlie."

Ellen's smile drooped.

"What's with the gloomy expression?"

"There is no Charlie."

"What happened? The last time I talked to you, you two had spent a night together."

"Mel spoiled everything."

"Mel? I thought you were through with him."

Ellen gave Libby a rundown of her fabulous night with Charlie and explained how Mel took her to dinner and tried to woo her with compliments and diamond earrings.

"So, you dumped Charlie for Mel, the man who every day of the year treats you like you-know-what?"

"It's more like Charlie dumped me."

"That doesn't sound like Charlie."

"Well, he didn't dump me. He's just backing off, giving me space to work things out."

"How do you feel about that?"

Ellen took a long sip of tea. "Lousy."

"Meaning?"

"Meaning I miss Charlie, but I'm still mixed up."

"Do you want to know what I sense about the situation?"

"Oh, yeah. I'm so glad you're back. I need your insights."

"I wish you would get your own insights, but I want to save my dearest friend the heartache, so here goes." Libby set her cup on the coffee table and shifted toward Ellen. "When you told me you were leaving Mel, I had these pictures flash through my mind. I saw you with a tall, curly-haired man Charlie's size, with the same ruddy complexion. I got the symbol of two hands interlocked together, which to me means something permanent."

Ellen wilted.

"That doesn't make you happy?"

"It doesn't un-mix my emotions," Ellen said. "Mel said all the right things. Plus, he reminded me I have to think about the kids. And I do. And get that disgusted look off your face."

"Have you forgotten about the discussion you had with your daughter?"

"No."

"It sounded to me like she was doing just fine with your decision to separate," Libby said. "So, don't let him guilt you into going back to a life of half-baked promises. Just compare how Charlie treats you with Mel's actions. *Then* make your decision. If you want my bottom-line advice, I say don't let Charlie get away."

"I hope you're listening to your own advice," Ellen said, "because Kipp is a great catch, too."

Just then the little girl in the big tee shirt came running across the room and climbed onto the couch next to Libby.

TWENTY-EIGHT

On his way home Kipp called Charlie on his cell phone. When Charlie found out about Kipp's plans to go to Seattle to the FBI field office, he volunteered to go with him.

Tuesday morning Charlie picked up Kipp, and they made the drive together. Kipp had to explain the details of his daughter's rescue, and Charlie tagged along to be a character witness for Kipp in case the FBI cast suspicions Kipp's way.

After hearing Kipp's story and questioning him for a while, they told Kipp they would contact the field office in Salt Lake City and send an agent to talk to Grace and Rebecca to verify the details and get a description of the couple who had kidnapped Kelly. They said they would be in contact with him later.

Satisfied everything was being done to apprehend the kidnappers, Kipp and Charlie left for home. When they arrived in Port Anderson, Kipp suggested they get something to eat at The Fish and Ale.

It was another warm summer day, typical of the Pacific Northwest in August. The air conditioner in Charlie's truck shielded them from the heat, but Kipp welcomed the open feel of the pub with its salty air. A few sailboats were tied up to the adjoining pier.

Instead of his usual seat at the bar, Kipp led Charlie to a table where they could have an unobstructed view of the harbor. Sam waved hello to Kipp when he passed by. The waitress took their order and brought them two ice waters.

Kipp glanced around to see if he recognized anyone. The place was beginning to fill with the early dinner crowd.

"We were so busy talking about your trip and the rescue, I forgot to ask about Tanya," Charlie said. "When's she coming to see Kelly?"

"I haven't talked to her yet," Kipp said. "Right now she's on a plane to Australia. I left a message at her hotel. Hopefully, she'll call soon. To tell you the truth, though, I'd rather have some time alone with Kelly before she gets here."

"Yeah, but she should know."

"I know that. But you know how she is. She'll want to take over, even if it's not in Kelly's best interest. She'll make everything about herself."

"What do you plan to do?"

"I'm not sure," Kipp said. "It all depends on Kelly and how she's doing. But I'll tell you, Charlie, it's taking every ounce of strength to keep from driving to Libby's and embracing my baby girl. I'm counting the minutes until I can see her again."

The waitress interrupted them with their order of hamburgers and fries. Charlie dumped a mound of ketchup on his plate. "Why don't you drive down this evening?"

"Libby told me to wait, and I trust her judgment. You should have seen how Kelly took to her. It was like they were mother and daughter, I swear."

"There's another reason to pursue that woman."

"I don't need any more reasons."

"So, what's stopping you?"

"Libby."

"Why? Did you put the moves on her and get shot down?"

"She won't even give me a chance to think about it." Kipp thought back on the last few days. "You know, Charlie, the woman is the most gentle, loving soul, but as soon as she begins to open up, she shifts into business mode, and I can't get close to her. I know she cares about me. We've had moments. I can feel it."

"She's had cancer. Did you know that?"

"Cancer?"

"Breast cancer. Ellen told me."

"Jesus, I had no idea."

"Yeah. From what Ellen said, she had to go through chemo and radiation, the works. She didn't have a mastectomy, but I guess she might as well have. They kept having to go in to remove suspicious areas, so you can imagine."

"Then that explains it."

"What?"

"She seemed overly modest on the trip. We had to share a room a couple of times, and she wouldn't even change into pajamas with me out of the room. Jesus, I had no idea."

"So, knowing that, how do you feel about things?"

"About getting to know Libby?"

"Well, yeah, being with a woman who's had that kind of surgery, with all the complications?"

"I don't know. It certainly doesn't change the great person she is."

"Yeah, but what about being intimate?"

"Hey, we're not anywhere near that." Kipp bit into his hamburger, chewed a while. "What about you and Ellen?"

Charlie gave him a thumbs-down. "Let's move on to another topic."

"That bad, huh?"

"Let's just say she's in the wounded-buffalo stage, the one I was in right after my divorce. I don't know which way she's going to turn next."

"Are you going to wait it out?"

"Don't know. It depends on her."

"You must really like her," Kipp said. "I haven't known you to spend a whole night with a woman since the divorce, unless you're holding out on me."

"That's the truth, but hell, why did I have to pick a woman with ten tons of baggage fresh out of a twenty-year marriage? If I'd never answered the call that night…"

"Why was she so scared, anyway?"

"The door was open when she got home. She thought it might be Libby's ex snooping around. You should have seen her brandishing that pistol. She looked like she had palsy, the way she was shaking." He chuckled.

"What is Libby doing with a gun?"

"Her ex. She didn't mention him?"

"In passing, but she didn't elaborate."

"I guess he's a real piece of work. Beat her up a number of times. Left her when she got the cancer."

"Jesus." More than ever, Kipp wanted to throw his arms around her, hug her close, protect her in some way.

"But the clinker?" Charlie said. "He's an ex-cop."

"She seems so strong, like she has it all together. What would she be doing with a man like that?"

"That was my thought," Charlie said. "Who would have known?"

At the thought of Libby's misfortune, Kipp lost his appetite and shoved the half-eaten burger aside. "Let's get out of here."

Charlie stuffed the last few fries in his mouth and followed Kipp to the bar where Kipp insisted on paying the bill.

Charlie dropped Kipp off at his house and headed back to Harbordale with the promise of being available whenever Kipp needed him.

Kipp looked forward to the end of the evening because he would be that much closer to seeing Kelly. He opened the door to a ringing phone.

Tanya greeted him from Sydney. "I got your message. You said it was urgent. Is it your parents?"

"It's Kelly. I've found her, Tannie."

"You did what?" She paused. "Oh, my God. Our baby, our baby. Is it true? Where? Where is she?"

Kipp had to stop her from getting hysterical, so he could give her the details about the kidnappers and the polygamist community. He told her about Grace and Rebecca. He told her about the rescue, leaving out Libby's part in it. He wanted to explain that detail in person.

By the time Kipp was finished with the story, Tanya was sniffling. "How did you know she was there?"

"I'll explain that when you get here. Can you get a flight out?"

"I just got here, Kipp. I'll have to see. Of course, I'll be there as soon as I can. Oh, Kipp, honey, our baby." She resumed sobbing.

"Can you take a cab from the airport?"

"Can't you pick me up?"

"Kelly's not ready to be thrown into a place like that." He didn't want to discuss Kelly's state of mind over the phone.

"Why not, Kipp? Why can't you and Kelly pick me up?"

"Tanya, trust me. It's better if you catch a cab and we wait here."

"I don't see why you two can't come!"

Already Kipp found himself getting irritated with her insensitive attitude. "Think of Kelly, Tanya. She's been through a lot."

"All right. All right. I'll call you when I get in. I love you, sweetie." She hung up.

Weary from this three-minute exchange, he kicked off his shoes, disrobed, and fell into bed early. The light from outside cast shadows on the rug, and children's voices sounded down the road. Despite the distractions, he hoped to sleep.

Mentally, he was drained, but he stayed awake long enough to calculate how much time he would have with Kelly before Tanya arrived. He hoped for at least a full day. It all depended on how Kelly responded to him. If she had difficulty, he would have to leave her with Libby, and he wondered how he was going to explain that situation to Kelly's own mother.

Libby had been a godsend. In the last few days, she had been more of a mother to Kelly than Tanya ever was.

He thought about everything Libby had gone through: the cancer, the abuse. She deserved so much more than that.

Now that he knew her secrets, her reasons for being so closed up, he wondered if he would ever have the opportunity to embrace her fully the way he wanted to. He'd always been with women who were near-perfect physically. Could he overlook Libby's surgery? He'd cross that bridge when he came to it—if he was ever given the chance.

TWENTY-NINE

The next day, when Kipp pulled up to Libby's house, Libby was standing in the yard, adjusting a sprinkler. The August sun had made a greenish gold patchwork of the lawn. He saw no sign of Kelly.

Libby waved. Her emerald blouse and shorts blended in with the environment, but her wide smile and her rich dark hair made her stand out.

His stomach fluttered. The excitement of seeing her mixed with the anticipation of seeing his daughter; it was difficult to separate the two. If he had not been so tired the night before, he would have wrestled the sheets, anxious for the morning light to wake him.

By the time he'd replaced his sunglasses with his wire-rims, Libby had turned on the water and was approaching the Jeep. He stole a glance in the rearview mirror, then stepped out to greet her. Without giving her time to protest, he gave her a warm hug and felt no resistance.

"You got your hair cut," she said. "It's much shorter."

His cheeks warmed. "I thought I might look more like the earlier pictures with me and Kelly together. If I could, I would have slapped on a mustache. Where is she?"

"With Ellen. They went to the store to exchange some clothes. Kelly is smaller than Ellen thought. She doesn't wear the usual size for her age. She's so tiny."

"That's how Tanya was when she was a little girl."

"Would you like some iced tea? I'll bring it out, and we can sit on the porch and wait."

"How did she do with you?"

"I'll get the tea and we'll talk." Libby walked up the sidewalk ahead of him.

Kipp held back, watching her navigate the porch steps. She carried more weight than Tanya. He balked at the comparison; there was no comparison. Libby might not have a model's figure, but she had so much more.

When the screen door shut, he returned to the Jeep to retrieve the stuffed bear, the key to the reading that had led to Kelly's rescue. On the porch he sat in one of the rattan chairs and laid the toy by his feet.

Libby came out, handed him a glass, and moved her chair closer to him.

"Do you think you should have let her go with Ellen?" Kipp said. "What if she gets overwhelmed in the store? She's never been exposed to anything like that."

"Ellen will take good care of her, and I think you're going to be surprised."

"Surprised about what?"

"Before I go on, I hope you don't mind that we cut her hair," Libby said. "Not short. Just the extra length. It was too straggly. They must have kept it in braids."

A twinge of jealousy rose in Kipp—not that Libby had cut Kelly's hair, but that she was having experiences with his daughter before he'd had a chance to get to know her again.

Libby, who had an uncanny way of reading him, set her glass down and took his hand. "Forgive me, Kipp. I'm just excited about Kelly's progress. I didn't mean to do anything to upset you."

He withdrew his hand. "I expected her to be here, that's all, not gal-livanting around town, getting clothes and haircuts. I wanted to do that." Hearing himself, he felt foolish, like a kid coveting another child's toy. "I'm sorry, Libby. I'm grateful for all your help. Honest."

"I really didn't think she'd be ready to venture out so soon, but she seems happy and willing."

"I thought it would take days, weeks."

"Let me tell you what happened."

Kipp eyed Libby. "Is this something I have to get prepared for, like when I saw you the first time?"

"Maybe. You seem pretty open now, but I know what happens when you don't want to hear something."

He hesitated, wondering if he should pursue this. "Okay. I'll bite. Tell me your impression of me."

"Your mind is like a rubber band," she said. "You stretch it and stretch it, and when it reaches the limits of understanding, that rubber band snaps back in an instant, and you close up and respond in anger."

Kipp leaned back, his eyes narrowing. She knew him so well.

"I just want you to keep an open mind when I tell you what happened yesterday," she said. "You need to know this before you see Kelly, and I don't want you to be upset when she gets here."

"What the hell did you do with her?"

Libby recoiled.

Kipp heated with embarrassment. "Point well-taken. I apologize, Libby. Please tell me the story."

"Do you trust me?"

"You know I do."

"You know I wouldn't do anything to harm her."

"Of course not. I think I'm still pumping adrenalin. Please go on."

Libby reached for Kipp's hand, which he willingly gave, and proceeded to tell him the details of her time with his daughter.

Not wanting the child to be traumatized from being alone in a strange environment, Libby had allowed the child to sleep in her bed. When Libby woke in the morning, the girl was asleep, snuggled next to her, making hushed breathing sounds. Libby moved to get up, but the child clung to her.

After breakfast, Ellen left them to go to town to buy clothes and to give Libby a chance to work with the child. In the beginning, Libby spent time playing with her and drawing pictures. She encouraged her to draw pictures of her mommy and daddy, but the child only drew mommy pictures.

Afterward, Libby sat with her on the couch and told her the story of a family with a mommy and daddy named Kipp and Tanya and a little girl named Kelly. She spoke gently, describing where they lived and everything she remembered about their lives she had learned from Kipp. The girl seemed to take it all in.

When Libby finished the story, the child asked her who the man was who brought her here. Libby showed her Kipp's picture. The little girl studied it for a while, then laid it on the table and asked no further questions.

Kipp interrupted the story. "That doesn't sound like much progress to me. Sounds like she blew me off."

"Let me finish," Libby said in a tone that made him wish he'd kept quiet. She continued the story.

Ellen had come home with a selection of clothes and shoes, and Libby interrupted the session to give the child time to absorb the new information and to try on the new outfits. Libby's shirt hung orphan-like on the girl, but most of the clothes Ellen bought did the same. They picked out the least baggy outfit, a pair of shorts and a tank top. Ellen agreed to exchange the rest in the morning.

After lunch and a walk in the forest, Libby coaxed the girl into the bedroom for an afternoon nap. She pulled the shades, darkening the room. With her hand resting on the girl's tummy, Libby took several deep breaths, focusing and allowing the healing energy to move through her into the child. She called on the child's angels and guides to help her heal and remember. Soon Kelly's eyelids drooped shut and her breathing steadied.

Once Libby closed her own eyes, faces of people unknown to her flashed across the screen of her mind. She sensed the room was overflowing with beings connected to Kelly.

Then the room was charged with electricity. Libby's body shuddered. She opened her eyes to a blue mist hovering in the corner. Before the image faded, she recognized the outline of the elderly woman she'd seen previously.

She stopped to take a breath. By this time in the story, Kipp was gripping her hand, encouraging her to go on.

Libby had carefully scooted to the edge of the bed and tiptoed out of the room. She took herself out of the picture and let whatever might happen occur between Kelly and her invisible helpers. She waited with Ellen in the living room.

An hour later, Kelly emerged from the bedroom, rubbing her eyes and mumbling. When she saw Libby and Ellen, her face lit up, and she climbed on the couch between them.

Libby asked her if she had a good sleep, and she responded with a request to see the photo of her and Kipp together. Studying it, she proceeded to recall a dream about a grandma visiting her and showing her her real mommy and daddy. She pointed to Kipp's image and said her daddy looked like the man in the picture.

Libby smiled at Kipp. "That's the story. Can you accept it, or are you going to fight it?"

His eyes filled with tears of joy. "How do you do it, Libby?"

"I don't do anything. I just facilitate, but the outcome is not up to me.

We'll see what happens when she sees you."

"Do I call her by her real name?"

"The grandmother in her dream told her her real name."

"How can I ever repay you for what you've done?"

"There's no need. Just remember, Kipp, she's been through two major traumas. First, being taken away from you and then being yanked out of a very unorthodox community. She has a lot to process."

"I know."

"Right now she seems happy and content, but she certainly could lapse back at any time. Do you plan to take her to a counselor?"

"I hadn't thought that far ahead."

"I think you should be aware of some things."

"Like what?"

"After an abduction, children who have been recovered can experience a number of problems, like interrupted sleep or excessive fright or concerns about being abducted again. She might revert back to wetting the bed or sucking her thumb. You saw how clingy she was to me."

He nodded.

"She might become that way with you. She might even get confused about her identity because of the name change. She could exhibit depression or anxiety. There are trust issues."

"Libby, you're scaring me."

"I don't mean to, but I think you should be prepared for anything. She's been under so much stress. The good thing about her abduction is that the community took good care of her, and from what Rebecca said, she wasn't moved from one location to another as so often happens in parental abductions. Anyway, my point is, you really should take her to a counselor as soon as possible. In fact, you should go, too."

"We can handle it."

"I don't think so, Kipp. Kelly needs to get professional help. She needs to be coaxed into opening up about her ordeal. She's been through so much. You both have. Right now everything is new to her, but I think the newness will wear off."

"Can't she talk to you? I could bring her here."

"I think it should be someone you don't know, but even if I could see her, that would be up to you and Tanya."

Kipp realized he had forgotten about Tanya and about having to include her input into everything concerning Kelly. He had not mentioned Libby's role in the rescue, and he had a distinct feeling Tanya would not approve of any of this.

It dawned on him that he and Libby had come together for Kelly's sake, and once he and Kelly left Libby's house, that would essentially be the end of his and Libby's need to see each other. He wanted to bring up the subject of a future together, in whatever form that might be, even if it only meant friendship. As far as he was concerned, the issue needed to be discussed, even if he had to risk the possibility of rejection. "What about you and me, Libby? Do you see anything for us?"

Libby bent over to wipe a smudge from her sneakers, but he knew she was avoiding eye contact. "What about you and Tanya? You both have a responsibility to make a home for Kelly. She needs you. She needs both of you."

Her words clutched his heart. Libby had voiced what he knew was true. For now there would be no Kipp and Libby. He had to get used to it. "We can still be friends, can't we? I can't imagine not hearing your voice. I can't imagine not seeing you."

When Libby rose, her eyes were moist. "I'll miss you, too, but it's Kelly's well-being you've got to concentrate on now."

He wanted to protest in some way, tell her he had room for both of them, but he could not deny Tanya's role, and he had to face the fact it would be awkward to spend time with Libby when Tanya was around.

It might confuse Kelly.

Ellen's car wound up the road, crunching gravel. The sun was beginning to slant in the horizon, casting light on Kipp's legs and warming his sandaled feet.

Waiting for the car to come to a halt, along with waiting for the sight of his daughter, gave Kipp the same feeling he'd had in the woods that night in Idaho. Spurts of adrenalin shot through him, and he wanted to lunge off the porch and take her in his arms, but apprehension about her reaction held him back. Glancing askance, he caught Libby watching him.

"You're nervous, aren't you?" she said.

He nodded, but he kept his eyes focused on the car.

Ellen got out first and waved to them. She was struggling to remove packages from the backseat when Kelly slowly made her way up the sidewalk. The shorts and tank top she had on earlier had been replaced by a similar lime outfit in a more appropriate size. Her golden curls, held back by two barrettes, fell just beyond her shoulders.

Kipp could not get over how much she had grown to look like Tanya, and how Libby and Ellen had transformed her from a little girl on the prairie to a modern-looking child. His feelings all in a turmoil, he smiled as she approached, yet lifted his glasses to wipe moisture from the corner of his eye.

When she reached the steps leading to the porch, she paused, shaded her eyes from the glare off the windows, and glanced up at Kipp. He froze, waiting for her reaction. Her gaze dropped to his feet, and she scrambled up the steps and grabbed the stuffed toy. "Baby bear." She held the bear to her chest and leaned into Kipp's leg.

He held his breath and squeezed his eyes shut to stop from crying out loud. He slowly knelt and put an arm around his daughter, not knowing for sure if she would accept the gesture. She shocked him by letting go of the toy, flinging her arms around his neck, and smothering him in an embrace. Overcome with happiness, he swept her up in his arms and held her close. When he heard her say Daddy, he started to weep. "I love you, baby," he managed to blubber through the tears.

He could have stayed in that moment forever, but she squirmed to reach for the bear. He lowered her to the ground, and she seized the toy. Kipp knelt again, and she leaned into him. He glanced up at Libby, whose face was as wet as his.

Ellen stood by with her arms full of packages. "Looks like you have a daughter. I'll go inside and put these down." The screen door banged shut behind her.

"Look what I got." The little girl pointed to her clothes.

"You look beautiful, Kelly," he said.

She cocked her head to one side. "I'm Kelly, huh? Do you want to see my picture?"

Through tears, Libby was smiling at him when they passed by. Inside, Kelly broke free from Kipp and ran to the dining room table. He followed her with his eyes and thought his heart would burst.

She returned to him with the photo he had left with Libby. She pointed to herself. "That's me." Then she glanced from the picture to Kipp. "You're my daddy." She rushed into his arms.

He wanted to cry again from sheer bliss, but once he let go of the pain that had been stored for so long, he worried he would never stop crying. He kissed her and nuzzled his face against her cheek. The smell of her skin and hair brought back memories of the baby he used to pack around in his arms not so very long ago.

"Look what we have here." Ellen had dug in a sack and come up with a Barbie doll.

Kelly squeezed Kipp's neck, wiggled out of his arms, and ran to the dining room table. She held the doll and grinned.

"What do you think?" Libby said.

"I'm shocked. She's acting normal, like any little girl would with a new toy and new clothes. I thought she'd not know what to make of it all. I thought she'd hang back, be more shy."

"I guess that's what deprivation will do. She's acting like she's been set free."

"What do you think she'll do when I take her home? Do you think she'll adjust okay?"

Libby hesitated before answering, and Kipp worried she was about to give him the bad news that Kelly's encouraging recovery was a fluke and that she would turn into the little girl Sarah at midnight.

"Do you have to go home today?" Libby said instead, while she busied herself straightening the magazines on the coffee table.

Kipp clutched her arm, forcing her to look at him. Her eyes brimmed with tears. "Isn't Kelly going to be okay with me?"

"Of course," she said. "But remember what I told you about the counseling. You have to be prepared for anything. You can always call me. You could stay here tonight, you and Kelly."

Kelly came into the room, smiling, and parked on the floor in front of them with her doll and her bear.

Ellen handed her the doll's outfits, stepped back with her hands on her hips. "She's such a sweet child. You should have seen her in the store. She wanted to touch everything."

That stab of jealousy erupted in Kipp—the wanting to be the first to have these experiences with his daughter—but he brushed it off. "Maybe we should get going." As soon as he said it, he panicked. Taking Kelly home was both exciting and terrifying, and for a moment he considered staying.

"What about something to eat?" Ellen said.

"Yes," Libby said. "You could even stay the night."

"I wish we could, but I'm not sure when Tanya will arrive. It could be the middle of the night. I want to have some time alone with Kelly before she shows up." Kipp turned to his daughter, who was now watching him. "Do you want to go home now, sweetheart?"

She scrambled to her feet and glanced from Kipp to Libby. "Can Libby go, too?"

Libby took her hand and held it against her leg. "Remember what we talked about this morning, about going home with your daddy?"

"Why can't you come, too?"

"Because I live here. I don't live with your daddy."

"But I want you to."

Libby looked pleadingly at Kipp for help.

"I wish she could come with us, too, Kelly, but we need to go home. Your real mommy is coming to see us."

"But I want Libby."

Kipp knelt beside her. "Honey, we'll see Libby again. We'll visit her, okay?"

Kelly's smile faded, her head lowered. She let go of Libby's hand. With that sullen look, she reminded Kipp of the person they would be seeing soon.

Ellen helped Kipp gather up the doll and its belongings. Kipp offered to pay for everything, but Ellen refused. She talked Kelly into taking the packages out to the Jeep with her, but before they were out the door, Kelly ran back to Libby and threw her arms around Libby's waist.

Libby returned the hug. "We'll see each other again, sweetie. Go on, now."

After Kelly ran out after Ellen, Kipp took Libby in his arms, and a rush of emotion overwhelmed him. Hovering in the warmth of her aura, he felt the tension from the conclusion of a long, hard-fought battle flow out of him. He held her close. He was tearing up again, and when he looked at Libby's face, he saw the tears in her eyes.

"You better go," she said. "She's waiting for you." She tried to take a step back, but he tightened his hold on her.

"I have to see you again, you know that."

"You and Kelly can visit."

"That's not what I meant." He lifted her chin and gave her a whispered kiss.

"We can't do this," she said.

"Why? Because of Tanya? I don't love Tanya. She'll be in my house because of Kelly. That's all."

"You have to give her a chance."

"Why?"

"Because of Kelly. She needs stability right now. She needs a mommy."

"I can't go where my heart won't go."

"You have to think of your daughter now."

"I am thinking of her. A fake marriage is not healthy for her, either."

"You have to focus on her now. Not us. It's not our time."

"When is our time?"

"I don't know." Libby pushed away. "You better go."

"Libby…"

She disappeared down the hallway. "Please go."

More than anything, he wanted to run after her and take her into his arms, but Kelly called out to him. He pulled a tissue from his pocket and dried his face. Before he stepped outside, he yelled down the hallway, "I'll be back, Libby."

Freeway traffic moved along steadily. The pavement was dry. It hadn't rained much this month. A month ago Libby had come into his life. It amazed him how strong his feelings were for her in such a short time. But at the moment he had to think about Kelly.

He had a difficult time keeping his eyes on the road. He stole glances at his daughter, who was strapped safely in the backseat. She played with the Barbie and the bear, and every once in a while, she asked where they were going. She seemed content.

His heart swelled with love, and for the time being, he let the past two years dissolve while he conjured up happier times. He pictured the house in Connecticut: the bright kitchen, the winding staircase, the tiny den off the living room. Kelly used to play on the floor with building blocks, and he would be hard at work at the computer, composing a story for a magazine, but from time to time he would stare at her and imagine her future, wondering if she would choose to become an architect or a lawyer.

His mind skipped to nighttime when he would carry her upstairs. She would pull out every item of clothing from her dresser drawer, looking for the perfect nightgown, and it would remind him she was Tanya's daughter. He would tuck her into bed, read her a story about bears, and watch her eyelids flutter shut.

After two years of hell, he was finally blessed with a full life. When he glanced toward the backseat again, Kelly asked about Libby, and he realized though his life was full, it was incomplete. Leaving Libby was heartbreaking, but he had to question whether or not his feelings toward her would be as strong once they were apart.

THIRTY

After Kipp left, Libby remained in her office. Astonished at how quickly she had become attached to Kelly and how much Kipp's departure was affecting her, she tried to reason with herself. Their time together had been amazingly short, and she didn't understand why her feelings about them were so intense. It was as if a part of her were being taken away. She had to get herself together before Ellen came back into the house, or Ellen, who had an uncanny way of seeing right through her, would hound her into talking about it. She was not up to that.

Ellen came into the room without knocking. "Hey, girl, why didn't you come out and… Oh, have you been crying?"

Libby brushed past her and into the kitchen to pour herself a glass of water.

Ellen's voice rang from the hallway. "Oh, Libby. I knew you felt something for Kipp. More than you let on. This is going to be really hard on you, isn't it?"

A rush of sadness lodged in Libby's chest. If she opened her mouth to speak, all that sadness would tumble out. She took her glass and went outside. Ellen followed. If ever Libby wanted to be alone, it was now, but she gave up trying and settled into one of the rattan chairs, stared at the winding driveway, and imagined the sight of Kipp's Jeep leaving the property.

Ellen sat, too. "It doesn't have to be over."

Libby took a deep breath and continued to stare off into the distance, into the green of the forest.

"Well, what are you going to do now? Just let him walk out of your life? Kids are resilient, you know. I bet Kipp won't be with his ex that long."

"Ellen, do we have to talk about it?"

"No, but if you don't, you'll explode."

"Look, Ellen, I don't know what's going to happen with them, but I do know right now they have to provide a stable home for Kelly."

"And why's that?" Ellen said. "She didn't have a stable home before she was kidnapped. Wouldn't they want to keep things as authentic as possible?"

"She needs to get reacquainted with her mother. That's the important thing now."

"Boy, it's hot today." Ellen wagged her hand, fanning herself. "If you ask me, that little girl will be on top of things in no time, and you and Kipp can get things going. And, by the way, where's your psychic radar? Can't you see what might happen with him and his ex?"

"It doesn't matter what happens."

"Yes, it does. The sooner she's out of the picture, the better for the two of you."

"Ellen, I can't think of that right now. I'm too tired from the week. Can we drop it?"

Ellen fanned herself again. "It's either the heat, or spending the morning with a six-year-old, but I'm bushed, too. I think I'll take a nap. What about you?" She stood and looked down at Libby, then moved toward the door.

Libby thought of asking Ellen about Charlie but decided against engaging her in any more conversation. Instead, she set her glass down, leaned back, and closed her eyes.

The sun's rays had crept up the porch and engulfed the chairs, making it too hot to sit much longer. For the moment, she basked in the heat, letting it warm her clear through, as if that might relieve the ache. But the ache was in her heart, and as in the past, only work would dull the pain.

Her work seemed like another world, a different reality from what she had just been through. She did not regret one minute of her time with Kipp, especially because of the outcome, but to have let her guard down and opened the door to her heart, if only a crack, was so reckless.

The last time she'd opened herself to those feelings was with Dan, and that had ended miserably. Not that Kipp was anything like Dan, but the pain from that relationship was etched in her mind, in the cells of her body, and the thought of it was enough to keep her heart closed forever.

Despite the heat, sudden chills ran up her spine. Out of the blue, Dan's face popped into her mind. Startled, she opened her eyes. She felt sick inside. These vibes had to have come from just thinking about him and from exhaustion. They were nothing prophetic. She shook the feeling off and went inside to check her work schedule.

The house was air-conditioned cool. She poured herself another glass of water, lingered at the kitchen sink, and watched a squirrel dart across the backyard and into a grove of fir trees. She loved the woods around her property. It provided her the peace and seclusion she craved.

She dabbed her face with a dampened paper towel and headed down the hallway. Ellen's door was ajar. She peeked inside and waited for a response, but Ellen was already asleep.

Upon entering her office, Libby was overwhelmed with an image of Kipp sitting in the recliner, not what she expected or wanted. She waved her arm to ward off any more impressions.

Next week her schedule was full, and she was grateful her mind would be occupied. She needed to close the door to her heart as soon as possible. She felt so vulnerable, so off-balance. She needed to get back on track.

She sat at her desk, staring out the window, her mind wandering. She relaxed to the point of believing a nap might be a good idea after all. Besides, in her office Kipp's presence was everywhere.

She closed her appointment book and slipped off her shoes. Entering the hallway, she felt a jab in the middle of her back, like an electric shock, a signal that something was trying to get her attention. She ignored the warning and continued to her bedroom.

As soon as she lay down, the pain struck again. Normally, after a warning, a flow of pictures would follow, but she was too worn out to pay attention. She took a few deep breaths to settle herself and willed her mind to calm down. The twittering of birds broke the silence before she drifted into a light sleep.

At first she thought the noise was in her dream—the faraway rumble of a car's engine—but the louder the sound, the more she knew it was real. A shot of electricity, running up her spine, jolted her to a waking state, and the fleeting glimpse of the face she feared most flashed before her. She stood by the side of the bed and froze.

This could not be happening. She hadn't seen or heard from him in so long she blamed a wild imagination fueled by fatigue to create something that was not there.

Her rational mind took over. She thought it might be Kipp. Perhaps he forgot something. That was it. For a fleeting second she glanced at the nightstand, at the pistol's hiding place, thought about taking it with her for safety's sake. But what if it were Kipp and Kelly? She left the pistol alone.

She hastened quietly from the room past Ellen's door. She didn't want to wake Ellen if it was a false alarm, and she prayed it was.

She reached the foyer before the doorbell rang and opened the door in time to see Dan, her ex-husband, climbing the porch stairs. Her first instinct was to lock the screen door, but he swung it open before she could react. She staggered back from the doorway. She couldn't bring herself to say anything.

He blocked her attempt to shut the door. She shifted her gaze to his rough, calloused hand. All the ways he'd used that hand to terrorize her flooded her memory. The smell of alcohol added to the images. She couldn't move and felt like a child awaiting punishment. Then she remembered thinking about him earlier and wondered if she had willed him to come.

"Hey, baby. Can I come in?" His baritone voice snapped her out of her trance.

One foot was already through the doorway. Why had he bothered to ask? She backed inside, and he advanced toward her. Medium in height and build, more wiry than muscular, he would appear non-threatening to any stranger, but Libby was no stranger. She knew what he was capable of.

"What do you want?"

He glanced around the room, then settled his alcoholic eyes on her. His fingers were shoved into the pockets of his jeans, his white tee shirt, the pocket bulging from a pack of cigarettes, was tucked inside. His ebony hair was buzzed close to his scalp, the way he'd worn it in the Marines. Even in the heat of the day he wore cowboy boots, the pointy kind, and the sight of them reminded Libby how sharp they could be in the soft flesh of the belly. She winced from the memory.

His tongue hung half out of his mouth while he sized her up and stopped at her chest. "You look good."

"What do you want, Dan?"

"Money."

"How much?"

"Coupla grand."

She'd loaned him money in the past, but that was years ago, and she thought with that loan he was finally out of her life. "I don't have that to give."

"You've got money." He scanned the room. "Look at this place."

"I thought you were married."

"It's not going so well."

"What do you need money for?"

"What's with the third degree? I just need it."

She sensed the belligerence she knew too well, and she wanted him out of her house, out of her life. She reached for her purse on the coffee table, dug out her wallet, and pulled out a wad of bills. "Take this and get out."

He snatched the money from her hand and leafed through the bills. His face, turning a purplish-red, changed to an ugly scowl. He stuffed the bills in his pocket. "What am I going to do with fifty bucks? I need two grand."

"I don't have it."

"I didn't drive across this fucking county to go away empty-handed." He grabbed her wrist. "Come on, let's go."

"Go where?"

"To the bank. I know you've got the money."

From the corner of her eye, Libby saw Ellen coming down the hallway, and she tried to warn her by shaking her head.

"Hey, what's going on?"

Dan twirled around and in the process dropped Libby's arm.

"What's all the commotion?"

He glanced from Ellen to Libby. "Hey, I get it. You've taken up with a woman. I should have known. You were always a cold fish in bed. Which one is the man in this relationship?"

"Get out."

He let out a howl. "My ex-wife is a fucking lesbian."

"You don't know what you're talking about, mister," Ellen said.

"Shut up." He turned to Libby. "I want the money, now. Let's go."

"I told you I don't have it."

Ellen swung around and jogged down the hallway.

"That's not what I want to hear from you, baby. Now, are you going to come with me, or do I have to make you. It's your call."

Struck by the wild look in Dan's eyes, Libby wanted to talk him down, anything to prevent riding in a car with him. "Why are you here? Where is your wife?"

"That's none of your goddamned business. Now, come on." He cocked his head toward the door.

"Why don't you sit down? I'll make you coffee."

He grabbed her wrist and held tight. "I don't want any goddamned coffee."

She was determined not to go anywhere with him. "Are you hungry? I could make you something to eat."

He tightened his grip and dragged her toward the door just as Ellen came barreling down the hallway with the pistol in her hand. "Let her go, asshole."

He narrowed his eyes and began to take quick, deep breaths, snorting like a bull, ready to charge.

"Ellen, put the gun down."

"You heard your fag lover, put it down," he said.

Ellen's face puckered, and she marched up to him and held the gun in his face. "You let her go and get out."

He shoved Libby sideways where she fell into the coffee table. He knocked the gun out of Ellen's hand and pushed her backward.

He quickly picked up the gun and held it on Ellen. "You fat bitch." He opened the chamber. "Stupid, too. It's not even loaded." He gripped the barrel, holding the gun like a hammer, and turned to Libby, who had recovered from the fall and was rubbing a sore leg. "What do you have a gun for?"

"What do you think?"

He laughed. "What good is it if it isn't loaded? Obviously, you don't know how to use it. You never were too bright. I'll just take it off your hands."

"Fine. Do what you want."

"Like I have to ask. Now, let's go get the money."

"She's not going anywhere with you," Ellen said.

"You're not only a stupid bitch, you're mouthy, too."

"Stop it, Dan. Don't talk to her that way."

He lunged at Libby, gripped a wad of her hair in his hand, and held the butt of the gun to her face. "Didn't I ever teach you not to tell me what to do?"

Libby's neck snapped backward from the yank of his hand. "You're hurting me."

Ellen flew at Dan, swinging. With Libby's hair in his grasp, he shoved Ellen away with his free hand. Ellen charged again. He kicked her back with the heel of his boot and swung Libby around, so she was between them. He held Libby's neck in an armlock. "Back off, dyke, if you don't want your lover hurt."

Ellen stopped cold.

"Now, this is what I want you to do. I want you to go in the bedroom and stay there until I say you can come out. Libby and I have some unfinished business to take care of before we leave. If you dare show your fat face, I'll hurt her so bad you won't be able to recognize her, then I'll come after you, got that?"

Ellen's face sank into a mixture of terror, sorrow, and defeat.

"Do what he says, Ellen."

"But, Libby."

"Just do what he says, please."

Ellen glanced toward the window, hesitated, then backed down the hallway and into her room. Libby prepared for the worst. Dan always made good on his threats, and a swirl of horrible memories overwhelmed her. Her body ached, anticipating the pain. She expected his heavy hand to come down on her, but instead, he backed her to the couch and made her sit with him.

He laid the gun on the table. "I want to see what they did to you."

When he touched the top of her blouse, she dug her nails into the flesh of his arm as hard as she could and used the time it took for him to register the pain to spring off the couch. He caught her arm, and when he stood up, he backhanded her across the face. She sucked in a pained breath.

"I didn't want to have to do that, baby, but you gave me no choice. After we're done here, we're getting the money."

"Please, Dan, don't."

"I'll have you, baby." His voice mellowed with those nauseating words he always said before he raped her.

As he pulled her to her knees, her body went limp. His arm, brushing against hers, was dangerously familiar. The stench of his body was mixed with the stink of tobacco and alcohol. Salty tears trickled into her mouth. She lost the strength to fight him. Sinking deeper and deeper into despair, she closed her eyes and prepared to leave her body.

An agonizing minute went by. She held still.

Dan suddenly let go of her hair and rushed to the window. She heard the sound of an approaching car.

When he turned around, his face had paled out. He checked the window again, then charged past Libby and bolted out the back door.

A second later the doorbell rang. Ellen galloped down the hallway and swung the door open. When a sheriff's deputy asked if she was the one who made the call, she ran to Libby's side. "Libby, are you all right?"

The deputy entered and made a sweeping view of the room. "What happened here, ma'am?" With the sound of an engine starting, he swung around to look outside.

Libby cried out, "Let him go."

The deputy turned back to Libby. "Do you want to tell me what happened?"

"My ex-husband."

"He assaulted her, can't you see that?" Ellen said.

"I need to hear it from you, ma'am."

"He came for money. We argued. He hit me."

"He threatened both of us," Ellen said.

Ellen and the deputy helped Libby off the floor and walked her to the sofa. He spotted the gun on the coffee table. "Is that your gun?"

"Yes."

"It's not loaded," Ellen said.

"Did he have this?"

"I got it out of the drawer to scare him, and he took it away from me," Ellen said.

"Did he threaten you with it?"

"He knocked it out of my hand and took it away from me. He was going to beat her with it."

The deputy focused on Libby. "You can press charges against him, ma'am. You have a good witness."

"I don't want to. I know all about the hotline for battered women and the shelters. I've been through this before."

"I'll arrange to have your injuries looked at."

"That's not necessary. He only hit me once. There are no other injuries. I'm just shook up."

"Libby…"

"I think you should be checked out, ma'am."

"I said no. I'm all right."

After taking Dan's full name and description, the deputy stepped outside to make a call. Another vehicle came up the driveway.

Ellen ran to the window. "Charlie's here. He's talking to the deputy." She opened the front door and waited until he came up the walkway and into the house. "Oh, Charlie, it was awful."

Charlie moved directly to Libby's side. "That's going to be a nasty bruise. Why don't you let me take you into town and get it looked at? It will help with evidence against him. You can press charges."

Libby held her palm to her face. Sitting here with a cop was like déjà vu. "I can't do that, Charlie. It will just make him angrier than he is now, and he'll want revenge. He's been in jail before, and it didn't do any good."

"But he assaulted you. That's a crime, and he should be punished."

"I won't press charges."

"Libby, don't be stubborn about this."

"I won't do it."

"At least get a restraining order against him," Ellen said.

"I've had those before. With him it doesn't help."

Ellen went into the kitchen, returned with an ice bag, and handed it to Libby. "You've got to do something, Charlie."

"She needs to press charges."

"What if he comes back?" Ellen's face was panic-stricken, and she exchanged glances with Charlie.

The thought of his return made Libby's throat tighten. They didn't know the seriousness of his visit, the threat of rape, and she kept it to herself. She could still smell his foul breath. She just wanted the nightmare to end.

The deputy came to the door, and he and Charlie had a discussion. The deputy left. Charlie came into the house.

"Should we call Kipp?" Ellen said.

Libby removed the ice bag from her cheek. "Don't be ridiculous."

"He might care what's happened to you."

"He has enough to worry about right now. I'm not his concern."

"I think you're mistaken."

"I'm just shook up a little. I just want to lie down and rest." When she got up, her legs wobbled, and she reached out to Charlie for support.

Ellen took her arm. "I'll walk her down to the bedroom and be back in a minute." Once they were in the bedroom, Ellen helped Libby lie down and draped an afghan over her. "I'm so sorry this happened. I feel like a fool, staying in my room like that."

"Don't beat yourself up. You had no choice. I'm just sorry he said those mean things to you."

"You know the old saying, sticks and stones…"

"You're a good friend, Ellen. You called 9-1-1 and Charlie, didn't you? You did exactly what you should have done."

"At least I did that. Get some rest. I'll be here when you wake up." Ellen leaned over and lightly kissed Libby's forehead. She closed the bedroom door on the way out.

THIRTY-ONE

ELLEN WIPED the corners of her eyes as she walked down the hallway. What a cruel man Libby had married. Ellen recalled how infatuated Libby was before the marriage, and she wondered how Libby could have been so taken in, especially with her psychic nature. Love was definitely blind.

In the heat of the moment, Ellen had used her cell phone to call Charlie, and now he was waiting for her in the living room. With Dan out of the picture and Libby in bed, Ellen and Charlie would be alone. She wished she had dressed in something other than shorts.

As Ellen entered the room, Charlie stood and smiled awkwardly at her and sat after she made herself comfortable. "Can you tell me the details?"

"It was awful, Charlie. After Kipp and Kelly left, I went into the bedroom to take a nap. I don't know how long I was in there because I fell asleep, but I woke up to voices, arguing. When I went to investigate, I saw him holding Libby's wrist and yelling at her. It was just awful."

"Then what happened?"

"When he saw me, he let her go, but he made these crude remarks about us being lovers. I ran to my room and called 9-1-1, then you. Then I got Libby's gun."

"What the hell were you going to do with Libby's gun?"

"What do you think I was going to do? He was threatening her."

"Jeez, Ellen, you're the one who could have been booked in jail."

"Well, I didn't get that chance because he knocked the gun out of my hand. Besides, it wasn't loaded."

"Jesus." He threw up his hands.

"Charlie, you weren't here. You have no idea what it felt like to be threatened by that maniac."

"I'm sorry, Ellen. I just wish you two would learn how to use a gun."

"Well, maybe if you'd teach me…"

"Maybe that wouldn't be a bad idea."

Ellen paused, wondering if Charlie was alluding to spending more time with her. "Anyway, he said all kinds of nasty things to me, and he grabbed Libby by the hair, so I charged him. I was going to beat him up really good."

Charlie smirked, was having a hard time keeping a straight face, and Ellen glared. "Charlie." He cleared his throat and his expression changed back to concern.

"He shoved me back with his boot and told me to stay in my room or he'd do something horrible to…" Libby's name caught in her throat. She sniffled, and Charlie offered her a hanky. "I feel so guilty because I just left her there with him. Lord knows what else he did to her."

Charlie scooted over and put his arm around her. "Hey, you did what you had to. It's called survival, babe. Besides, if you had defied him, he might have done something terrible to you. What did he come here for, anyway? What were they arguing about?"

"Money. He smelled like a booze hound. He probably needed money for alcohol."

"I bet drugs. People don't do stupid things for alcohol. They do it for drugs."

"He looked half-crazed. His eyes were on fire. I never saw anyone like that."

"He was probably higher than a kite. When was the last time she saw him?"

"I don't know. Maybe two, three years ago."

"He must have been pretty desperate to seek her out after all that time. I'm going to make a call."

Ellen held him back. "She doesn't want you to."

"I need to call the sheriff's office and find out if they caught up with the guy." He patted her knee and left to use the phone in his car.

From where Ellen was sitting, she had a good view of Charlie striding down the sidewalk. Dressed in dark slacks and a short-sleeved, white shirt, he looked distinguished, all business. He swaggered a little when he walked.

With the crisis passed, her thoughts drifted to her relationship, or non-relationship, with Charlie. He had come to their rescue at a moment's notice, and that was sexy. The man was sexy.

She weighed the shoulds in her life with the wants: she should go home and be a good wife, but she wanted to be loved by someone who respected her and treated her like a queen, someone like Charlie.

Charlie came into the house, carrying a duffel bag. "I made the call, and you're not going to believe this, but he's already been stopped."

"What happened?"

"He tore out of here like a wild man, and I guess he kept driving the same way when he got spotted."

"Will he go to jail?"

"He's in jail." Charlie dropped his bag in the foyer and sat with her. "Is the guy married?"

"Yes, but no doubt she's a battered woman."

"I'm worried about when he gets out," Charlie said. "He might turn his attention to Libby again."

"Why so? Law enforcement was here. Why would he chance it?"

"Who's the last person he was with before his life went in the toilet?"

"That wasn't her fault."

"The way a guy like that thinks is not rational. He'll blame her for his latest problems."

"Why not his wife?"

"In his mind Libby is still one of his possessions," Charlie said. "She always will be. Remember, it was the cancer that parted them. He'd probably still be here if it wasn't for that. Now that her health is better, I bet he's turned his sights on her again."

"But he's married, and he came for money."

"I'm not saying he didn't need the money," Charlie said, "but I bet that wasn't the only reason he came here. His present marriage has been a diversion, and now that it's a mess, which I bet it is, he needs Libby. She's made something of herself, she lives comfortably, and he can't stand the thought of her having any kind of success."

"But it's been a long time. Why would he even think she'd put up with him?"

"When was the last time she saw him?"

"Like I said, two, three years ago."

"And what happened then?"

"He wanted money, same as this time."

"And did she give it to him?"

"Yes, but he didn't hurt her."

"It makes sense that he would come back again if he knew he could still intimidate her. I just don't think he'd come back here if he didn't have an ulterior motive, like coming back into her life again."

"You sound like one of those FBI profilers."

"I've just been around it enough. These guys are real manipulators. They're not even human."

Ellen nodded toward the duffel bag. "What's that for?"

"The bag? I called in and took the last couple of hours off. I thought I might camp out here tonight. I've got stuff in there I might need in the morning."

Ellen furrowed her brow. "Do you think he'll come back?"

"Not tonight, but you two have been through a lot, and I don't want you to be here alone. I want you to feel safe. I'll camp out on the couch, if that's okay."

She let out a relieved sigh. "You don't know how grateful I am, and I'm sure Libby will feel the same, but if you're staying, I'm going to make you dinner."

"I could take you and Libby out."

"Normally, we'd jump at the chance, but I don't think Libby will want to go out anywhere tonight, not after what happened." Ellen tapped the side of her face. "Swollen cheek?"

"Jeez, that was insensitive of me," he said. "Of course, she wouldn't. Then let me help you with dinner."

"That's a deal. Let's see what we can scrounge up."

All the way to the kitchen, she sensed him following her with his eyes, which dredged up those nasty, self-conscious feelings about her weight. She shooed those feelings away and searched the pantry for dinner ideas, but when she turned around, he was staring at her.

"I don't have time to thaw anything, but how about macaroni and cheese? I have a great recipe I got from my grandmother. It's a pretty beefed-up recipe."

"Sounds fine to me."

"Great." She rounded up noodles, cottage cheese, eggs, and cheddar.

"What can I do?"

She found a grater in one of the kitchen drawers. "You can grate the cheese." She gave him a plate and took a bowl from the shelf.

After she put water on the stove for the macaroni, she sidled up to Charlie at one of the counters. He grated the cheddar while she mixed up the cottage cheese and eggs.

"How am I doing?"

She stole a glance and chuckled.

"What's so funny?"

"You have to ask how you're doing? You're only grating cheese."

"Hey, I know how you women are."

Ellen stopped what she was doing and placed a hand on her hip. "Oh, really. Tell me."

The grimace on Charlie's face was a sure sign he knew he had stepped into a giant black hole. "I just meant," he stammered, "women like precision, and men can be slobs, you know."

"I'll have to think about that." She ambled to the stove to check on the water and returned to the counter.

"Have you given it some thought? Am I back in good graces?"

"Mmm… I'll let you know."

"Yeah, well, I'm real worried." He grinned.

Ellen nudged him with her elbow. He nudged her back.

She shifted her attention to the stove until the noodles were simmering. When she sauntered back to Charlie and discovered what he had done—grated a huge pile of cheese, way too much for the casserole—she started laughing.

"What's so funny?"

"Let's just say women like precision, but men like everything big. You know, like big guns, big trucks, enough cheese for an army."

Charlie's face reddened. "What's the matter? You don't like my big mountain of cheese? I thought you women liked it big."

Ellen thought she might have to pee, she cackled so hard. Charlie let go with a roar, and without missing a beat, he grasped her in a big bear hug. She howled, pounding his chest. They were so into each other, they didn't hear Libby enter the room.

"Hello, you two."

Ellen broke out of Charlie's arms.

"Don't stop on my account," Libby said. "It's nice to hear laughter around here."

"Oh, honey, we're sorry if we woke you."

"Don't be. I'm getting hungry."

Ellen put the finishing touches on the casserole and stuck it in the microwave. She threw a salad together while Libby and Charlie set the table. Soon they sat down to eat.

Libby's bruised face was a reminder of their terrifying afternoon, and the conversation was more subdued than it would have been. When Ellen mentioned to Libby that Charlie would be staying the night, Libby looked at Ellen quizzically.

"I'm sleeping on the couch," Charlie volunteered.

"Oh, I don't mind if you two sleep together in Ellen's room," Libby said. "That won't bother me."

Charlie and Ellen glanced at one another. "Honey, Charlie needs to sleep on the couch, just in case."

"You don't think he'll come back, do you?"

Charlie put his hand on Libby's. "He's in jail now, but after what you two have been through, I want you to feel safe."

Libby's eyes softened. "You're such a good person, Charlie. Thank you. And thank you for coming this afternoon."

"Oh my God, Charlie, I don't think I even thanked you for doing that," Ellen said.

"I think you did," he said.

"Well, this is an official thank you."

"I feel like a real hero."

"Yes, and you'd make someone a real catch."

Ellen shot Libby an I-don't-want-you-to-say-another-word look before Libby excused herself. With Charlie's help, Ellen cleared the table and set the dishes in the sink.

Libby held a bag filled with ice. "I'm going to take a bath and go to bed. I'm bushed."

"And still strung out, I bet. Do you want me to run your water or wash your back?"

"Thanks, but I don't need any help. I'll be fine. Can you and Charlie entertain yourselves?" She managed a smile.

Charlie grinned. "That won't be a problem." And Ellen tweaked his cheek.

"By the way," Libby said on her way out of the kitchen, "the sofa folds out into a queen-sized bed."

Ellen wrinkled her nose at Libby. "Scoot."

Though Charlie insisted he could sleep on the sofa cushions, Ellen helped him make up the bed.

"Why don't you stay up and watch TV with me? I don't think I can get to sleep right away."

"I don't think I can sleep either," Ellen said.

She turned down the air conditioner, tossed him a pillow, and grabbed the remote. He patted the seat next to him. She leaned against the sofa back, alongside Charlie, and stretched out her legs. He aimed his arm around her to take the remote out of her hand and left his arm draped over her shoulders.

She snuggled into him. "This feels good."

"It feels right."

"I'm beginning to think so."

He gave her shoulder a squeeze, powered on the TV, and turned the volume low.

"I'm worried about Libby. I wish we could let Kipp know what happened."

"I can call him," he said.

"She doesn't want him to know, but I think he cares about her."

"He's head-over-hills."

"Really?"

"The timing's lousy with his ex there and his daughter needing all his attention."

"Still. He should know."

"What about your situation?"

"I'm certainly not going to leave Libby here by herself."

"Does that mean you're not going back to Mel?"

"I didn't say that."

Charlie leaned sideways, dragging his arm with him.

"Hey." She pitched his arm back. "I didn't say I was. Maybe if you court me a little, I might be convinced to stay for good."

Charlie kissed her forehead, then he switched the channel to the local news.

⤬

Ellen had forgotten to close the curtains, and the morning light streamed through the picture windows. Voices, chattering on the TV, were mixed with Charlie's snores. She and Charlie were lying on the sofa bed fully clothed, snuggled next to each other.

Her mouth was dry, her tongue felt like sandpaper, and she suspected her breath could move an army; she longed for a glass of water.

Before she could inch off the couch without disturbing him, he swung his arm over her and yawned. "What time is it?"

"Six."

"I guess we fell asleep."

"Looks that way."

He leaned in to kiss her and got a mouth full of hair. "What's wrong?"

She turned back and pointed to her mouth. "I don't want to kill you."

"That's an old excuse." He held her close and kissed her squarely on the mouth.

She could feel him against her, and he was definitely aroused. Her own body tingled, and she anticipated being with him that way again. She couldn't remember the last time she felt that way about Mel.

"Man, you feel good. I better get up, if I still can."

Snickering, she watched him stand and make the necessary adjustments. "Can you believe we actually fell asleep last night?"

"That means we owe each other a roll in the hay."

"You're on, fella."

"That means you'll go out with me again?"

"What do you mean again?"

Charlie hesitated. "I guess I owe you a real date, don't I?"

"Yep. And I'm going to hold you to it." She got up and smoothed the wrinkles in her blouse. "Do you want to take a shower, or have some coffee?"

"Naw. I think I'll go home and clean up there before I go to work."

Ellen walked him to the door and they embraced. "Thanks again, big guy."

"I can tell you're still concerned."

"Does it show?"

"You're holding on awfully tight, and your body's pretty tense."

"You sure know how to read people."

"That's my job."

"I think it's more than that. You're a sensitive man."

"Don't tell anybody, or it'll ruin my reputation as a bad-boy cop."

She gave him a playful jab. "You're a funny cop, too."

"Look, I'll call you when I get to the station," he said. "I'll check on our friend's status and let you know what they've done with him. That way you and Libby can rest easier. I'm going to check in with you every hour. If you go out somewhere, you call me and let me know where you are. Leave a message. Okay?"

She saluted him. "Yes, sir."

"I mean it. And keep the doors locked, and don't answer the doorbell for anyone you don't know. I don't trust that joker."

"You're a jewel." She reached up and gave him a quick kiss.

He picked up his duffel bag and left her lingering in the doorway until he drove away.

When she turned around, Libby was standing back behind her in her bathrobe and slippers. "Has Charlie gone?"

"Hi, honey. Yeah, he's gone home and then he's going to work, but he's going to keep tabs on us. Did you sleep well? Let me look at you." Ellen examined Libby's face. "It's going to be okay. Just a little bruising. The ice helped."

"It's still sore. I had a hard time calming down last night. I kept seeing his face."

"A real nightmare, wasn't it? Let me make you some tea." Wandering into the kitchen, she said, "Looks like Charlie and I are going to see each other again."

"I guess there is some good to come out of all this."

The phone rang, and they both jumped.

"I'll get it." When Ellen picked up, she was relieved to hear Charlie's voice. Afterward, she told Libby, "Charlie found out that they got Dan on a DUI. He won't have a license for a while. So, we can rest easy."

Libby sighed. "Maybe that will be the end of it."

Ellen debated whether or not to tell Libby about her and Charlie's earlier discussion concerning Dan, and how Charlie thought Dan might be focusing on Libby again, but she decided not to upset her. "We both think Kipp should know."

Libby frowned. "I'm not his concern, Ellen. I'm not sure I ever will be."

THIRTY-TWO

Kipp rose early Thursday morning, anticipating Tanya's arrival. He had mixed feelings about her coming so soon, since he would have preferred more time alone with their daughter. Kelly seemed to accept him, but he wished he had more time to cement their relationship before adding another person to the mix, even if that person was her mother. Tanya wasn't the most grounded person in the universe, and he feared her flightiness would somehow upset the child, who, more than anything, needed stability.

Before taking a shower, he looked in on her. He had moved his computer desk into a corner of the living room and made up the extra bed for her because he wanted her to have her own room as she'd had in Connecticut. She was sleeping soundly, clutching the toy bear. His heart swelled to the bursting point. In that moment, it was as if no time had gone by at all.

He dressed, made his bed, and straightened up the living room. He was in the kitchen washing dishes when he heard the patter off little feet cross the linoleum floor. When he turned, Kelly was next to him. He wiped his hands on a towel and knelt beside her. She hugged his neck. He swept her up in his arms and swung her around, producing a spattering of giggles, a sound he had not heard in a very long time.

"Where's my mommy?"

He showed her Tanya's picture. "This is Mommy, and she'll be here soon."

Kelly held the photo, then cocked her head. "Where's my other mommy?"

This took him by surprise. If he'd anticipated her questions, he hadn't prepared the answers, and he wasn't sure what to say. He thought of Libby and wished she were here to coach him. She had warned him Kelly might need extra help adjusting.

He sat her on the couch and decided to wing it. "I'm going to tell you a story." He cradled her with his arm. "Once upon a time there was a little girl who lived with her daddy in a house far away from here. One day she went to stay with some people who loved her very much. They took good care of her until her real mommy and daddy could bring her home." He cringed at his feeble attempt, wishing Libby were here to help him.

Kelly stared at him with widened eyes, the hazel color reminiscent of her mother's.

"You're that little girl, honey, and your other mommy was taking care of you for me until I could bring you home. Do you understand?" Feeling totally inadequate, he held his breath and waited for her response.

"Oh." She climbed off the sofa and took his hand. "I'm hungry."

Relieved for the time being, he let her lead him into the kitchen. She certainly had a way of bringing simplicity to chaos. Still, Libby's warning about the need for counseling lingered in the back of his mind.

Kelly climbed up on a stool. Kipp fixed her a bowl of Cheerios and resumed washing the dishes. She used to be chatty and animated, but now she only asked a few questions before lapsing into silence. Her behavior, even though normal under the circumstances, concerned him, and again Libby came to mind.

"Where's Libby?"

The timing of her question astounded him. "Libby's at her house."

"Can we go there?"

"Not today, honey. Your mommy is coming soon."

The doorbell rang. Kipp grabbed a towel and headed for the door. Kelly swiveled around to look. He turned the lock, and Tanya barged through the doorway in hot pink jeans and tee shirt and gave Kipp a quick hug. When Kelly slid off the stool, Tanya bounded toward her and scooped her up in her arms. "My baby. My baby." Kelly let out a high-pitched wail, struggled to the floor, and ran to her room. Tanya gasped and began to cry.

With Tanya's grand entrance, Kipp's fears were materializing before his eyes. He didn't know which one to comfort first, but he ran after Kelly, who was sitting on the bed, clutching the bear. He sat beside her and rubbed her back. "It's okay, sweetheart. Daddy's here."

Tanya stood in the doorway, sniffling.

Kipp cast Tanya a stern look. "This is your mommy, Kelly. She missed you very much. She didn't mean to scare you. If she promises to tiptoe over here very slowly and hold out her hand, will you say hello?"

Kelly nodded, staring at the floor. Tanya knelt in front of her and offered an open palm. Kelly tentatively laid her hand in Tanya's.

"Oh, baby, I'm sorry I scared you. I'm your mommy, and I love you." But Kelly wouldn't look at her, and Tanya glanced at Kipp, hurt.

Kipp gave Kelly a squeeze. "Do you want to finish your cereal?"

Kelly skirted Tanya and dashed out of the room.

"God, Kipp, I didn't realize how bad it was."

"What the hell did you think it was going to be like? I tried to warn you, but you had to charge in here like a—"

"I don't want to argue with you."

"Just take it easy, okay? Be sensitive for once in your life, and think about your daughter for a change."

"I've thought about her every day for two years."

"What about the first four years of her life?"

Tanya stood tall, her shoulders back. "I'm not going to have this discussion, Kipp. So drop it, and go get my bags."

Glad for the breather, Kipp brought in Tanya's luggage. Tanya tagged along to his bedroom.

"I'll take the couch."

"The couch?" She laid her arms on his shoulders. "Don't you think we should sleep together?"

He brushed her arms away.

"What about Kelly?"

"What does Kelly have to do with our sleeping together?"

"If she sees her mommy and daddy together, it will feel more like the real thing, like before."

He held her at arm's length. "Aren't you forgetting about the years you weren't living with us before she was kidnapped? That's what's normal to her."

"But, Kipp, I've missed you, and I want us to be a family again. This is the perfect opportunity to get back together, you and me."

"And what about Kelly?"

"You know I meant the three of us. We could be a family again."

"And how many men have you slept with in the last six months? No, I take that back. In the last two weeks."

"Oh, stop it, Kipp."

Kipp huffed. "I'm taking the couch."

Tanya watched in silence while he gathered his clothes from the dresser drawers and stacked his tee shirts and underwear on the upper shelf in the closet. He pushed his shirts and slacks aside to make room for her clothes.

"You didn't tell me how you found her."

Kipp weighed just how much to tell her about Libby and decided to remain cautious. "Remember the psychic I told you about?"

"You didn't!"

"She gave me the direction to go in."

"Who is this psychic?"

"She works for the FBI." He lied so he wouldn't have to explain anything else about her.

"She? Was she with you when you found her?"

"Jesus, Tanya, what difference does that make? She saved our daughter."

Tanya's lips fell into a pout.

Kipp placed his hands on her shoulders and looked directly into her eyes. "Listen to me, okay? We need to think about Kelly now. Nothing else matters. Let's try to be civil to each other and stop arguing, for her sake."

"Tell yourself that." Tanya pushed his hands off and exited the room, pulling her hair into a ponytail.

❦

In the morning Kipp opened the blinds to the backyard. Several chickadees were hopping the branches of the maple tree and flying into the birdbath.

He squeezed the muscles in his neck, working out the kinks from the cramped, lumpy sofa. Even though Tanya had fussed about the sleeping arrangements, she'd given in and slept in his bed alone.

Tanya's silvery, oversized purse was plunked in the middle of his desk, and her white jacket was splayed over his leather chair. She had been here less than twenty-four hours, and already the two-bedroom house was beginning to feel crowded in more ways than one.

Kelly traipsed into the room in her pale pink nightgown and tugged on his jeans. He took her in his arms and pointed outside. "See the chickadees in the birdbath? They like to take baths, too."

When she tired of watching the birds, she rubbed the stubble on his face, as her toddler-self used to do, which warmed his heart. "Where's Libby?"

"Remember I told you she's at her house?"

"Why can't I go see her?"

"She's busy right now. We'll visit her again one day. Why do you want to see Libby?"

"She's nice."

"So is your mommy."

"Not like Libby."

He kissed her cheek. "Let's get you some breakfast." He turned and faced Tanya, who was standing on the far side of the room in one of his tee shirts.

She held out her arms. "Come here, baby. Let me make you some eggs."

"I don't like eggs."

"Fine. Cereal, then." Tanya spun around and disappeared into the kitchen.

"Go with your mommy." Kipp put Kelly down, and she wandered silently after Tanya.

He left them in the kitchen and went into the bedroom to get a shirt. He was rummaging through his clothes and picking out socks and underwear when he sensed Tanya's presence in the room.

She closed the door. "What's with this Libby person?"

Kipp pulled a cotton shirt off a hanger, ignoring her.

"Who is she?"

"I told you. She's an FBI agent."

Tanya stationed herself in front of him and searched his eyes. "You're lying. I just had a little talk with our daughter, and she told me you've been to this woman's house. What FBI agent would let you do that?"

"So what if she's not an agent?"

"What are you doing taking Kelly to another woman's house when you knew I was coming? All she talks about is Libby. Libby this and Libby that. Did you sleep with her?"

"That's none of your business."

"Kelly said the three of you rode in the car together and went to her house. How many days were you with this woman?"

"She helped me bring Kelly home."

"And now she's trying to take my place."

"Don't be absurd."

"Well, I'm not going to compete with her or anybody else." She stormed out of the room.

Kipp jogged after her, worried she might upset Kelly. He glanced in Kelly's room. It was empty. In the living room, he panicked. She was nowhere around. His heart quickened.

"What's wrong with you?" Tanya was rummaging in her purse.

"Where's Kelly?"

"She's in the backyard."

He rushed to the window and spotted Kelly circling the birdbath. "And you left her out there alone? What the hell were you thinking?"

"Don't raise your voice to me. She's fine."

"I don't want her out of our sight, especially when she's in the yard."

"You're overreacting."

Kipp gazed at Tanya in disbelief and slammed the door on his way outside.

❧

A week later Kipp was drinking a cup of coffee in the kitchen, waiting for Tanya and Kelly to wake up. The house was dismal on overcast days, and he snapped on the overhead light.

He reflected on the week past, evaluating Tanya's reunion with their daughter. Kelly's initial reluctance had given way to an acceptance of sorts.

Tanya had actually spent an entire afternoon in the bedroom, playing dolls with Kelly. Kelly seemed to warm up to her mother, but Kipp had a hard time believing it was anything beyond a superficial attempt on Kelly's part. In that respect mother and daughter mirrored each other.

But Kelly hung on to her memories of Libby. He thought she would forget in time, but daily she reminded him that Libby had been a part of their lives, and these little reminders kept Libby in the front of his mind, not just the way she looked—although that was high on his list of how he remembered her—but the way she could reach into his soul and understand him.

Since Tanya's arrival, he'd taken it upon himself to get up early to be alone without any distractions. If he could not be with Libby in person, at least he could capture her in his thoughts.

This morning Tanya and Kelly were sleeping in, and it was almost nine. They had been out late the night before. At Tanya's insistence, he had taken them to dinner at the Space Needle in celebration of Kelly's return.

He listened for any stirrings, but there were no footsteps or voices. Satisfied they were still asleep, he called his editor. The polygamist community was going to make a very interesting story. Jerry answered on the second ring.

"It's your long-lost writer."

"Kipp?"

"The one and only."

"How goes it? You sound pretty chipper."

"You bet I do. I found Kelly."

"You found her? Where? Is she okay?"

"She's doing as well as can be expected. At least she's not hurt."

"That's great. That's great. Where the hell did you find her?"

"That's what I want to write about." Kipp told Jerry everything about the religious cult and Kelly's rescue. "I want to blow that community wide open."

"That is one remarkable story. How soon do you think you could have your article ready?"

"The FBI is involved now, and I don't want to do anything to hinder their investigation. I also want to be careful about how much personal detail I put into the story. I have to protect Kelly. I'll have the story ready as soon as they give me the green light."

"You've got to give me some lead time."

"You'll have it. I'll keep in touch."

Kipp gave him a rundown on Kelly's progress before he hung up. Then he called Charlie, who asked him about Kelly.

"I think she's making progress, but she's still timid. She has her moments."

"Are you going to register her for school this year?"

"She's still getting oriented to being home. She'll need to be evaluated, but I'll probably homeschool her this year."

"Did Tanya ever show up?"

"Yeah, she's here."

"How's that going?"

"Not so well at first. You know how she is. But Kelly's beginning to accept her."

"How about you? Has she wormed her way into your bed?"

"If there wasn't a child in the house, I'd tell you to f-off."

"I guess that answers my question, and I'm glad. You don't want to get tangled up in that mess again. Have you heard from the FBI?"

"No, but I'm worried about when they do catch up with Kelly's abductors. If they want her to testify, it will be too traumatic."

"They know how to handle those matters in a delicate way. I don't think you have to worry."

"I sure could use Libby's advice. Kelly sure misses her."

Charlie laughed. "That's a good one."

"She does."

"Yeah, and who else misses her?"

"You know, you're taking advantage of my no-swearing dilemma. But I admit it. I do miss her. Have you seen her lately?"

"Not since I was there on a call."

"A call? What kind of a call?"

There was silence on Charlie's end.

"Charlie?"

"Yeah, I'm here. Libby didn't want me to say anything to you." He got quiet again.

"What is it, Charlie? If it concerns Libby, I want to know."

"Okay, but you'll have to tell her you twisted my arm."

"Just tell me."

The story of Libby's ordeal with her ex-husband flowed out of Charlie as if he'd been given truth serum: the call from Ellen, Libby's bruised face, Dan's eventual escape and his time in jail.

Kipp fell silent until Charlie assured him Libby was not seriously hurt. "How is she now?"

"From what Ellen says, she's working and carrying on as if nothing happened," Charlie said. "But there was a block of time when Ellen wasn't in the room, and she doesn't know the extent of his threats, and Libby won't talk about it. I've seen this with victims all the time. They won't talk. They just deny. They won't press charges. She didn't want to press charges."

Kipp heard most of Charlie's words, something about pressing charges, but all he could do was picture Libby's face. His heart went out to her. His hand formed into a rock-hard fist, and he wished he could slam it into the face of the madman she called her ex-husband.

After Charlie finished his tirade on victims and abuse, he told Kipp another call was coming in. They agreed to keep in touch.

Kipp contemplated phoning Libby, but Kelly came around the corner, rubbing her eyes, and for the time being he had to set his idea aside. "Hi, baby bear. Time for breakfast?" He stroked her silky blond hair. "Does Kelly want cereal or pancakes this morning?"

She looked around the room, seemed disoriented. "I'm Sarah. Where's my other daddy?"

"Oh, baby." Kipp knelt and held her. Tears welled up, and his heart gripped with pain. "You're Kelly, honey. Sarah was the name you had for a while, but now you're Kelly, remember?" His inept explanation brought to mind Libby's warning, and he knew at that moment they would need help. He kissed his daughter on the cheek and hugged her close.

Tanya waltzed into the kitchen in another one of Kipp's tee shirts and stopped short, eyeing the two of them together. She bounded over and draped her arms over Kipp's shoulders. "Thanks for taking us out last night." She tried to kiss him, but he turned away.

After breakfast Kipp helped Kelly dress for the day. He made a note to take her shopping for clothes since Tanya hadn't made the effort. She seemed oblivious to Kelly's needs, which didn't surprise him. Little by little, the old patterns were emerging.

While Tanya showered, he put *Cinderella* in the DVD player. Kelly rewarded him with a crooked smile and an appreciative kiss. They both settled on the couch.

Kipp, after his and Tanya's first arguments, made it a rule to keep their heated discussions away from Kelly, so when Tanya came into the room and gestured for Kipp to join her in the bedroom, he made sure the doors were locked and left his daughter's side.

The curtains were drawn, and Tanya eased the door partway shut so only a slice of light from the hallway filtered through. "I'm leaving for Sydney tomorrow."

To Kipp, her announcement was a kick in the gut, and if he spoke now he knew he would fly into a rage.

"I know this is a surprise to you. We didn't discuss it, but I need to go back and finish the shoot. I promised them. Besides, I have a contract to fulfill."

A number of words came to his mind, none of which were complimentary.

"It will only be for a few days."

"When did you make this decision, or had you planned this all along?"

"Only last night."

"Is that what that call was about? I heard your phone ring."

"My photographer needs me to finish up."

"Your photographer needs you. What about your daughter? She needs you. She's still confused about her identity. In fact, she came into the kitchen this morning calling herself Sarah."

"She'll get over it. Besides, I'll only be gone a few days, a week tops."

He came so close to shaking some sense into her, his own body shuddered. "This is so typical of you, Tanya. I don't know what I was thinking. I had it in my head that being with Kelly after her ordeal might spark some maternal instinct in you, but I was so wrong."

"You're so unfair."

"That little girl needs you more than ever."

"And what about you? Do you need me? If you do, I haven't seen it."

"This is not about us, Tanya. It's about the welfare of our daughter. When is this going to register with you?"

Tanya turned her back on Kipp and pulled a suitcase from the closet. Kipp left the room.

THIRTY-THREE

KELLY LAY in her bed and stared at the streaks of light on the ceiling. Her daddy thought she slept through the night, but that wasn't true. She woke up two times, maybe three. She had dreams, dreams full of people, so many people in her nighttime dreams. She was lined up with other children, marched to breakfast and dinner, marched to bed in one large room, marched to a big white building with girls in braids and long dresses. There were dreams of car trips and mommies. There were so many mommies. But they all went away. That's what scared her most of all.

Last night in the hallway she had listened to Mommy tell Daddy she was going away today. Why did her mommies always leave her?

She rolled on her side and glanced around the room. On the wall next to the window was a bookshelf filled with her daddy's books. On a chair next to the bookcase was her mommy's sweater. She brought the sweater back to bed, held it to her face, and inhaled a big whiff of flowery-scented softness. She stuffed the sweater under her pillow, hiding it from view. That way, every night she would remember her mommy in case she never returned.

She closed her eyes so tight no light could sneak through, and Libby's face popped into the darkness. She wished she could see Libby again.

She heard voices. When she got up and opened the door, her mommy was coming down the hallway with a suitcase in her hand.

"Hi, baby." Her mommy set the bag down and whisked past her into her room. She looked around at everything. "Have you seen my pink sweater?" She charged to the bed where a bit of sleeve peeked out from under the pillow. "What's it doing here?" She draped the sweater over her arm and ruffled Kelly's hair. "I'm very late, baby. I don't want to miss my flight. I'll see you in a few days." She hurried out of the room.

Her daddy stood in the doorway. "Come here, sweetie." She ran into his arms and laid her head on his shoulder. She loved her daddy.

⌒⌇⌒

Kipp held Kelly tight. After the front door closed, he wiped a tear from her cheek. "Don't cry, baby bear. I'm here, and I love you." On an impulse, he said, "Would you like to visit Libby today?"

Her eyes brightened, and she squeezed his neck so tight he had a difficult time swallowing. It was the first time she'd reacted this positive all week. He helped her bathe and dress and fixed her pancakes with her favorite blueberry syrup.

While she ate, he called Libby and prayed she would be home because he didn't want to disappoint his daughter; she had suffered enough disappointment for one day. Ellen answered, and though Libby was out running errands, she encouraged him to come anyway. She knew Libby would want to see them, and she was anxious to see Kelly, too.

⌒⌇⌒

The sun broke through the clouds, and its rays stretched into the forest. It had sprinkled earlier in the morning, and beads of moisture on the fir needles twinkled like Christmas lights.

As soon as they turned onto the gravel road leading to Libby's house, Kelly's body language changed; she jerked to attention and peered out the window. He knew he had made the right decision. Being with Libby would be a shot in the arm for both of them.

Before the Jeep came to a complete halt, Kelly tugged on the seatbelt in an attempt to free herself, snapped the clasp open, and turned her attention to the door handle. Kipp hurried around the car and opened the door. Without a word, she scooted around him and up the sidewalk. By the time Kipp reached her side, she was trying to pry open the screen door.

Kipp was about to slow her down when the front door opened, and Libby greeted them with a smile. He opened the screen door. Kelly squeezed through the space and tumbled into Libby's outstretched arms.

Kipp stood back and observed. The change in Kelly's behavior, from the timidity she displayed around Tanya to the enthusiasm and warmth she exhibited with Libby, was obvious, and it was a sad commentary on how his ex-wife related to their daughter.

Libby had knelt to embrace Kelly, but when she rose and was eye-level with Kipp, her bruises were evident: a yellow rim around her eye and faded streaks running the length of her cheek. He couldn't help staring, and she instinctively brought her hand to her face, hiding it.

"Daddy, can we stay here with Libby?"

Distracted, he looked toward the rocking chair where Kelly had made herself comfortable. "For a while, baby."

"I want to stay here and sleep with Libby. You can, too."

Kipp and Libby exchanged amused glances.

"We have to sleep at our house, Kelly, but let's have a nice afternoon with Libby, okay?"

Kelly left the rocker, climbed on the sofa where Kipp and Libby had settled, and nestled into Libby's side. She peered up at Libby. "What happened to your face?"

"I fell down and hurt myself."

"I fell, too."

"When did you fall, sweetie?"

"In the barn where the cows were."

Once again, Kipp exchanged looks with Libby. It was the first time he had heard Kelly say anything about the community she'd lived in. He and Tanya never had a barnyard with animals.

"Do you want to tell us about the barn, Kelly?" Libby said gently.

She hitched a shoulder. "Do you like my daddy?"

"Of course I do."

"My daddy has a house, but my mommy went away."

Libby looked to Kipp. He explained Tanya's absence as positively as possible. He kept his opinions to himself. He didn't want to upset Kelly.

Ellen came in from the backyard. "Well, look who's here." And Kelly ran to her and hugged her around the waist.

"This is the happiest I've seen her since I brought her home," Kipp said.

"She likes it here because she gets great big chocolate chip cookies. Isn't that right? I've got a batch in the oven, and you can help me put the last batch on the cookie sheet."

Kelly's smile widened, and she tugged on Ellen's hand.

"We'll go into the kitchen and rattle around, so your daddy and Libby can talk."

Left alone with Libby, Kipp examined her face. "Charlie told me your ex showed up and—"

"He told you? I asked him not to say anything because you have enough to think about."

"Didn't you think I'd want to know? I care about you."

"I really don't want to talk about it."

"You said something about the guy on our trip, but you didn't tell me he was an abuser."

"He drinks. He gets angry. That's all."

"It's more than that, Libby. I don't like to see you hurt this way. If I had been here, I would have killed the rotten—"

Libby put her fingers to his lips.

He held and kissed her hand. "I've missed you." Until that moment he hadn't realized how much she meant to him.

Seeing Ellen enter the room, Kipp immediately let go of Libby's hand. Ellen broke into a huge grin. "Don't mind me." She set two cups of coffee on the table and hustled back to the kitchen.

"Kelly's not relating very well to her mother, is she."

"Just as I thought it would be," Kipp said. "They never bonded when she was a baby, so I didn't think it would be any different. But I was hoping."

"Maybe if you give it more time."

"Tanya's thirty-one years old. She's had six years to change, but her work means more to her than her daughter. It always has. I don't know why I pushed her into getting pregnant."

Libby touched Kipp's cheek, and he held and kissed her hand again. "You have to let go of the past," she said. "It serves no purpose."

"Why don't you do your psychic thing on me, and we'll see where this is going to take us?"

"You mean you and Tanya?"

"I'm talking about you and me, Libby."

"I wish I could tell you."

"Don't you have any feelings about it?"

"Don't you?"

Kelly skipped into the room and displayed hands covered in cookie dough. "Daddy, I'm making cookies."

"I see that, honey."

She ran back into the kitchen, and Libby smiled. "She's so sweet. So, tell me about your plans to go to Connecticut."

"You are psychic."

"It was just a hunch. You two have roots there."

"Tanya wants us to move back to the farmhouse. She thinks Kelly will do better where she used to live."

"How do you feel about it?"

"I don't think the location will make a difference. I think it's Tanya. But you heard Kelly talk about barns and cows. She's getting mixed up about the past and the present."

"That seems normal to me. It's still fresh in her mind. You need to let her talk about everything without any restrictions, even if the subject is painful for you."

"You need to help me with her, Libby. You're the only one I trust."

"I would love to, but she has a mother."

"You should be her mother." Kipp moved an arm over Libby's shoulder, and she flinched, obviously in pain. He quickly drew back. "I'm sorry."

She looked away.

"What did the bastard do to you?"

"It's nothing. Let's go see what your daughter's up to." She strode from the room.

That was the Libby he was accustomed to—the woman who could put the walls up in the blink of an eye. Someday, if he were lucky, he hoped to ease those walls down once and for all.

He wandered toward the sounds of laughter. Kelly was handing a cookie to Libby with an expression of sheer joy.

"Doesn't your daddy get one?"

Kelly snatched another cookie from a plate on the counter and offered it to Kipp. "Ellen said we could take cookies home, right, Ellen?"

"That's right, dear."

The doorbell rang, and Libby glanced at her watch. "Is it that time already?" She excused herself to answer the door.

A man's voice boomed from the foyer. "Hiya, babe. Boy, am I glad you could squeeze me in today. You're number one on my list. You know that, don't ya? When are you going to let me take you away from all this?"

"Oh, Gabe."

"At least let me take you to dinner. Say, what happened to you?"

"Just a run-in with the closet door."

"Musta hurt."

Curious, Kipp had moved to the doorway to put a face to the voice. Kelly stood beside him, staring up at the man, quiet for the first time since their arrival.

After Libby introduced everyone, she told Gabe she would meet him in her office, and he went down the hallway, whistling. She said to Kipp, "I've got to do this reading, and I have a phone reading after that. I'll be about two hours. I didn't know you were coming, or I would have cancelled."

"We should get going, anyway, before the traffic gets bad."

Kelly squeezed Kipp's hand. "No, Daddy. We can stay here and sleep with Libby."

"We have to go, honey. Libby has work to do. We'll come back again."

Libby gave Kelly a hug. "Thanks for coming, sweetie. You take good care of your daddy, okay?"

"Okay."

"I have to go now."

Kipp longed to hug her, but if he did, he feared he might cause her pain. He searched her eyes, hoping for a clue to her innermost feelings. No words passed between them. She squeezed his arm and fled down the hall.

While Ellen wrapped up a stack of cookies, Kipp leaned against the counter. "So, who's this guy Gabe?"

"Just an appointment."

"Has he ever taken her out to dinner?"

"Once or twice."

If Ellen was trying to pique his interest, she'd succeeded. He said, "I thought she didn't date clients."

"Do I detect a bit of jealousy?"

"Just want to know."

Ellen slid the cookies into a paper bag. "She went out to dinner with him before he became a client, nothing more, but he's not her type."

Satisfied he could let go of that concern, Kipp took the bag of cookies from Ellen and handed it to Kelly. "Ready to go?"

Kelly held on to Ellen's hand and declared, "I want to stay here."

"Not today, honey. Maybe another time."

"That's right, Kelly. Your daddy will be back here again. I'd bet my chocolate chip cookies on it." Ellen walked them outside.

"Have you seen Charlie?"

"We haven't seen each other much since Libby's ex was here. He had to work overtime on a case last weekend. But we've talked every night. He owes me a date."

"I'm sure he's good for it. He's a good guy."

"I know. Believe me, I know."

"I hope it works out for you two."

"If your psychic friend has anything to say about it, it will."

They were halfway to the car when Kipp said to Ellen, "I wish she could predict our future."

⚬⚬⚬

Libby hung up the phone, ending the reading for a woman in California, and leaned back in her chair. The wind had picked up, and the tree limbs swayed in a hypnotic dance outside her window. Kipp was in the forefront of her mind, and she wished he had decided to stay.

Ellen tapped on her door. "I've got everything on the table. Are you hungry?"

"I can eat." Libby went into the kitchen with Ellen. "I think it's going to rain again. We sure could use it."

"If this was November, I'd have your head examined." Ellen made a place for the tuna casserole on the table. "You know, that man is in love with you."

"Who, Gabe?"

"You know who I mean. The gorgeous hunk who was here a couple of hours ago."

Libby dished up her plate.

"Well, aren't you going to jump all over me and tell me I'm full of horse manure?"

Libby gave her a carefree shrug.

"I can tell a lot from that little gesture. That wasn't a not-interested shrug. That was a don't-look-now-but-I'm-falling-for-him shrug."

"Oh, Ellen…"

"So, how are we going to get you two together?"

"I've only known him a month or so."

"Hey, I only knew Charlie a week, and we've already done the nasty."

"Kipp's got responsibilities right now… and Tanya."

"I'd like to meet that woman. She sounds like a real winner, a real mother-of-the-year type."

"She's still Kelly's mother."

"If she wasn't in the picture, would you consider dating Kipp?"

"Maybe."

"At least that's not a negative. We're definitely making progress."

THIRTY-FOUR

The date was Friday, September 14th, a week after Kipp and Kelly visited Libby, and Kipp was sitting at his desk, jotting down ideas for the article he planned to write about the polygamist cult. Kelly sat on the floor next to him, drawing pictures.

Earlier in the day a call had come in from Special Agent Watcomb, who gave Kipp an update on the couple who had taken his daughter. From interviews the FBI discovered they had fled to Canada shortly after leaving Kelly in Grand. The FBI told him they would be working with the Canadian authorities to locate the couple, and they would be in touch with Kipp as soon as they had more information.

Kipp moved to the floor beside Kelly and asked her about the picture she was drawing. She pointed to the stick figures of men and women and explained to him that she had daddies and mommies. She pointed to a figure of a woman off to the side and asked him how to spell Libby's name. At that moment Kipp decided to write his article without mentioning Kelly's rescue, without mentioning her at all. She had suffered enough trauma already, and he didn't want to expose her to any media attention.

He hugged her to him. "It's almost time for bed, baby bear. Why don't you get your nightgown, and I'll run you a bath." When Kipp rose, he heard voices outside.

Tanya came through the doorway. "Hello, sweetheart." She dropped her bags and gave Kipp a hug.

He moved out of her embrace. "I didn't know you were coming home tonight."

"I couldn't wait to see my little girl." She smoothed Kelly's hair and glanced at the drawings. "Who's in the picture, honey?"

"All my mommies and daddies."

"And who is this?" Tanya pointed to the lone figure set apart from the others.

"That's Libby."

"Who is Libby, Kelly?"

"You don't have to talk about her," Kipp said.

"Yes, you do, honey. Mommy wants to know all about Libby."

"Tanya, leave it be."

"She's nice," Kelly said. "We went to her house and had cookies."

"Did you." Tanya was looking at Kipp, annoyed.

"Chocolate chip cookies."

"Go get your nightgown, Kelly," Kipp said.

Kelly ran off, returned with her nightgown, and handed it to Kipp.

"Let's get you a bath."

Tanya tossed her purse on the couch. "Let me give her a bath and put her to bed."

Kipp gripped Kelly's hand and moved around Tanya.

"Let me do it, please." Her expression was soft, almost sad.

Maybe she was ready to be a mother to Kelly. Kipp knelt beside his daughter. "Your mommy wants to put you to bed tonight. Is that okay with you?"

Kelly peered up at her mother, smiling, and Kipp gave Kelly a squeeze. While Tanya and Kelly were in the bathroom, he read the evening paper. After her bath, Kelly gave him a kiss and went off to bed.

Kipp continued reading, but kept an ear out for Kelly's voice. It was hard for him to relinquish his role as the person responsible for tucking his daughter in bed. He missed reading her a story, but he didn't want to discourage Tanya's attempt at mothering. He had worn two hats, both father and mother, the first four years of her life before she was kidnapped, and he had to admit he didn't relish sharing those duties with Tanya.

He kept checking his watch, and finally Tanya tiptoed into the room. "She's asleep. I don't know how you do it. She asks to be read the same passages over and over. It's so exasperating." She settled next to him and ran her fingers up and down his arm.

He laid the paper aside and picked up her luggage. "It's getting late."

She followed him to the bedroom and closed the door. "I want to talk to you."

"About what? Oh, let me guess."

"Why are you taking Kelly to see this Libby woman?"

He pulled his pajamas from the closet shelf and grabbed his robe.

"She's not Kelly's mother, Kipp. I am. And I don't think you should be confusing Kelly like this."

"She's a friend, Tanya. Can't Kelly have a friend?"

"Not when I'm around."

"Well, you weren't around, were you?"

"I have a job, Kipp, and if you remember, before Kelly was taken away, I was paying child support."

"Laying down cash doesn't make you a good mother."

"That's not fair at all."

"What is?"

"What about me? I want to be your wife again, and Kelly's mother."

He stared at her in disbelief. "It's too late for us, Tanya. One too many affairs too late, or have you forgotten?" He turned away and gathered his slippers.

Backing against the door, she blocked his exit. "Why can't you give me another chance?"

"Move out of my way."

Her golden hair glistened in the light, and he was so close to her he could smell her lemony perfume. He stood solid, staring at her, until she slid away from the door.

"Kipp, don't do this," she yelled after him as he strode down the hallway.

❧

On Monday morning, after Tanya heard Kipp moving about, she got out of bed and did her Yoga routine: the Sun Salutation. When she heard water running in the bathroom, she slipped into the kitchen and put on a pot of coffee. Barefoot, she had on Kipp's tee shirt from yesterday over her undies. Having the shirt touch her skin made her feel closer to him.

She sipped her coffee, and while she idly skimmed the stray papers on the counter, a business card caught her eye. She didn't recognize the company's name—New Horizons—but when she turned it over, Libby's name and address were written in Kipp's handwriting. She copied down the information and stuck it in her purse just as Kipp wandered out of the bathroom in sweatpants and no shirt.

He walked past her in search of his glasses, and she jumped at the chance to block his path and pull him into an embrace. The feel of his bare chest gave her chills. She wanted him. She kissed him while rubbing her hand over his chest. His hands went to her waist. She sensed a hesitation in him, as if he might be having second thoughts about loving her, but instead he gave her a slight push.

"Kipp, why can't you let yourself go and give in to your feelings?" She followed him into the kitchen.

"You don't know anything about my feelings."

"I want to. You almost kissed me back. You had to be feeling something then." She tried for another embrace, but he turned his back to her and poured himself a cup of coffee. "I need more than this."

"Your being here isn't about you, Tanya. It's about Kelly." He took his cup to the living room.

She waited until he was seated at his desk. "I'm going shopping in Seattle today. I didn't bring enough clothes with me. Do you need the car?"

"Take it." He draped an arm over the back of his chair. "Why don't you take Kelly? She needs clothes, too."

"She'd be bored in the big department stores. I might be all day. She'll just get tired. Besides, I want to leave soon." She left the room before he could argue with her. The scowl on his face was bad enough.

By the time she'd showered and dressed, Kelly was in the kitchen eating cereal. Tanya gave her a quick hug and kiss.

Kelly scooted off the stool and scurried to the door after her mother. "Where you going, Mommy?"

"I'm going to the city for a long day of shopping. It's not for little girls. But I'll be back before you go to bed."

Once she was outside, Tanya took in a deep breath, filling her lungs with the cool, fresh air. The day was gray and depressing, but not as depressing as Kipp's house or his miserable attitude. This whole situation was stifling. She needed this time alone, free to do whatever she pleased. And what she wished more than anything was to find this Libby person and set her straight: Kipp was her man and Kelly was her daughter. She was not going to stand by and let them be lured away by another woman.

She took the freeway south instead of north to Seattle. At the first Harbordale exit, she stopped at a gas station, asked for directions, and drove on in search of Libby's house.

Kipp hadn't said it in so many words, but she could sense there was something between him and Libby. The joyful look on Kelly's face every time Libby's name was mentioned hadn't escaped her. She wasn't sure what she would say to this woman, but she had to get a look at her, size her up, make her understand that Kelly had a mother and Kipp had a wife, an ex-wife, yes, but Tanya planned to change that status.

In the past she'd made mistakes, but that part of her life was over. Being so close to Kipp again, in the physical sense, brought back the feelings she'd had for him when they first met. Many men had breezed through her life in the last six years—photographers, professional athletes, businessmen—but none compared to Kipp. It had taken her so long to realize what a prize he was. She wanted him back. Having Kelly home again was the perfect inroad, and she intended to use the opportunity to her advantage.

She turned into Libby's driveway. The house—a simple rambler— was unexceptional, and Tanya was relieved to know she didn't have to compete in that area. The property was lush and wild, and she couldn't comprehend why a person would choose to live in the dense, dark woods. Kipp's location was secluded enough, and she planned to convince him to move back east.

Tanya relaxed when a chunky woman in sweatpants and tee shirt answered the door. If this was Libby, her trip to Harbordale had been pointless.

"Can I help you?"

"I'm Tanya Reed, Kipp Reed's wife."

"I've seen you in the magazine ads." She folded her arms. "I'm Ellen. If you're looking for Libby, she's away, teaching a workshop in Minneapolis. She won't be back for a couple of days."

"Then I'll come back another time."

"Since you've come all this way, why don't you come in for a minute? I'll make you some tea, and we can talk."

"Why not?" At least she could check out Libby's house.

While she waited for Ellen to bring the tea, she inspected the room and tried to get a sense of the woman she was beginning to suspect held Kipp's heart. The furnishings were modest, nothing expensive, but a lovely blend of muted colors. There were pottery pieces tucked into various corners, and everything fit in with the natural scheme of things. Soft-toned paintings of flowers and birds graced the walls. Though not Tanya's style, the décor was pleasant enough.

She hoped to find photos on the walls, but there were none. Disappointed, she checked the coffee table for other clues to Libby's personality. The magazines were nature-oriented, not one had anything to do with fashion or entertainment. When she riffled through the *National Geographic*, a photo fell out of a woman in jeans with long, straight hair sitting on a rock overlooking ocean waters. Upon Ellen's sudden return, Tanya dropped the picture.

Ellen set a teacup on the coffee table. "That's Libby, taken about six years ago. She's a knockout, isn't she?"

"I suppose."

"Her hair's shorter now, and it makes her even more beautiful. So, why did you come to see her?"

"Can I ask you a question first?"

"Shoot."

"Are you Libby's sister?"

"We're best friends."

"Well, my business is with Libby."

"I didn't know she had any business with you. She didn't mention it."

"I came on a whim."

"What for?"

"It's between her and me." This woman was getting on Tanya's nerves.

"So, how's Kelly?"

Tanya moved toward the foyer. "I really should go."

"Is Kelly getting used to you? I heard she's struggling a little."

"Just who told you that?"

"Kipp mentioned it to Libby."

"He shouldn't have because we're doing just fine. All three of us."

"That's not what Kipp implied."

The muscles in Tanya's neck tensed.

"You should have seen Kipp and Libby and Kelly. They looked so natural together. You should be happy for your *ex*-family."

The emphasis on the *ex* made Tanya livid. This woman had no right to make those observations. "Kipp and Kelly are my family, get it? And you might as well relay that message to your friend. In fact, you can tell her to stay out of our lives." She swung the door open and glared at Ellen. "And you know what else? I don't want her to talk to Kipp ever again. You can tell her that, too." She slammed the door on her way out.

That Libby woman was not going to have Kipp if she had anything to do with it. Tanya mulled the situation over and over. At the end of Slater Road, she spotted the Harbordale Mall. It wasn't Seattle, but it would have to do.

❧

By the time Tanya arrived back in Port Anderson, it was getting dark, and she struggled to open the door to the house with an armload of packages. Kipp and Kelly were sitting on the floor with their backs against the couch, watching TV. Kelly was dressed for bed, and an empty pizza box lay open on the coffee table.

"Hi, you two." She set the packages on Kipp's desk. "I see you ate dinner."

Kelly stared at her mother in silence.

"Are you hungry?" Kipp said.

"I picked something up in town."

"How was Seattle?"

"Busy. The traffic was horrendous. Wait until you see what I bought you, Kelly." Tanya rummaged through a shopping bag and held up a pair of white pants and a hot pink top. "Just like Mommy's. Do you like it?"

Kelly scrambled to her feet and grabbed for the pants.

Tanya jerked them out of her reach. "No, no, don't touch. You'll get them dirty. Look, honey, look what else I bought you." From another bag she pulled out a teddy bear. "You can throw that old dirty one away."

Kelly's frown deepened. "I don't want that bear. I want my bear." She dashed out of the room, crying.

Kipp leaped up, but Tanya motioned for him to stay put. "Let me handle this." She noticed the astonished look on his face before she hurried after Kelly.

A few minutes later she came out of Kelly's room. "I told her I'd get rid of the new bear, but she still wanted to go to bed. There's no pleasing her."

Kipp sighed in disgust and left the room to kiss his daughter goodnight. Tanya slipped off her shoes and sat on the couch with her legs curled under. Nothing she did seemed to please him either. This was so hard.

When he returned to the living room, he said, "I think we need to talk about how things are going."

"I have something to discuss with you, too."

"I want to know what your plans are, Tanya?"

"What do you mean?"

"Are you going back to New York, or are you planning to stay here?"

"That's what I wanted to talk to you about," she said. "You know my work is in New York, and I have to get back there soon. I haven't changed my mind. I still want you and Kelly to move back to Connecticut."

"Kelly and I are staying here."

"You know I have to go back to work."

"Then you should go."

"I want us to be a family again, Kipp. Kelly needs me."

"From what I've observed, I think she would do better if you weren't here."

"Are you trying to hurt me? Because if you are, you're doing a good job."

"I thought it would be good to have her mother here, but she never knew you before she was kidnapped. She's been on edge ever since you got here. She needs time to adjust to the way things were, and let's face it, you weren't in her life."

"God, Kipp, twist the knife why don't you."

"I'm not saying this to hurt you, Tanya. I'm thinking of Kelly and what's best for her. She barely knew you back then, and she needs time to adjust back to how it used to be when it was just her and me."

"If we're placing the blame here, I think you should share some of it. Maybe if you had thought about your wife a little more, things would be different now. Ever since Kelly was born, it's been all about Kelly." From the look on Kipp's face, she wished she hadn't said those words, and this wasn't the direction she wanted the discussion to go. "I'm sorry. I didn't mean that. I want to get to know her better. I want to start over, Kipp, with Kelly and you."

"That's not going to happen."

"Let me try, please. I've made mistakes in the past. I know that. But I want to change. I still love you."

Kipp sat down and removed his glasses. He leaned forward and rubbed his eyes.

"Please, Kipp."

He looked at her. "When was the last time you were with a man?"

"I don't know."

"Come on, Tanya, was it in Australia?"

"Maybe."

"Last week?"

"What difference does that make? I needed someone to love me. You wouldn't. I've given it some thought, and I'm willing to put that in the past. Besides, you've had your flings."

"I haven't been with anyone in a long time and certainly not one after the other."

"What about Libby? I'm sure you've slept with her."

"She and I are just friends."

"Who's lying now? You know, I don't like you and Kelly spending time with her, like you were a family."

"Is that what Ellen told you?"

Tanya's face heated. She hated getting caught. That Ellen was a hag.

"She called me after you left."

"That figures," she said. "I don't care, Kipp. I wanted to see the person who is stealing my family. I had a right to."

"There's no use talking to you. I'm going to turn in." Kipp went into the bathroom and shut the door.

Tanya went into the bedroom and took everything off, including her underwear, and pulled on one of Kipp's shirts with his smell all over it. She hugged it to her body. When he came into the room after his pajamas, she embraced him in desperation. "Make love to me, Kipp. You'll change your mind, and remember everything we had together. I can make you happy."

He peeled her arms away. "I know what you want, Tanya, but do you know what I want? I want you to go back to New York, back to your life there, and leave us alone, just like before. That's what I want."

She sat on the bed and watched him walk away. Maybe he was right. She wasn't cut out to be a mother with all the toys and the storytelling and the peanut butter sandwiches. When she grew up, she hadn't had a role model, unless a drunken mother was someone to look up to, but then she'd walked out, leaving Tanya with an indifferent stepfather. Tanya had men who adored her, fans who worshipped her, but still she wanted the one man she couldn't have. She decided to take a different approach.

❧

Tanya got up early the next morning. She called a cab on her cell phone and hauled her bags into the living room.

Kipp rolled over on the sofa and reached for his glasses. "What are you doing?"

"What does it look like? I'm going back to New York just like you want me to. Doesn't that make you happy? Because that's all I ever wanted to do."

"It's your call."

"My call? I don't think so. You want me out of your life, and I'm going."

"Aren't you going to say goodbye to your daughter?"

"Oh, I don't think I'll have to."

Kipp struggled to sit up.

"When I get back to New York, I'm hiring the best lawyer I can find, and I'm going to fight you for full custody."

"We've already been down that road, remember?"

"Yes, but things have changed." She picked up her purse and jacket. "I think the judge will see it my way when he finds out Kelly was missing for two years, and the ex-husband won't let the poor, distraught mother spend time with her." She studied Kipp's face to see whether she'd made the impression she was aiming for. Sufficiently satisfied as she saw the pain, the worry, the fear, she opened the door and picked up her bags. "You'll hear from my attorney."

She stepped outside and closed the door. She hated leaving on these terms, but it was the only way to get his attention. If there was even a remote chance of losing Kelly, Kipp would think about the lawsuit, come to his senses, and come back to her. She was sure of it.

THIRTY-FIVE

LIBBY WOKE Saturday morning to the drip, drip of the downspout outside her bedroom window. The week had been sunny, even in Minneapolis, but she welcomed the rain. She snuggled under the covers and planned a leisurely morning in bed to relax from the busy week. Besides the workshop, she'd done phone readings and a healing session.

She drifted back to sleep, and woke to the phone ringing. She vaguely heard Ellen's voice. It was now ten. She slipped on her robe, wandered into the kitchen, and asked Ellen about the call.

Ellen poured Libby a cup of coffee. "That was Kipp."

"Is Kelly all right?"

"She's fine, and she wants to see you."

Libby sat at the table, hugging her cup. "What did you tell him?"

"I said to come on down."

"I don't know if that's a good idea after what you told me about Tanya's visit."

Ellen brought her cup to the table. "Not to worry. She's not in the picture anymore. And, oh, by the way, Kipp wants to see you, too."

"Back up a minute. What about Tanya?"

"She up and went back to New York. Kipp said he'd explain when they got here. He wants to take you out to dinner."

"Ellen, why didn't you tell him I'd call him back?"

"I saved you the call. I told him I'd babysit Kelly."

"What about your date with Charlie?"

"He'll understand. We'll both watch her."

The full impact of being with Kipp again finally sank in. Libby hurried to the sink to deposit her cup. "When is he coming?"

"You can relax. They won't be here until five. I told him I'd feed Kelly. So, you can just take your time. Go soak in the tub, and make yourself as sweet as pie."

"But I hate to ruin your time with Charlie."

Ellen joined Libby at the sink. "Charlie's not going anywhere, and neither am I."

"What are you saying?"

"I'm saying that I made an appointment with a young lawyer, a good-looking one, I might add, who is supposed to be topnotch on divorce and family issues. I'm going through with it."

Libby gave Ellen a squeeze. "That's wonderful, Ellen. What turned the tide?"

"Someone named Charlie," Ellen said. "I haven't heard from Mel since he was here last. I know I shouldn't jump into a relationship right away, but my life has been empty for a long time now. You knew that. And Charlie has given me more in the short time we've been together than I had in my whole marriage. We connect on every level, and he accepts me just the way I am." She grinned at Libby. "You knew this would happen, didn't you?"

"I had my hunches."

"You had more than that. You're the best psychic friend a girl could ever have. You see it, but you don't push. That's what I love about you. Plus, you've let me stay here and mooch off you for way too long now."

"I've loved having you here. And I don't know what would have happened if you hadn't been here when Dan showed up. You saved my life."

"I'm so glad I was here. Do you think he'll come back?"

"I just don't know for sure."

"That doesn't make me feel very confident."

"I'd like to say I'll never see him again, but my gut tells me otherwise."

"Well, you've got me and Charlie on your side. And Kipp."

At the sound of his name she felt a fluttering in her stomach. "Kipp? What am I going to wear?"

"Wear that slinky, black thing."

Libby was on her way to the bathroom. "That's too dressy."

"He said to dress up," Ellen yelled after her. "Anyway, whatever you wear will knock him over."

❧

In the late afternoon Libby was putting the finishing touches on her makeup, wondering how she had managed to come to this point in her life. Had something pushed her and Kipp together, or was it just a quirk of fate? The image of Kipp's grandmother came to mind and how the persistent visions had propelled them into an adventure, leading them to Kelly and to discovering one another.

The jittery feeling in her gut was plain, old-fashioned nerves. This felt like a first date, even though they had already spent hours together. If her psychic antenna was working at all, she sensed this evening was going to mean more to both of them than either could imagine.

Ellen's voice rang out, "They're here."

Libby checked her appearance one last time. The makeup concealed what was left of the bruising. Her hair swept her chin and curled around her cheeks. Her silk dress seemed too snug around the bodice but obscured what it needed to hide. Still, she tied a colorful scarf around her neck and let it hang down. She slipped on a pair of black heels.

When Libby made her entrance, Ellen and Kipp stopped talking and both stared. Kelly let go of her daddy's hand and ran open-armed to Libby. Libby bent to embrace her.

"Be careful of Libby's pretty dress," Kipp said.

"She can't hurt this."

"You look sensational."

"You're pretty," Kelly said.

"Thank you, sweetie." Libby glanced at Kipp, then back at Kelly. "Are you going to be okay staying here while your daddy and I go out?"

Kelly nodded.

"She'll be all right with Auntie Ellen. We're going to bake cookies again."

Kelly ran to Ellen and took her hand.

"I guess I don't have anything to worry about," Kipp said.

"You certainly don't. In fact, Charlie will be here shortly. He's going to spend the evening with us, so we have all the protection we need."

"Are you ready to go, Libby?" Kipp helped her on with her coat.

Kelly ran back to Kipp and flung her arms around his waist. "You'll come back, won't you, Daddy?"

Kipp gave Kelly a hug. "You don't have to worry about that, baby bear. Libby and I will be back soon."

"I'll put her to bed in my room," Ellen said. "You two take your time and have fun."

When they stopped to turn left at the main road, Libby touched Kipp's arm. "We don't have to go, you know. I can feel how hard this is on you, leaving her."

"It shows, huh? I don't like leaving her. I never will. But I can't be by her side every day of her life. Little excursions will make the bigger ones seem easier. Besides, I can't think of anyone I'd rather make this maiden voyage with than you."

Once Kipp turned onto the freeway north, Libby asked about Tanya's departure.

"She had to go back to work, the usual excuse."

"Is she coming back?"

"I thought you'd know the answer to that, being a master psychic and all."

"I haven't had time to key in to your situation."

"You mean you haven't thought about me day and night?"

"I wouldn't admit it if I had."

"So you don't really have a feeling for what Tanya is going to do?"

"I can only imagine she is going to put up a fight."

"What makes you say that?"

"From what Ellen told me, she wants you back."

"And she'll do anything."

"Like trying to take Kelly away from you."

"See, you did know."

"That wasn't too hard to figure out," Libby said. "She can't do that, can she?"

"She'll have to do it over my dead body. But I know how her mind works. She's bluffing. She thinks that will scare me enough to run back to her."

"I wouldn't dismiss it, Kipp."

"Is that the psychic talking?"

"Desperate people do desperate things."

"Can't you get a reading on this?"

Libby stared at the cars up ahead with Kipp glancing at her from time to time. "Well, my feeling is she will try, maybe even start proceedings, cause you a few headaches, but nothing—"

"Not tonight. I don't want to spoil our evening." He drove a while in silence as if he were pondering something.

"How's Kelly been?"

"I'm not sure how to answer that. It's like you said, she clings to me.

She always wants to know where I am. She gets quiet. She sometimes gets her names mixed up. It's heartbreaking."

"Didn't the three of you see a counselor?"

Kipp didn't respond.

"Kipp, you know what I told you, and I wouldn't say it if it wasn't important. You need to get professional help as soon as possible. Kelly needs it."

"We've got you now. You can help her."

"I'll do whatever I can, but you and Kelly need to see someone you don't know personally. I hate shoulds, but in this case I feel it's tremendously important. You should both go. There are support groups, too. I can give you the name of a counselor."

"I know you're right, Libby. She is having problems. It's just so hard for me to ask for help. I've always taken care of everything myself. I guess I'm stubborn that way."

"I know how you are, Kipp. Believe me, I know."

He glanced at her, grinning. "I'll call Monday." He turned his attention to the road and drove without saying a word.

Libby had the feeling he wanted to talk to her about something besides Kelly because he was too quiet. She wanted to prompt him, she knew it concerned her ex-husband, but she waited. He reached over and squeezed her hand.

"You want to know about Dan, don't you?"

"Can you always read people's minds?"

"I just know I haven't been open about that situation, and maybe you need to know."

"Only if you want to talk about it."

"Go ahead and ask me."

Kipp made the appropriate exit toward Port Anderson and put the Jeep on cruise control. "Do you feel comfortable talking about him?"

"He's always in the back of my mind. I always wonder when he'll come back."

"I don't want to upset you, but how did you ever get mixed up with a guy like that? I mean, with your gift of reading people so well, couldn't you see it?"

"I don't know how to explain it. He wasn't that way when I met him. I guess I didn't read the signs."

"You mean there were signs?"

"When I think back on it, I did have clues," she said. "After we were married, he started belittling me. The emotional abuse was so subtle at first, so hit-and-miss. Then it got worse, and the physical abuse gradually entered the picture and increased over time. I was in love. I got caught up in trying to keep things stable. I lost my own compass for a while. By that time, he had an emotional grip on me. I didn't know who I was. I thought I could change him back to the person he was when we met. Believe it or not, Kipp, I'm like everyone else. I have issues to work through like every other person on this planet, or I wouldn't be here."

"I'm so sorry that happened to you. You don't deserve it."

"No one does."

Kipp motored on toward the Narrows Bridge, quiet all the way.

Libby shifted, looking at him. "You have something else on your mind, don't you? What is it?"

Kipp started to speak, then hesitated.

"Please. Just say it."

"Okay, but if I'm out of line, just tell me." He reached for Libby's hand. "Charlie told me you had cancer."

"Breast cancer, yes. Five years ago."

"He also said—"

"The surgery didn't go well?"

"He said they had to go in more than once."

"Things didn't turn out as well as I would have liked." She withdrew her hand. "If you don't want to go any further with this…"

Kipp reached for her hand again. "I'm not saying that at all."

The exit to Port Anderson came into view. As they reached the edge of the hill leading into town, sunshine had broken through the clouds, and the sun's rays stretched far across the harbor.

"I hope you didn't mind coming all the way back here. This restaurant serves outstanding seafood. It's quaint and intimate."

"I'm sure it's lovely."

"But we've got time to kill before dinner. Would you like to get a drink beforehand?"

"I don't drink anymore, but is your house far from here?"

"Just up the hill."

"Why don't we wait there? I'd love to see where you and Kelly live."

As soon as they entered his house, he locked arms around her waist. "I've wanted to do this for a long time." He kissed her cheek, her neck, and nuzzled his head against hers. "Mmm… I better stop before I forget I'm a gentleman."

"I don't know if I want you to."

"Come on." He took her hand and gave her a tour of the house, ending in the doorway of the master bedroom.

Libby scanned the modest furnishings: dresser, chair, nightstand, and double bed.

"Tanya slept in here." He lifted her chin. "If you're asking, I didn't sleep with her."

Though Libby wouldn't have asked, she was relieved. They stood in the doorway holding hands, and Libby knew once they crossed the threshold to the bedroom, they would have to cross a threshold in their relationship. And what Kipp discovered about her might turn him away. She worried about taking that chance, but in her heart she had to overcome that barrier; she had to find out if he would still want her.

She squeezed his hand. He looked into her eyes, and they both knew the meaning of that one small gesture.

He removed her coat, draped it across a chair, and lit a white candle, left by Tanya on the nightstand. The flame cast a soft orange hue and quivering shadows along the wall.

She sat anxiously on the edge of the bed while he laid his sport coat aside. Her hands were like ice. He unknotted his tie, laid it across his jacket, and unbuttoned the top buttons of his shirt. He placed his cell phone on the nightstand.

He sat beside her, cupped an arm over her shoulder, drawing her to him. "We can still make it to dinner."

She shook her head. Dinner meant nothing to her, but what would happen in the next few minutes would mean everything. "Please."

As soon as she reached for the zipper's clasp, he moved her hand away, took hold of the clasp himself, and inched it toward her waist. Taking his time, he slid the dress off her shoulders, exposing her slip and bra. She sucked a breath in. He hesitated. Fighting the panicky feeling, she nodded, giving her consent for him to go further. He edged the straps off her shoulders and down to her elbows. He removed her scarf, exposing her breasts in the golden light.

To shield herself from his reaction, she closed her eyes. Clenching her teeth, holding her breath, she felt his fingers tracing the scars and folds of the disfigured breast, felt him move on to stroke the other. Her breath quickened, not from the panic that welled within her, but from the softness of his touch. Heady with the scent of his cologne, she nearly melted.

"They're beautiful," he whispered.

He kissed each breast, and the emotion flowed out of her from deep inside: first, a heaving, then the sobs. Tears washed over her cheeks.

He unbuttoned his shirt, pulled her to her feet, and pressed her against his bare chest. "It doesn't matter, Libby. It doesn't matter at all. I'll love you, no matter what."

She clung to him. "I love you, too, Kipp. It's been such a long time since I've felt this way."

He handed her a wad of tissue, gathered from a box on the nightstand and slid her straps up over her shoulders. "I want to make love to you, but I know how emotional this has been, and I don't want to overload you."

"What about dinner?" She couldn't suppress a grin.

He laughed, as the time was such that they'd lost their reservations. "We can always go down the hill to the pub."

Libby kicked off her shoes and let her dress fall to the floor. "I have a better idea."

"Are you sure? I'm serious about this. We can wait." But he took her in his arms. "Maybe not." He pushed her hair aside and kissed her cheek and neck. She leaned into him and swayed with him. "Mmm… You feel so good." He leaned to the side and pulled back the bedspread and slipped off his shoes.

Libby lay on the bed and made room for him to cuddle with her. He ran his palm up and down the flesh of her arm. She rested in the feel of his touch, then woke to the sense of his finger grazing her cheek.

"I can't believe I dozed off."

"I'm really wowing you, aren't I?"

"I'm sorry."

"Don't be," he said. "You've been tense for a long time. You're going to learn you don't have to be afraid of men. You can trust me, and you can relax from now on."

She fingered his chest, playing with the curly blond hairs.

"Whew. It's been a long time."

"Me, too, but I bet you'd like to get back to Kelly."

He kissed her forehead. "You read me so well. While you were dozing,

I couldn't stop thinking about her wanting to know if I was coming back." He glanced at the clock. "What a wonderful date I am. I bring you to my bed, and I'd rather leave than make love to you. But, look, Libby, I don't want to rush this. When we make love, I want to give you 100 percent."

"We have plenty of time."

"Then we have something to look forward to, and believe me, I look forward to loving you." He pressed the small of her back. "Don't ever forget how much I want you."

"Let's go and see Kelly."

He moved off the bed and helped Libby up. She stepped into her dress, and he reached around from the front and worked the zipper up her back. He hugged her against him and ran his hands up and down her spine. "I'm having second thoughts. I want to go, but I want to stay."

Their lips touched and they kissed deeply. His cologne overwhelmed her again. She hungered for his touch, and by the feel of his body pressing into her, he more than hungered for her. She closed her eyes and imagined their naked bodies entwined. She whispered in his ear, "Let's go see your daughter." But it took every ounce of willpower to let go of him.

⁕

At Libby's house Kipp parked next to Charlie's truck. Lights from the TV flickered through the curtains. Before they went inside, he took Libby into his arms and kissed her. "I can't believe how this happened."

"You can thank your grandmother."

He looked puzzled, then smiled in recognition. "Those mysterious visions."

Libby kissed his cheek. "Visions of hope."

He opened the door, and Ellen came toward them with a huge smile on her face. "Have we got good news for you. I mean, Charlie does. Tell 'em, Charlie."

Charlie got up from the couch. "Yeah, Libby. Seems your ex is going to be in jail for quite some time. Got him on a drug charge."

"Isn't that great, honey?" Ellen gave Libby a hug.

"This has been quite a day." Libby glanced at Kipp.

"Why are you home so early? I thought you'd be out half the night," Ellen said.

"How was Kelly?" Kipp said.

"She woke up a couple of times and wanted to know where you were, but she seemed satisfied when I assured her you were coming back soon."

Charlie shook Kipp's hand. "Hey, buddy, I haven't seen you in a while."

"We're going to have to remedy that."

"It looks like the five of us will be seeing a lot of each other," Ellen said.

"This is amazing," Libby said. "The four of us, and Kelly."

"As if you didn't know," Ellen said.

Libby waved her off.

"How was dinner?"

Kipp and Libby exchanged glances.

"You mean you didn't get dinner? Man, I couldn't go without dinner."

"Oh, Charlie." Ellen gave Libby a smug grin. "Kipp, why don't you go look in on Kelly? I know you're dying to. And I'll make us some popcorn. We can watch a movie together, or our resident psychic can give us all readings."

"Ellen, you never stop."

Kipp wandered toward Ellen's bedroom while Charlie looked through Libby's movie collection.

Ellen grabbed Libby's arm and led her into the kitchen. "Okay, spill."

Libby whispered, "It's going to be all right."

"That's rather vague. Can you be more specific?"

"He saw them, and everything's okay." A surge of emotion just about overpowered her, but she held it back.

"I knew it," Ellen said. "I told you he's a good man. I knew him to be that way in high school. We've both got good men." She hugged Libby. "Why don't you look in on Kelly, too? She asked if you were going to be her new mommy."

"She did?"

"She likes the idea. She told me she likes you better than any mommy she ever had."

Libby held her hand over her heart. "That sweet thing."

"If you play your cards right, girl, you'll have that child you've always wanted. Now, go on."

Libby entered Ellen's bedroom as quietly as she could, and Kipp rose from the bed. "She woke up for a minute and wondered where you were. I told her you were here, and you were going to be with us for a long time." He held Libby and kissed her. "She loves you, and so do I. So, what does my psychic say about that?"

"She says she feels very, very blessed, and she sees a long and happy future for the three of us."

THIRTY-SIX

THREE WEEKS LATER Kipp was on his way to Harbordale from Seattle where he had spent the afternoon at the Federal Building. Special Agent Watcomb had called and asked him to come to the FBI office because there were new leads in his daughter's kidnapping case.

The sky was dirty dishwater gray and threatening rain, but the weather didn't dampen Kipp's spirit; he was too charged with a jumble of emotions to sink into melancholy. He had much to tell Libby.

As he approached her house, she stepped up to the picture window and waved to him, her smile radiating a welcoming warmth. She disappeared, and the screen door opened. He barely made it inside before she caught him in an embrace.

He pressed the small of her back, drawing her close. "I've missed you," he whispered in her ear, then kissed her.

"It's only been two days."

He stroked her hair and looked into her mysterious blue eyes. "Two days too long."

"I've had this underlying agitation all morning," she said, "and now I know why. It's you. I can feel your energy. It's electrified. What's happened? What did they tell you?"

"Let's sit down."

"Let me get you something to drink." She went into the kitchen and returned with a tall glass of cold well water.

He laid his jacket on the rocker and sat at the table. She sat near him. Despite the dismal day, the house was bright from the large windows and skylights.

"Are you done working for the day?"

"I just finished up with my last client. Do you need to call about Kelly?"

"I called from Seattle before I left," he said. "Charlie and Ellen are building a tree house for her when she visits. They're all having a wonderful time."

"Then tell me what happened."

Kipp took a long drink of water, quenching the thirst he'd developed on the drive back. "I don't know where to begin."

"You said they had a new lead."

"They found one of the kidnappers."

"How? Where?"

"They showed me a picture of a woman. She looked young, no more than thirty, thirty-five. They asked me if I recognized her, which I didn't."

"How did they find her?"

"They mentioned interviewing Rebecca and Grace. Other than that, they didn't get specific, except they did tell me the woman had ties to the town of Grand. They must have tracked her down."

"I thought they told you the kidnappers fled to Canada."

"That's what they said, but something changed."

"What about the other kidnapper. I saw two, a man and a woman."

"They told me there were others involved besides those two. And then they started questioning me about Tanya. They asked me all the old questions they'd asked before—where she was, who she was with, who her friends were, how she acted at the time."

"Tanya."

"They wanted to know what her behavior was like before and after Kelly came home. What kind of mother she was. They even asked about our relationship. They wanted to know how close we were. Of course, I had to tell them about her recent threat to sue me for custody."

"I can't believe you had to answer all those questions again."

"By then I had the feeling they thought she was a prime suspect, and I asked them as much. Instead of answering me, they showed me a picture of a man—well-dressed, trim haircut—a Wall Street type. I'd vaguely remembered seeing a man who looked like that talking to Tanya at a party once. Then Agent Watcomb asked me pointblank if I had any reason to believe Tanya would hire someone to kidnap Kelly."

"Oh, Kipp, they really thought that? What about the lie detector test?"

"I asked him about that, too," Kipp said. "He just gave me a sharp look and said polygraphs aren't always infallible. If they held a belief about her involvement, I wanted to know why they didn't pursue it before. He said they'd been watching her back then for about six months, but she was never seen with a child. Then the trail went cold. I'm just glad I had someone in Charlie's position to vouch for me. But now, with one of the kidnappers in custody, they have more to go on. She must be giving them names."

"Do you think Tanya is capable of such a thing?"

"I don't want to think that. It's too painful for me to even go there," Kipp said. "But, Libby, I wondered why you didn't pick up on the fact that there were others involved."

Libby paused to consider. "When I got the impressions of the kidnappers, the picture was fuzzy. Their facial features weren't clear at all. That indicated to me I was supposed to focus on getting Kelly back, not on finding the kidnappers. I don't know why I didn't pick up on Tanya—I think I just couldn't imagine a mother being that cold. Could you?"

"Normally, I'd say no," he said, "but today I heard on the news a woman threw her child in the Hudson River just to get back at her ex. I think Tanya may have been focused on getting to me through some crazy scheme with Kelly." He took another swallow of water and stared at the table top, lost in the possibility of Tanya's complicity in such a horrendous act of having their daughter kidnapped.

Libby touched his arm. "Kipp?"

He shook loose from his thoughts. "I was thinking back on the time Tanya and I spent together and her relationship with Kelly. She never loved that child as a mother would. I think I told you that. She was into her own dream world of fancy clothes, fast cars, and men. I remember, after we split up, how she kept hounding me to take her back. It was always 'I love you, Kipp. I want us to be together, Kipp. Please, Kipp.' I mean, she really turned up the heat. It was suffocating. But I wouldn't budge. After the abduction, she seemed obsessed with my lack of warmth toward her. That's one reason we argued so much. Then after Kelly's return and we were together, she wouldn't stop nagging me about being a family again, but I saw the jealousy in her eyes whenever I held Kelly or paid attention to her. Tanya's a selfish woman. I saw right through her. It hurts to think she would mastermind the kidnapping of her own child, but is she capable?" He paused. "I'm afraid I'd have to say yes."

"Why would she do it, Kipp?"

He shook his head. "I guess in her own twisted mind, the only thing keeping us apart was Kelly."

"Kipp, that's so sad. She will have ruined her life. But you seem so level about this. Knowing you as I do, I'd think you'd be bursting with anger."

"All the way here I went through every emotion imaginable, but right now, I don't know how I feel. I'm not excusing what she did when I say this, but when I think about her past, she had a tough upbringing and practically had to beg for everything she got, even love. Then she grew up to be this incredibly beautiful woman and suddenly she had everything, even a beautiful child. She wasn't stable enough to handle it. But am I angry? Anger is too mild a word."

Libby rose from her chair, draped her arms over Kipp's shoulders, and gave him a hug.

"How do you think this is going to play out, Libby?"

She got quiet, and he could feel her breathing deepen. Finally, she said, "I'll be honest with you. I had chills running up my spine when you asked me earlier if I thought Tanya could have done it. Let's just say, I don't think you're ever going to have to worry about that custody suit." She gave him another hug. "No matter what, I'll be here to help you through any fallout from this."

He got up and embraced her, the fragrance of roses captivating him again.

"I know what will make you feel better," she said.

He lifted his eyebrows, wondering what she had in mind.

She took his hand, led him to the rocking chair, and handed him his jacket. "Let's go see your daughter."

With an amused smile he slid his arm around her waist and tugged her close. "You mean our daughter."